**Here's what critics are saying about
Gemma Halliday's Wine & Dine Mysteries:**

"I rank *A Sip Before Dying* as one of my favorite fun reads.
I say to Gemma Halliday, well done. She wrote a mystery
that encompassed suspense flavored with romantic notions,
while giving us a heroine to make us smile."
—*The Book Breeze Magazine*

"Gemma Halliday's signature well-written story filled with
wonderful characters is just what I expected. All in all, this
is the beginning of a great cozy series no one should miss!"
—*Kings River Life Magazine*

"I've always enjoyed the writing style and comfortable tone
of Gemma novels and this one fits in perfectly. From the
first page, the author pulled me in...when all was said and
done, I enjoyed this delightfully engaging tale and I can't
wait to spend more time with Emmy, Ava and their
friends."
—*Dru's Book Musings*

"This is a great cozy mystery, and I highly recommend it!"
—*Book Review Crew*

"I could not put *A Sip Before Dying* by Gemma Halliday
down. Once I started reading it, I was hooked!!"
—*Cozy Mystery Book Reviews*

BOOKS BY GEMMA HALLIDAY

High Heels Mysteries
Spying in High Heels
Killer in High Heels
Undercover in High Heels
Christmas in High Heels
(short story)
Alibi in High Heels
Mayhem in High Heels
Honeymoon in High Heels
(short story)
Sweetheart in High Heels
(short story)
Fearless in High Heels
Danger in High Heels
Homicide in High Heels
Deadly in High Heels
Suspect in High Heels
Peril in High Heels
Jeopardy in High Heels

Wine & Dine Mysteries
A Sip Before Dying
Chocolate Covered Death
Victim in the Vineyard
Marriage, Merlot & Murder
Death in Wine Country
Fashion, Rosé & Foul Play
Witness at the Winery

**Hollywood Headlines
Mysteries**
Hollywood Scandals
Hollywood Secrets
Hollywood Confessions
Hollywood Holiday
(short story)
Hollywood Deception

Marty Hudson Mysteries
Sherlock Holmes and the Case
of the Brash Blonde
Sherlock Holmes and the Case
of the Disappearing Diva
Sherlock Holmes and the Case
of the Wealthy Widow

Tahoe Tessie Mysteries
Luck Be A Lady
Hey Big Spender
Baby It's Cold Outside
(holiday short story)

Jamie Bond Mysteries
Unbreakable Bond
Secret Bond
Bond Bombshell
(short story)
Lethal Bond
Dangerous Bond
Bond Ambition
(short story)
Fatal Bond
Deadly Bond

**Hartley Grace Featherstone
Mysteries**
Deadly Cool
Social Suicide
Wicked Games

Other Works
Play Dead
Viva Las Vegas
A High Heels Haunting
Watching You (short story)
Confessions of a Bombshell
Bandit (short story)

DEATH IN WINE COUNTRY

a Wine & Dine mystery

GEMMA HALLIDAY

Dedicated to Zack, who loves bacon more than anyone I know.

CHAPTER ONE

————

Carrie Cross smiled back at me, her alabaster skin even more radiant in the late afternoon sunlight than it was on daytime television. While both she and her alter ego, Stormy Winters, the character she played on the soap opera *Carefree Hearts*, were California natives, that was where the similarities between the two ended. Unlike Stormy, who lived up to her name on every episode, Carrie was more like a Disney Princess—kind, upbeat, and possessing a sort of flawless beauty that made one wonder if she was real or airbrushed. Currently, Carrie's deep brown eyes shone with excitement as she led the way up the unpaved path to her new house. Her long blonde hair shimmered with every move, and her figure-hugging dress did what it was made to do, showing her slim frame off to perfection.

"So, what do you think, Emmy?" she asked me, her voice full of enthusiasm. "Isn't it just the perfect vacation home?"

The sun dropped lower in the sky as evening approached, bouncing its color across the cream colored craftsman style building, and my eyes roamed the lush acreage that sprawled toward the backdrop of shady oak trees and scattered tall pines. On the far side of the home, a large stone fire pit was the centerpiece to ten Adirondack chairs complete with sumptuous cushions, the flames roaring already for the evening ahead.

"It's stunning," I agreed, taking it all in.

"I know it's a bit excessive for a second home," Carrie admitted, eyes straying to the two-story five-bedroom house. "But my filming schedule is just so hectic, and I really do need a place to unwind and relax. And, you know, Bert has been such a whiz with the investments he's made for me that, well…I think we're going to be very happy here."

Carrie beamed as her french bulldog, Barkley, dashed between her legs, rolling onto his side in the thick grass. "I know we still have to put some finishing touches on it," she continued, "but we're mostly there. I want to paint the upstairs guest rooms still, and we need to replace the old security system." She paused. "I mean, not that it doesn't work, but it only has a couple of cameras—one at the property entrance and one at the front door. Bert said there are a lot of fans who don't understand boundaries, so he's upgrading to a whole smart home system. It's better to be safe than sorry."

On that point, I agreed. While Carrie wasn't exactly at the Hollywood royalty level of stardom, I knew her character had gotten her fair share of fan mail—sometimes praising her and sometimes not quite understanding the lines between her villainous character and the reality of Carrie the actress. So I was glad her husband, Bert, had an eye on her protection.

I'd first met Carrie when I'd been working as a personal chef in Los Angeles, right after graduating from the CIA. (Just not *that* CIA—the Culinary Institute of America. Though, I'd put my knife skills up against any federal agent's.) Carrie had been gracious enough to hire me to cater a cast party for her, despite my lack of résumé at the time. We'd gotten along so well that she'd ended up being a regular client. I'd done monthly dinner parties for her and her friends, as well as several more cast parties. We'd both been sad to part ways when I'd moved back home to run my family's small winery, Oak Valley Vineyards, but thanks to social media, we'd kept in touch since then. So when Carrie had decided to purchase a vacation home in Wine Country, the first thing she'd done once the papers were signed was call me to help her plan a housewarming party designed to showcase her new "rustic" country home. And maybe make her LA friends just a smidgeon jealous in the process.

"I know a couple of people I could refer you to for installing a security system," I told her, thinking of the handyman we'd used to fix our electrical panel last month. Oak Valley Vineyards had been in my family for generations, and it was starting to show it—needing just about a new everything all the time.

"Thanks! I'll take you up on that. I mean, not that you have a lot of crime up here in Wine Country," Carrie went on. "I personally think Bert just wants to play with some new gadgets." She laughed, the sound light and tinkling, almost like a song. "But I suppose he can afford them. Oh, I will never get enough of this view!" She finally paused for a breath as she spread her arms wide in a dramatic gesture that took in the distant rolling hills full of grapevines just starting to bud as spring crept up on us.

"That makes two of us," I told her honestly. While I'd been reluctant to leave my burgeoning career in LA for the relative quiet of Sonoma, I had to admit the scenery was a huge plus. That, and with my mom's health failing, I'd had little choice. But I shoved those less-than-party-worthy thoughts aside as I focused on Carrie's running monologue again.

"I had really wanted to have the party outside here, but Bert said it's just too cold still, even if we rented heaters. I suppose he's right—he usually is!—but I'd love to have my birthday party out here next month. Oh! You could cater that too, right, Emmy?"

"I'd be happy to," I replied, meaning it as I mentally pictured my accountant, Gene Schultz, giving me a double thumbs-up. He'd been hounding me to finish my quarterly taxes, which might have been an easier task for me to do if I had enough money in our bank account to actually pay them. As it was, we were looking at having to file extensions and incur penalties that in no time would start eating up any profits we made. But the revenue from this catering gig would help. And if Carrie had regular work? Who knew. We might even see black in our account books next quarter!

Carrie clapped, lifting up onto her tiptoes, her delight evident. "Oh, I've missed your cooking. The company I hired to do the last cast party was just so generic, you know? Tartare this and sashimi that. It's all been done! I know you will really wow everyone tonight."

Suddenly I was a bit worried at living up to her expectations. I had, in fact, put a tartare on the menu. Granted, it was a vegan one—one of Carrie's requests. Apparently her LA friends didn't "do" meat, dairy, or gluten. Which I'd feared only left cooking with air, but I was CIA trained, after all—I could even make air taste good. "I'll do my best," I promised.

"Most of the cast are flying in, and some of the network mucky-mucks, of course. Must play nice to the powers that be." She winked at me. "So I want everything to be perfect, you know? Just really dazzle them with all that Wine Country has to offer." She took my hand and squeezed it, her grin upping in wattage. "This is going to be so fun!"

"Maybe I should get a look at the kitchen and get started," I offered, trying not to let the pressure get to me.

"Oh, you're going to love it. That was one place I insisted Bert stay out of the renovations and leave it all to me." She winked again. "It's a total chef's dream!"

Some of the trepidation started to melt away as the chef in me "dreamed" big.

"But, before we go inside, I have to show you Dante."

I raised one eyebrow, wondering who or what Dante was. I didn't get a chance to ask, as Carrie was off and running again.

"Bert wanted to give me an early birthday present, and when I found Dante, I knew I just had to have him. He only arrived a couple of days ago, and he's quite wild, but he's so beautiful, and I love him already," she gushed.

"Wild?" I asked, following her as she led the way around the back of the house toward a large barn and horse corral a few yards away.

"Uh-huh." Carrie glanced back at me, eyes shining. "Isn't that crazy? Like, an actual wild horse. It's straight out of a movie, right?"

"A horse. I didn't know you rode," I told her. From what I'd remembered of Carrie, she'd been more of a mimosas-at-noon kind of gal than a doing-anything-that-might-result-in-dirt-in-her-manicure girl. Barkley was about as close to wildlife as she'd gotten.

"Oh, I don't. Yet. But I'm all in on this country vacation thing. I read an article in *Vanity Fair* that said horseback riding is very relaxing." She nodded sagely. "And Dante won't be wild for long. Tripp will have that horsy as tame as a bunny in no time."

I didn't have the opportunity to ask who Tripp was, as we approached a dirt filled arena that caused my heart rate to speed up. Or more accurately, it was the stallion galloping wildly that caused my heart rate to spike. A man in a cowboy hat stood in the center of the arena, a rope loosely slung in his hand. Dust billowed behind the horse's hooves as it stomped the ground, its mane whipping in his wake.

"That's Tripp there," Carrie said as she scooped Barkley up in her arms, pointing to the either brave or stupid man egging on the stallion. "Tripp Jones…you've heard of him?"

I shook my head. While our property was just under ten acres, all of that land was allocated to either vineyards or the winery buildings. Horses were something I had little experience with. "I take it he's a local?" I asked.

Carrie nodded. "He's known as a horse whisperer. My costar, Harper, recommended him to me. Her family has their own estate over in Napa. I knew that as soon as Tripp met Dante, he would have no trouble taming him."

The chestnut colored horse with the black mane must have caught our scent on the wind, as he appeared to spook and kick up his back legs. His head was bowed as he bucked, and I had my doubts as to how easy Tripp's job was going to be.

"Just wait until the guests see this," Carrie said, eyes sparkling. "Like, nobody in LA has a wild horse, right?"

I had to admit, I hadn't seen them trotting around Beverly Hills during my residency there.

Barkley let out a yap, and the horse whisperer turned, shooting an annoyed glare our way. While his expression was not necessarily welcoming, the rest of him was surprisingly easy on the eyes. He appeared about my age—somewhere in the twenty-nine-ish zone—and his Wranglers were slung low on his hips, held in place with a large silver buckle. His flannel shirt flapped open, showing off a white T-shirt that was plastered tight against his toned torso, and the skin on his forearms and face was a sun-kissed bronze. He had Bad Boy written all over him, and I wondered if Bert had approved this particular hire.

Carrie waved, oblivious to the man's scowl. "Tripp, come meet my friend Emmy."

He obliged, turning and making his way out of the corral and leaving Dante on his own. The animal settled down to a brisk walk, though he pawed at the ground as he passed us, as if almost daring us to mess with him.

"How is he?" Carrie eagerly asked Tripp as he came up to us from the other side of the fence.

"Wild." His voice was deep and had a clipped quality.

"I'm sure you'll have him whipped into shape in no time."

Tripp frowned. "I don't whip any animal. Never have and never will."

"Oh! I didn't mean that literally." Carrie let out her tinkling laugh again. "I just meant that you'd have him behaving. I mean, that's what you do, right? Whisper sweet nothings to them and all that." Carrie shot him a knowing grin.

But Tripp seemed to have no reaction to her song-like laughter or her wide smile, his expression neutral as he replied, "Something like that." His eyes flitted toward me, and I could feel him giving me a quick appraisal.

"Oh, sorry. Tripp, this is my friend Emmeline Oak. She owns a winery nearby."

"Please, call me Emmy," I said.

Tripp touched the rim of his hat and nodded in my direction.

"Emmy's going to be catering the party tonight," Carrie went on. "When you're done here, you should come up to the house. Practically everyone in Hollywood will be there!"

While I knew that was a slight exaggeration, I could see the idea causing Tripp's frown to reappear. "Don't think it's really my crowd, ma'am," he said.

But Carrie waved him off. "Oh, don't be silly. A real life cowboy? You'll be the most popular man in the room!"

Tripp did more scowling, clearly unconvinced.

Dante completed another circle of the arena, kicking indignant dust our way as he passed by, and Barkley let out a yip toward the large beast. Which caused Dante to rear forward, kicking up his back legs in response.

"You need to keep that dog away from here," Tripp said. "If it gets kicked by Dante, it'll be the end of it."

Carrie protectively pulled Barkley tight against her chest, smoothing his short hair. "Dante wouldn't hurt my baby."

I doubted that. Dante looked ready to hurt anyone or thing that got near him. For all Tripp's hard demeanor, I had to hand it to him in the bravery department. You couldn't pay me to step into that arena with Dante.

"Maybe you could show me the kitchen now?" I suggested, nudging Carrie.

"Right. Of course. Let's get this party rolling, huh?" she said, putting her breezy smile back on as she turned to lead the way to the house.

*   *   *

After showing me the lay of the land in her culinary haven—which was, as promised, a dream to a chef like myself—Carrie left me to prep as she went upstairs to the master suite to get herself party ready. I was well into slicing up a plate of raw veggies to look like a garden, complete with flowered radishes and cherry tomatoes, when my sous-chef for the evening arrived. Ava Barnett, my best friend, had graciously agreed to help me serve, and I was pretty sure it was only halfway because she was a massive *Carefree Hearts* fan.

Ava and I had known each other since we were teenagers, and I often thought of Ava more like a sister than best friend. Some people even said we looked similar. We were both somewhere in the size eight realm, even if Ava's size eight was all athletic lines and mine was more dessert-loving curves. We both wore our blonde hair long, though Ava's was silky smooth and picture perfect in any weather, while mine tended to range from wavy to frizzy to downright Einsteinish, depending on the day and amount of hair products I had on hand. And while I usually preferred to keep it simple in the wardrobe arena, with jeans, T-shirts, and the occasional pair of high heels to jazz things up, Ava's style was a feminine bo-ho chic that always felt light and timeless.

"Sorry I'm late," she said, rushing into the room. Her floral dress billowed around her knees as she gave me a quick hug that enveloped me in a cloud of peachy lotion. Ava owned her own jewelry shop, Silver Girl, in downtown Sonoma, and her arms jingled with her latest creations as she plopped her bag onto the counter. "I couldn't decide what to wear. I mean, just the idea of meeting him had me flustered."

"*Him*?" I asked, raising an eyebrow her way.

"Nolan Becker." The name was said on a sigh.

I shook my head. "Should I know him?"

Ava gave me a horrified look. "Uh, yeah! Nolan *Becker*?" She reached into her bag and pulled out a copy of *Soap Opera Digest*. "He plays Dr. Drake Dubois."

I glanced at the page in her hand, a classically tall, dark, and handsome guy in a white clinical coat staring back at me. "He's cute," I admitted.

"Girlfriend, that's like saying bacon is *kinda* tasty."

I couldn't help a grin. Ava was well aware of my love affair with bacon.

"Dr. Dubois is beyond cute," she went on. "He's hot. Like, volcanic. You should see him on the show. He has smoldering looks down to a science."

"Down, girl," I joked.

"Oh, there will be no down if Nolan shows up. You know my mother always wanted me to marry a doctor."

I shot her a look. "Your mother gave me a Ruth Bader Ginsberg doll for Christmas. *Feminist* is her middle name. There is no way she dreamed of you *marrying* a doctor."

Ava grinned. "Okay, fine. So she wanted me to *be* a doctor. But one look at my chemistry grades killed that dream, so I'm pretty sure marrying is as close as she's gonna get."

"You know this guy only *plays* a doctor, right?"

She waved me off. "Details. I'm not the picky type."

I had to laugh. "Well as long as you're the serving type, that's all I care about tonight."

"And exactly what are we serving?" Ava asked, thankfully changing focus as she took an apron from my box of supplies and tied it around her waist.

I handed a copy of the night's menu to Ava.

"We'll start with mini almond flour blini's with carrot lox, then we'll do sweet potato canapés with mung bean sprouts and tofu teriyaki tartare. After that, we'll bring out Wine Marinated Stuffed Mushrooms, eggplant scallops, and small cups of butternut squash and porcini mushroom risotto."

Ava frowned. "All vegan, huh?"

"And gluten-free. It's what Carrie wanted." I shrugged.

She shrugged. "Well, if anyone can pull it off, it's you."

I grinned, appreciating the vote of confidence.

"And the wines?" Ava asked.

"I've brought a few bottles of our Petite Sirah, and plenty of the Chardonnay that I'm hoping will pair with the risotto, and the Zinfandel with the mushrooms."

Ava nodded her approval. "Sounds delightful. If missing meat." She grinned.

"One can hope. Now, let's get cooking. The guests will be here before we know it."

CHAPTER TWO

———

Ava was just setting out the last plate of canapés when I removed my chef's coat in favor of the simple black A-line dress I'd selected for serving duties. The dress was a bit more fitted than the last time I'd worn it, but then I'd been doing a lot of taste testing of late, so that was sadly to be expected. I made a mental note to look into this vegan thing later, if only for a few days to get the dress back to moderately formfitting instead of suck-it-in fitting. I slipped my feet into my stilettos. At least they still went on easily.

Carrie pushed through the kitchen doors and rushed toward me, smothering me with the latest scent from Tiffany's.

"Emmy, is everything ready?" She looked immaculately put together in her Gucci raspberry red knee-length cocktail dress. I'd heard a lot about that dress, and I'd admit that it was worth the money she'd told me she had spent on it. A black band enhanced her tiny waist, and the red silk accentuated her painted lips. She'd done the smoky eye thing and tied her hair up in an elegant chignon, emphasizing her long neck and smooth skin. The only hint at her anxiety was sitting in her eyes, as her lashes batted at excess speed.

"Relax. Everything is ready to go as soon as you give the cue."

"Fantastic." She took a deep calming breath as her husband, Bert, entered the kitchen behind her.

"Carrie, what have you done with Barkley for the night?" Bert asked.

"He's locked in the bedroom. I've left some meditation music playing softly so that he won't get freaked out by the sounds of the party. And I've taken Tripp's warning seriously. He can't go anywhere near Dante, so we have to keep a close eye on him."

"Good thinking." Bert placed his arm around her shoulders and lightly kissed her temple. "Now, I need a drink before our guests arrive." He turned to acknowledge me for the first time since stepping into the room. "Emmy, which of your wines do you recommend?"

Bert and Carrie had only married a couple of months before I'd left LA, and I'd first met him when I'd catered their wedding. Bert had the handsome Prince Harry thing happening, with the sandy ginger hair and blue-gray eyes. He kept his face cleanly shaven, accentuating the boyish features that had made him a child star. *Home with the Hendersons* had been one of my favorite television shows as a kid. His character, Little Bertie, had coined the catch phrase "You know it, Mama!" complete with a cheeky wink, and I'd driven my mom crazy by copying it at every opportunity. As far as I knew, Bert had left acting in his childhood, but apparently he still ran in the same social circles, as I remembered Carrie saying she'd met him at a party at her agent's house just a few months before they'd wed. These days he was more on the financial end of things. Carrie had described him as a "whiz with money," and I knew he handled all her finances, making investments with her portfolio that had apparently been paying off big time. Big enough to afford the home that I knew had to have set her back a number well into the seven figures, knowing the current California real estate market.

"I brought a couple of bottles of our Petite Sirah," I told him. "It's a red that we only do small runs on." I had an uncorked bottle close by and poured him a glass.

Instead of inhaling the aroma and allowing the liquid to slowly hit his palate in order to get the full taste of the wine, he downed the glass, finishing with a smack of his lips.

"Nice stuff. Your friend knows her booze, Care," he told his wife.

I held my smile in place with no small effort as I poured more "booze" into the empty glass he held toward me. I'd just topped it off when Ava rushed into the kitchen, her cheeks flushed with excitement.

"He's here! He just pulled up in the driveway." She stopped as she spotted Carrie and Bert. "Sorry, I um, thought Emmy was alone."

Carrie didn't bat an eyelash. Instead she asked, "Who's here?"

Ava recovered from her faux pas and grinned as she removed her apron, throwing it back into my supply box. "Nolan Becker. He's driving a flashy little sports car, and he looks good enough to eat."

"He looks that way even without the sports car." Carrie smiled.

"You are so lucky to work with him every day," Ava gushed.

Bert snorted, but no one seemed to pay it any attention.

"Would you like to meet him?" Carrie asked.

"I would kill to meet Dr. Drake Dubois," Ava said.

Carrie laughed. "Well, I assure you *Nolan* is nothing like his character."

"Oh. Right," Ava said, looking slightly deflated.

Carrie leaned in close and winked at Ava. "He's hotter."

Ava grinned and might have even swooned a little.

Bert downed the rest of his "booze" and grunted again as he set the glass on the counter with a thump. "Perhaps we should greet our guests," he suggested, taking Carrie by the arm.

Ava and I followed the couple into the living room, where we watched them welcome Nolan—which had Ava almost passing out—as well as a couple of other men who'd arrived at the same time. We'd just had time to offer drinks to the newcomers when several more guests followed, a steady stream entering until the expansive room seemed to echo with the din of chattering voices, tinkling wineglasses, and laughter, as the crowd enjoyed Carrie's hospitality and hopefully our food as well.

"He kissed my hand," Ava said, sidling up alongside me, a Chardonnay bottle in her hand.

"He?" I asked.

"Nolan. Carrie introduced us, and I swear the man actually kissed my hand." She looked down at the appendage as if it were anointed.

"Let me guess—you're never washing it again?" I teased.

"Wash it? Honey, I may just enshrine it for all time." She paused. "His lips were so soft," she said, eyes going across the room to the man in question, who was presently swirling the last of his Chardonnay in a glass as he chatted with a slim woman in a green sequined cocktail dress. "I wonder who he's dating at the moment. The magazines are always quiet about that."

I shrugged. "I guess he likes to keep his personal life personal."

"He could have any woman he wants, I bet." Ava's eyes glazed over, as if mentally doodling her name in hearts with his.

"Is that bottle empty?" I asked, gesturing to the one in her hand in an effort to pull her back to reality.

"Uh-huh." She placed it on the side table we'd set up as a makeshift bar and pulled her phone from her pocket, bringing up a social media site.

"I wonder if Nolan would accept a friend request from me," she said, scrolling.

"I bet he'd accept a fresh glass of Chardonnay," I hinted.

But she was deep in social media and ignored me. "Oh, did you see Harper Bishop's selfie with a glass of the Zin?" she asked me, holding the phone for me to see.

Apparently Harper and the woman in the sequined dress were one and the same, the photo showing her standing by the large fireplace with the caption *Livin my best life in Wine Country*. I had to admit, the bottle of wine in the background with our label clearly visible was nice publicity.

"No, I hadn't seen that." I paused. "Because I'm working," I said, hoping she got the hint this time as I shoved an uncorked bottle of Chardonnay her way.

"Oh, so am I! I'm reposting every single mention that has been made from this party. So far your Zin has the most likes. You need to keep plenty of stock of that one. After tonight, you'll be getting loads of orders."

I said a silent prayer that she was right.

"Anyway, Harper was the most enthusiastic about it," Ava continued. "I hope she's not driving home later, because I've already poured her far more than the legal limit, and if the tabloids are correct, she's already been pulled over for a DUI."

I shook my head. "No, Carrie told me that both Harper and Nolan are staying here for the weekend. So there's no need to worry about how many times we refill their glasses."

At the mention of "Dr. Drake Dubois's" real name, Ava gave a dreamy sigh. "I wonder which room he's staying in."

"You wouldn't?" I laughed, knowing exactly what was running through Ava's mind.

"It would only be a tiny peek," she confessed on a grin, hurriedly pushing her phone into her pocket as Carrie stepped up to us, the sequined Harper Bishop trailing behind her.

"Everything is amazing, Emmy," Carrie said, the previous anxiety in her eyes gone—though thanks to a flawless party or a couple glasses of Oak Valley wines, I wasn't sure. Likely both.

"I'm glad the guests are enjoying themselves," I told her.

"Oh, we are," Harper piped up, her voice throaty in a Lauren Bacall way that felt the polar opposite to Carrie's perky one.

"Emmy, have you met Harper?" Carrie asked, turning to her companion.

Harper Bishop was probably the most classically beautiful woman I had ever met up close. Her high cheek bones, dazzling green eyes, and full lips looked as though they came straight from the gods. Yet I knew that you only got a body like hers from hours in the gym, no carbs, no fat, and no fun. And possibly a little help from a scalpel.

"Harper's my sister. Well, she plays my sister on the show, but we're so close, I tell everyone we're actually sisters." Carrie let out one of her tinkling laughs, putting her arm around the other woman's shoulder. "Anyway, I guess I should actually say, *played* my sister on the show. Her character had a slight incident recently and got herself killed."

"You're kidding!" Ava said, the bombshell clearly not one that had been leaked in *Soap Opera Digest* yet.

Harper gave a throaty laugh, flicking her luscious dark hair over her shoulder. "Yes, sad but true. This is one carefree heart that's stopped beating."

"But I'm sure your departure will have the highest ratings of the season," Carrie said, ever the one with silver linings up her sleeve.

"Oh?" Ava asked, her inner fangirl peeking out. "How does Allegra die?" She paused, turning to me to explain. "Allegra is Harper's character."

"In a thrift store, of all places. I mean, as if Allegra would shop thrift." Harper ran her hands over her emerald green designer label dress that I knew probably cost more than my car.

"What happens in the thrift store?" Ava asked on a breath, clearly completely enthralled.

Carrie leaned in close, ready to tell a secret that hadn't yet aired.

"Well, Allegra lost all her money in a bad investment and is poor now, only she didn't want everyone to know, so she was sneaking around the thrift store buying secondhand designer dresses and pretending they were new. But she didn't see the orange peel that had been discarded on the floor. She slipped and broke her ankle and was taken to the hospital. The nurse in the ER made an error and gave her the wrong medication. Allegra had an allergic reaction and died. Despite Doctor Drake's efforts to save her. Only the medication mix-up wasn't an accident at all. No. The nurse was none other than her arch nemesis, Abyssinia, in disguise."

Wow.

I struggled to stifle the grin I felt bubbling in my throat, not only at the unbelievable storyline but at Carrie's dramatic retelling.

"A thrift shop! Demoralizing, really," Harper said. "The producers' last dig at me, I suppose."

"I think the fans will love it. Even if they will miss you terribly," Carrie assured her.

"Yes, well, there's that." Harper smoothed an imaginary stray piece of fluff from her designer dress as Bert approached from behind.

"Harper, darling, what's this I hear? You're out of a job?" he joked.

"Oh ha-ha. Very funny, Little Bertie." Her tone matched his teasing one, but I could see an undercurrent of something else flitting behind her eyes. "But I tell you both, it's a blessing really. I needed some downtime."

"There's a bright side to everything, isn't there?" Carrie said.

"Yes, think of all that extra beauty sleep you'll be able to get now," Bert said, chuckling at his own wit. He glanced my way just long enough to see the bottle of Sirah in my hand and held out his empty glass.

Reluctantly, I filled it as a fourth joined their little trio.

"Well, you can't say I didn't try my best to save you." Nolan Becker approached the group of friends at our popular wine table, addressing Harper. "But even Dr. Dubois can only do so much."

He gave her a wide smile that flashed a dimple at the side of his cheek, giving him a mischievously boyish look. Bright blue eyes, tall, dark hair in a stylish cut, and clothes that spoke to both expensive taste and the money to afford it. Despite the fact that I usually went for the more rugged type, I couldn't help admitting he was strikingly good-looking.

"Well, at least we know the producers love *you*, Nolan," Harper responded, playfully swatting his arm. "Though, I have to say that scene where you declared your undying love to my dead body was very touching."

"It brought a tear to my eye," confessed Carrie earnestly.

"Some of my finest work." Nolan grinned, rolling his hand with an over exaggerated bow.

Ava looked about ready to faint. Or jump his bones. Maybe both.

"Well, I'm sure the *Carefree Hearts* fandom will be sorry to see Allegra go," added Bert, sipping from his third (or fourth?) glass. "But what do they say? All good things must come to an end, my dear Harper." He saluted her with his wineglass. "No matter how expensively gorgeous they are."

"Oh, Bert, stop. You're embarrassing me," Harper said, sending him a coy smile. Though, again, I caught some sort of look being exchanged between them that didn't quite jibe with their words.

"I hate to interrupt, but it looks like Eric is getting ready to leave," Carrie said, seemingly oblivious to any tension under the words of her husband and faux sister, as her gaze turned toward the door. I spied an older man in dark slacks putting on his jacket. "We should say goodbye."

Harper scoffed. "Why would I want to say goodbye to a network exec who basically just fired me?"

Carrie tilted her head to the side. "Come on, now, Harper. You know there are no hard feelings."

"Yes, come on, Harper," Bert teased. "Make nice with the gentry."

Harper rolled her eyes but complied, following Carrie as the host gave Ava and me an apologetic look.

Almost as soon as they walked away, another couple approached, looking for more Chardonnay. As I poured for them, my eyes strayed to Carrie and her entourage again as they met Eric From the Network at the door. I noticed as soon as Bert shook the man's hand, he faded away into the crowd. Carrie chatted in earnest with the exec, while Harper, on the other hand, barely gave the man a wan smile before her eyes followed Bert across the room.

"This is really delightful," the woman in front of me said, pulling my attention back to my task at hand. She was a bit older than the rest of Carrie's guests, though dressed just as stylishly. Her dark hair shot with gray was pulled into a low ponytail, and her husband appeared to be bored—possibly there out of obligation more than interest.

"Thank you. This was a particularly good year for us," I said, gesturing to the bottle.

"Well, it's lovely. Do you happen to produce any other whites?"

"We do," I told her. "We have a very nice Pinot Grigio this year. We only brought a couple of bottles with us, but I'd be happy to open one if you'd like to try it?"

"Please," she said, nodding vigorously.

I glanced around, noting we must have left them in the kitchen. I was about to ask Ava to fetch one, when I realized there was one member of Carrie's group who hadn't joined the goodbye party at the door—Nolan Becker, who at the moment was being flirted with by my serving help. Though, the way that

Nolan was smiling down at her and maybe even flirting back a little, I didn't have the heart to break it up.

"Let me just slip into the kitchen and grab a bottle for you," I told the woman. "I'll be right back."

"Thank you," she called as I retraced my steps to do just that.

Which took me a few minutes, as I realized the crowd had grown, spilling from the great room into the den, and even despite the chill in the air, out onto the back patios and around the blazing fire pit. I mumbled quite a few *excuse me*'s and *pardon me*'s as I bumped elbows with people and slid between laughing groups of Carrie's friends before I finally reached the kitchen and found the bottles of our Pinot Grigio. I grabbed two by the necks and, instead of shoving my way through the crowd again, decided to go around the back of the house and slip in through the side door. A little chillier, but probably faster. I wasn't sure how long my white wine loving woman would wait.

As soon as I pushed out the back door, a blast of cold air hit me, and I almost rethought my strategy. Instead, I quickly jogged as fast as my three inch heels would allow along the side of the building, toward the side door. I was shivering by the time I slipped back inside, coming into a small mudroom. From my earlier tour of the house with Carrie, I knew the hallway to the left led back to the great room—I could hear the sounds of the party at a dull roar. To my right was a stairway that led up to the second floor, where the bedrooms were located. I took a step toward the hallway, when a familiar voice caught my attention, coming from the stairwell above.

"…know why I'm asking, Bertie."

It was Harper, Carrie's former costar. And apparently she was with Carrie's husband. Despite my waiting wine lover, curiosity got the better of me, and I paused.

"Keep your voice down," I heard Bert say.

"What, you think *Carrie* will hear me?" Harper taunted with a throaty laugh.

I should have walked away. Back to the party. Minded my own business.

But something in the way Harper had looked at Bertie before, spurred me to climb the first couple of steps up the staircase, until I spied Harper on the landing above me, leaning in close to Bert.

Very close.

Close enough that I felt my breath catch in my throat in anticipation she might kiss him.

"This is not the time, Harper," Bert said. The tone in his voice sounded more irritated than amorous, but it was hard to tell the expression on his face from my angle.

I suddenly felt like I was eavesdropping on some very private moment. I was just about to retreat, when Harper pulled back.

"It is the perfect time. Come, Bertie, you know you wouldn't want your darling wife to come looking for us."

"Leave her out of this," Bert hissed.

But Harper threw her head back and laughed at him again. "Happy to, sweetie. You know what I want."

Then I watched her give him the same coy smile I'd seen earlier before taking him by the hand and leading him out of my sight.

I bit my lip, not liking what I'd just witnessed. Granted, it was *possible* the two could have been discussing anything. But I couldn't imagine a circumstance when I'd be that close with one of my coworkers' husbands. Correction: an *innocent* circumstance. Suddenly I felt terrible for Carrie.

My mind was still bouncing between unpleasant possibilities when I got back to the bar. Only my white wine drinker was missing.

"Where did the woman go?" I asked Ava.

"Huh?" she said, tearing her gaze away from Dr. Drake Dubois.

"The woman with the ponytail. She wanted to taste the Pinot Grigio."

But Ava just looked at me with a blank expression. "Sorry. I didn't notice."

I was about to chastise my daydreaming sidekick, when Nolan turned his boyish smile on me. "Now, Ava here tells me that you are the lady I need to speak to about purchasing a case of this wine."

I suddenly understood why Ava found him so dreamy.

* * *

It was a little after 1:00 a.m. by the time I loaded the last of my equipment into the back of my Jeep and released a contented sigh. The night had been a resounding success. Everyone had raved about the food, but more importantly they now knew the name of Oak Valley Vineyards, and I'd heard at least a couple of them say they'd be coming in for a tasting soon. Plus, at least according to Ava, photos of the event were trending on social media, which could only be a good thing if anyone else captured a glimpse of our wine in their selfies.

I'd sent Ava home about half an hour prior, thanking her for her help by doing the cleanup on my own. She'd been dying to tell her mom all the gossip she had learned from the cast of *Carefree Hearts*. I had a feeling fantasies of Nolan Becker would be invading her dreams that night.

I closed the trunk of my car and smiled into the darkness. In the distance Carrie's horse, Dante, roared, an imposing noise that sounded like a demon howling at the moon.

Tripp definitely had his work cut out for him with that animal. Horse whisperer or not, that thing looked dangerous to me. Personally, I thought whoever Bert had purchased Dante from had taken him for a fool.

I was about to make my way into the house, ready to check that I had everything, when the yapping sound of Barkley echoed through the night air. I spun just in time to see the little dog zip from the door that I had inadvertently left open and disappear into the darkness, his yap leading him all the way to Dante.

Oh crap.

Carrie loved that dog. Tripp's words of warning echoed in my head. If Barkley was headed toward Dante, the little guy didn't stand a chance.

Simultaneously kicking my heels off and grabbing my phone, I switched the flashlight on. I then sprinted across the lawn into the darkness, toward the corral.

Dante's roars upped as they competed with Barkley's yaps.

"Barkley!" I yelled. "Barkley, come here, boy." I didn't want to scare the dog, but it was hard to keep the fear from my voice. "Barkley please, please stay away from that horse!" I had no idea what I was going to do if he was already in the corral. Would I face a wild horse to save a dog? I guessed I was about to find out.

The closer I got, the louder his yaps were, but my heart missed a whole beat as his yaps turned into a high-pitched yelp.

"Oh, no."

I just made it to the corral as Barkley ran toward me, his tail between his legs.

Scooping him in my arms, I scanned him with the flashlight, grateful I couldn't see any telltale signs that he'd been hurt. I pulled him close, releasing a deep breath and hoping Dante had just given him a fright.

I allowed my light to scan Dante, just to make sure no damage was done to him either, when something sparkly in the corner of the corral caught my attention.

Scanning my flashlight toward it, the glitter of sequins shone back.

I felt my breath catch, fear renewing in my chest as I moved closer and realized that the sequins were attached to a person...one who was lying on her back, limbs splayed in an awkward position, muddy hoofprints littering her sparkling emerald dress that only hours ago had been the talk of the party.

Harper Bishop.

And, unlike a Hollywood script, I could tell from the lifeless stare in her eyes, there'd be no miraculous recovery for her.

Harper Bishop was dead.

CHAPTER THREE

———

I sat on the edge of one of the Adirondack chairs on the damp lawn and pulled my jacket tight against my body, shutting out the cool night air that was causing the goose bumps to crawl up my skin. At least I told myself they were from the cool air and not... I shook my head, trying my best to block out the image. I'd stopped shaking, and the tears had thankfully dried up, but I knew that the lifeless stare of Harper Bishop would haunt my dreams for a very long time.

I squeezed my eyelids shut, hoping to erase the picture that seemed burned on my retinas, but the red and blue lights flashing over the corral made ignoring my surroundings impossible. I reluctantly opened them again, taking in the uniformed officers, crime scene techs, and emergency medical staff crawling over the area like a flood of ants.

The night air crackled with the chatter of police radios, the occasional siren as new personnel showed up, and the angry sounds of Dante playing a background symphony to the organized chaos.

After finding poor Harper, I vaguely remembered screaming, running, and somehow managing to get Barkley safely inside the house. My noise must have alerted the last of the party guests that something was wrong, as Carrie, Bert, and the handful of holdouts had come running into the kitchen, where I feared I'd been in a near hysterical state. Someone had called 9-1-1, and as soon as the police had arrived, they'd separated us all—ostensibly to calm everyone down, but in reality I had a bad feeling it was to question witnesses. With a tragic accident like this at the home of minor celebrities, the police would want to make sure procedure was properly followed at all times. Especially once the press learned about it.

I could only imagine what Carrie was going through. The last I'd seen her, she'd been sobbing into Bert's shoulder as he'd led her to the den, reassuring her that everything was going to be alright. As I watched the coroner zip a black body bag closed, concealing Harper from view, I wondered what his definition of *alright* was.

Dante's loud snorting and whinnying sounded from the far side of the corral. Animal Control had attempted to round him up as soon as they'd arrived on scene—the police officers not able to even approach the body safely until they had. Now I could hear him kicking at the metal trailer they'd put him in, crying for release. Even though Dante was clearly a killer, I hoped they took him somewhere safe.

As I watched the handlers secure the trailer, I noticed a new vehicle approaching the scene, pulling up alongside the barn before shutting off its lights. A black SUV. And as the car door opened, I realized I knew the driver. Tall, broad shoulders, dark hair that hung just a little too long on his neck, and dark eyes with soft hazel flecks that quickly roved the area, assessing the scene. They stopped when they landed on me, and he made quick strides toward me.

"Emmy," he said as soon as he was within earshot.

"Grant," I greeted him back.

Detective Christopher Grant, Sonoma County Sheriff's VCI Unit—Violent Crimes Investigations. Which, I guessed an accidental death by trampling counted as. I had to admit, the scene I'd witnessed had spoken of violence, even if the perpetrator of the crime was not strictly human in this case.

Grant sat in the chair next to me and reached out to take one of my trembling hands in his. "You okay?" he asked, Cop Mode suspended for a brief moment as his eyes filled with concern.

While Grant and I weren't strangers, the exact label that fit our relationship was elusive. To say I was "seeing him" would imply contact on a regular basis—and between his job and my winery, that hadn't yet happened. There had been a few romantic hints here and there, but neither of us had pushed them into a definable territory. While part of me wouldn't mind seeing more of Grant—literally and figuratively—I got the impression he was the kind of guy who didn't do commitment to anything outside of a badge. Grant was a lot like Dante—wild and dangerous. And if a girl got too close, I had a feeling she was liable to have her heart trampled on.

But that didn't mean I didn't appreciate the warmth in his eyes and the comforting strength of his hand holding mine.

"I'm kinda okay," I said, trying to make my voice sound steadier than it felt.

"Only kinda?" He attempted a smile for my benefit.

The gesture had tears bubbling up in my throat again. To be fair, I'd been doing better until he'd sat next to me with his big brown sympathetic eyes.

"Come here." Grant put his strong arm around my shoulder and pulled me hard against him. The aroma of masculinity combined with his musky aftershave settled in my belly, and I pulled myself together.

"Think you can tell me what happened here?" he asked softy.

I nodded, taking a deep breath. "I think so."

"What time did you find the body?" Grant asked, removing his arm from my shoulder. The cold night air immediately took its place, making me shiver again as I tried to think back through the fog of shock and emotion.

"Maybe around one. The party was winding down, and I was cleaning up. I was loading the last of my catering equipment into my Jeep, when Barkley got out."

"Barkley?"

"Carrie's dog."

"You know Carrie well?" he asked, pulling out the little notebook he always kept in his back pocket.

"I used to. I catered for her a lot when I lived in LA. She just bought this place." I gestured to the building looming behind me, looking sad and eerie bathed in the flashing lights.

Grant nodded. "They told me there was some sort of housewarming party going on tonight."

"That's right," I confirmed. "Carrie invited a lot of her friends from LA up. Most are staying somewhere downtown, but

Harper was supposed to sleep here." I thought again of how overwhelmed poor Carrie must feel right now. How had she described Harper...like her sister? I thought of Ava, and how I'd feel if anything ever happened to her.

"When was the last time you saw her?" Grant asked, pulling me out of my thoughts.

"Carrie?"

"Harper," he said gently, a small frown forming between his brows.

"Oh. Right. Um, I'm not sure. She was with Bert earlier..." I trailed off, not sure how much of that I should share. With Harper dead, did it even matter what had gone on between her and Bert? And honestly, all I'd seen were two people upstairs. For all I knew, Bert could have been showing Harper to her guest room. Whatever it had been, Carrie didn't need to deal with that right now.

If Grant had an idea I was holding something back, he didn't indicate it. "When was that?"

"I don't know. Maybe eleven or so." I paused. "Why?"

"Just trying to establish a timeline."

I bit my lip. "Harper'd had a lot to drink. Ava said she'd poured her several glasses."

He looked up from his notes to meet my gaze. "Oh?"

I nodded. "You think she wandered into the corral by mistake?"

Grant took a deep breath. I knew he was a just-the-facts type of person and guessing was something he rarely did. "It's possible," he conceded.

"But you don't think likely?"

"At this point, we're exploring all angles." He paused. "But would you have walked into that corral with that horse?"

"No," I said. "But I haven't had as many glasses of wine as she did. Maybe she just wanted to look at Dante and fell in?"

"Maybe." His eyes were back on his notes.

"Did she die right away?" I asked, almost not wanting to know the answer. But the idea of her suffering gnawed at me.

When Grant looked up, the softness was back in his eyes. "The ME will know more once he gets her back to his office. But his best guess is she expired quickly."

Expired. Like she was a piece of meat left on the counter too long. "Does he know when she…expired?" I asked.

"Liver temp indicates around midnight. But again—"

"He'll know more when he gets her back to his office," I finished for him,

Grant gave me a tight smile. "Right."

I pulled my jacket closer around me again, trying not to imagine Harper's perfect body on a cold slab in a morgue.

I must not have tried hard enough, as Grant's eyebrows drew down in concern again. "You should go home," he said. "I know where to find you if I have any more questions."

"You sure?" I asked, glancing back at the house. As much as I felt I should stay for Carrie, I knew there was nothing I could do to help the situation now. Besides, she had Bert. And Nolan. And whatever other friends had lingered at the party. It wasn't as if she was alone.

Grant nodded. "Definitely," he said, rising and helping me to my feet as well. "I'll have one of the officers drive you home."

I was about to protest that I could make it home on my own, but to be perfectly honest, in that moment I wasn't 100% sure I could. "Thanks," I said instead, accepting the quick squeeze he gave my hand before he turned and went back into Cop Mode.

* * *

The sun streamed in through the crack in my curtains, alerting me to the fact that the day had started without me. I yawned as I checked the time on my bedside clock. 8:30. That was an hour later than I'd intended to stay in bed. Then again, as fitful as my night had been, I wasn't surprised. I rubbed my eyes, trying to get the sleep out of them as I stumbled out of bed and into the bathroom.

One hot shower later, I was starting to feel human again, even if once fully awake my thoughts again wandered to the events of the previous night.

After one uniformed officer had driven me home, accompanied by another who'd delivered my Jeep to my doorstep as well, I'd gone to bed on autopilot, too exhausted to even think. But Harper had haunted my dreams, and I couldn't help wondering what she'd been doing at the horse corral in the first place.

Had she wanted to see Dante? Even, heaven forbid, gone into the corral with the intention of petting him? Riding him? Maybe she hadn't realized how wild he was. I mean, it had been painfully clear to me in the daylight, but with enough alcohol in her system, in the dark, and with a little over-confidence to go with it, maybe it had felt like a good idea to her at the time. Hadn't Carrie said Harper had been the one to recommend Tripp to her—maybe Harper had dealt with unruly horses in the past and thought she could handle this one?

I shook my head, thinking that whatever her reasons for being there had been, dying the way she had was awful.

I did a quick makeup routine. Then I decided I didn't have the energy to work my hair into something presentable and threw it up into a messy bun instead. I grabbed a pair of jeans and knee-high boots with a stud detail, topping the outfit off with a simple cream colored V-neck T-shirt. Satisfied that at least I could be seen in public, I made my way into the morning.

Oak Valley Vineyards consisted of just over ten acres of grapevines of several varieties, majestic oak trees, rolling hills, and the main winery buildings that jutted up against a small gravel parking lot at the end of our long tree-lined driveway. The cluster of low Spanish styled buildings had been built by generations of my family over the years, including our wine cellar, which had lovingly been nicknamed The Cave by my namesake, Grandma Emmeline. My two-bedroom cottage that sat at the back of the buildings, nestled among the oak trees, had been built by my grandfather years before. It held a lot of fond memories, upgraded plumbing and AC, and it was pretty close to my version of perfect, even if it was on the small side of "cozy" and the closets left much to be desired.

Striding along the stone pathway between the buildings, I enjoyed the crisp feel of the morning air before stepping into the main kitchen. While my cottage had its own small kitchen, I rarely used it for more than a coffeemaker. Why would I, when I had a well-appointed modern commercial one just steps away?

Especially when the bigger one was brimming with the scents of Conchita's concoctions. As was the case that day as I stepped inside, the mingling scents of cinnamon and vanilla hitting my nostrils.

"Good morning, Emmy," Conchita Villareal sang, stowing a container of orange juice in the side-by-side refrigerator.

"Is it?" I asked, heavy on the sarcasm.

But she just nodded, her salt and pepper hair bobbing up and down in its usual bun at the nape of her plump neck. Conchita's warm brown skin glowed with her efforts of looking after us all. Married to our vineyard manager, Hector, she was as much a part of Oak Valley Vineyards as the buildings themselves. Hector had been there longer than I had, and I'd been the flower girl at his wedding to Conchita. I considered them more family than staff.

"You look tired," Conchita said, eyes going to the bags under my eyes that my quick makeup job had apparently failed to cover.

"Thanks," I mumbled, still doing my sarcasm routine.

"Let me fix you something to eat, *mija*." Conchita fussed over me like a second mother. Not that I complained. I'd hoped to have my own mother fussing over me for many more years than I'd gotten, but life had intervened. So I welcomed what I could get.

"No thanks. I'll just have some coffee," I said. While the cinnamon and vanilla scents were both soothing and familiar, I wasn't sure my churning stomach could handle food yet. And there was that smidge-too-tight dress to take into consideration too.

She clucked her tongue but moved to the coffeepot as I pulled a mug from the overhead cupboard.

"Coffee will rot your stomach," she warned, pouring me a steaming mug of the liquid anyway.

"That's the least of my worries." I grimaced and reached into another cupboard for a painkiller, swallowing two of the over-the-counter tablets dry.

Conchita tutted once again, but knew she was wasting her breath lecturing me about it.

"How did the party go last night?" she asked instead. "I want all the details, especially those of Nolan Becker. Is he as handsome in real life?"

"Ava seems to think so." I sat on the nearest stool, making a mental note to call her later. I'd texted her the briefest of updates before falling into bed the night before, but I knew she'd want the in-person version soon.

"I don't suppose he took his shirt off during the party, huh? He had it off in a hot tub scene last week on the show. Whew!" Conchita fanned herself. "Sent me into hot flashes for the rest of the afternoon!"

I chuckled. "No, Nolan kept his clothes on. But, he was the least eventful part of the evening." I paused. "The night did not end well."

"Oh? What happened?" Apparently Conchita had not tuned in to the news that morning, because I was sure Harper's death was probably on every outlet in America by now.

By the time I had brought Conchita up to date with the events of the previous night, she was sitting opposite me, sipping from her own cup of coffee.

"Poor Harper," she said, shaking her head. "It's a reminder that life is too short to not enjoy what we love."

"Amen to that." I raised my mug and clinked it against hers. Then we sat in silence for a few minutes, each in our own thoughts. Mine wandered toward Harper, wondering if she'd lived her life to the fullest—enjoyed what she'd loved while she'd had the opportunity.

"Anyway," I said, rising and setting my empty coffee mug in the sink, "I wanted to duck over to Carrie's to check on her. Unless anything here needs my immediate attention?"

Conchita shook her head. "No, Jean Luc just stocked the tasting room, and Eddie has the day off." She gave me a knowing grin. "So everything should run smoothly here."

Jean Luc Gasteon was my sommelier—French, finicky, and as knowledgeable about wine as any man I'd ever met. I had no doubt he could run our tasting room blindfolded with one hand tied behind his back if he wanted to. Eddie Bliss, my winery manager, on the other hand, was the exact opposite—as inept as he was jovial and about as quick to catch on to the winemaking business as a sloth being chased by a snail. Eddie had come to me after a long career as a househusband to his partner, Curtis, and while he'd been completely unqualified for the job, he'd been the only person willing to do it for what I could afford to pay. Plus, the customers seemed to enjoy his friendly nature and snappy wardrobe enough that they were usually willing to overlook minor details like him pouring them the wrong wines.

Usually. Though, I had to admit, I'd worry less about my absence that morning without Eddie on the grounds.

"Would you mind finalizing the menu for the weekend brunch for me?" I asked her, already gathering my purse.

She nodded. "*Sí*. Of course. You go to your friend. Don't worry about us here."

I gave her a grateful smile before I headed back out to my Jeep.

* * *

The Sonoma Valley wasn't large, and it was mostly made up of wineries and weekend estates. Those who lived there full time either owned a winery, worked for a winery, or were part of one of the many businesses that relied on winery driven tourism. The valley's part-timers were often Silicon Valley millionaires—enjoying their vacation homes—and those who flocked to the many bed and breakfasts that their trade kept afloat.

The beauty of the valley was something that I would never tire of. The backdrop of mountains, contrasting against the soft rolling hills and patchwork of vineyards, soothed my nerves as I lowered my window to enjoy the warming spring air.

However, as I checked my reflection in the rearview mirror a few moments later, I quickly wound the window back up. The breeze seemed to be having a detrimental effect on my current hairstyle—which was much more "messy" than "bun" now.

Using one hand to steer and one hand to smooth my hair down, I slowed my Jeep and turned onto Carrie's street.

A bevy of vehicles was parked on both sides of the road, almost blocking the drive to the estate. Slowly moving past them, I noted the dozen or so men snapping their cameras in my direction. Only once they'd had a good look at me, however, they put their cameras away. I took a guess they were paparazzi, and as I was a non-celebrity, it seemed I was of no interest to them.

I gave them a finger wave regardless and made my way past them to where a uniformed officer was standing guard at the driveway entrance. I rolled down my window again and gave him my name, saying I was a friend of Carrie's. It took him a moment of chatting into his radio before I was apparently approved to enter.

As I continued up the paved driveway, I noted the front of the house held almost as many vehicles as the street had, though these were largely white sedans marked as belonging to the Sonoma County Sheriff. I did spot Grant's black SUV as well, and I pulled my Jeep to a stop behind it.

I'd only just gotten out of my car when the front door opened and Carrie came rushing out, grabbing me in a fierce hug.

"Oh Emmy! I'm so happy to see you."

She didn't look happy. In fact, she looked as if she'd been awake most of the night crying, her eyes red, puffy, and sans makeup.

"How are you?" I asked, even though it felt a ridiculous question under the circumstances.

"I don't even know," she answered, her voice cracking. "It's all been such a shock."

"How did you even know I was here?" I asked as I beeped my car locked.

"I've been watching the drive from upstairs. Can you believe how many reporters have gotten wind of Harper's death already? They've been camped out down there since four this morning." She gestured down the driveway, frowning.

"It seems like the police have them under control."

Carrie shrugged. "Physically maybe, but you should see what they've printed."

"That bad?" I asked, following her inside the house.

She nodded. "Some guy at the *Sonoma Index-Tribune* led with the headline 'Horse Hates on Harper.'"

I cringed. "Let me guess, Bradley Wu?" I'd had a few run-ins in the past with the syndicated food columnist turned Sonoma county gossip who had a flair for the dramatic and an affinity for alliteration.

"I don't know. I didn't pay attention. It's all just too much, you know?"

I put an arm around her shoulders. "I'm so sorry."

She patted my hand before leading the way into the kitchen. "They started knocking on the door before the sun was even up," she continued. "Only when Bert called the police did they move off the property for fear of being charged with trespassing. Not that it's stopped all of them." She sat heavily on a stool and rested her elbows on the marble counter, rubbing her face with her hands.

"Is there anything I can do?" I asked.

"What can any of us do now?" Tears brimmed behind her lashes before she dissolved into a sobbing mess, dropping her head into her hands.

I moved to her and pulled her close, hoping that at least the warmth of another human could fill some of the void she was feeling. Only when she had regained some control of her breathing did I release my hold.

"Can I get you some coffee?" I asked, knowing that a hot drink often helped.

She nodded. "Make it an Irish please."

I grinned. Now there was the woman I knew.

From spending the hours that I had the previous evening in her kitchen, I already knew my way around it. I quickly made two cups of coffee—one Irish Coffee laced with whiskey for her and one regular cup loaded with cream and sugar for me.

"I'd invite you to sit on the terrace," Carrie explained as I handed her drink to her, "but the view isn't up to par this morning. I have no idea what the police are doing down at the corral, but there's been someone here all night."

"They're probably still gathering evidence." This wasn't the first time I'd seen Grant in action, and I knew he was thorough.

"Evidence of what? I mean, it's clear what happened."

"What do *you* think happened?" I asked softly. I was curious about her assessment of her friend's mental state, but I didn't want to upset her further.

Carrie licked her lips. "Well, Harper must have wandered down there by mistake, right? I mean, maybe she didn't realize how wild Dante was. Or maybe she just walked into his pen by accident."

I nodded. I'd gone over those possibilities too.

"I just can't believe she's gone," Carrie said, her voice sounding small. "This time yesterday I was showing her the guest room. She was so full of life."

I had no words, so I just continued to hold her hand.

"Do you know what I'm most worried about now?" she finally said.

"What's that?"

"Dante. Animal Control removed him from the property, and I have no idea where they've have taken him or what they're going to do to him. I mean, they wouldn't..." She trailed off, licking her lips again. "Like, put him down or something, would they?"

I shrugged. Honestly, I had no idea.

"Dante didn't mean to hurt Harper," Carrie pressed. "He would have just been scared. This is a new home for him, and he didn't know any of us. For Harper to have wandered into his corral in the middle of the night, he would have been petrified. It wasn't his fault, and he doesn't deserve to die for acting on instinct."

I hurriedly grabbed a box of tissues from the corner of the room as Carrie once again threatened tears.

"Carrie, where's Bert?" I asked, hoping for some backup to comfort her.

She shrugged, sniffing into a tissue. "I think he and Nolan went down to the corral. He wanted to make sure that the police weren't damaging any property." She took a long sip of her coffee, which seemed to calm her—though whether it was the warmth or the alcohol, I wasn't sure. "Bert's taking all of this pretty hard," she told me.

"Oh?" I tried to keep my voice neutral even as my mind flipped back to seeing him slip upstairs with Harper at the party.

Carrie nodded. "He feels responsible. You know, it happening at our party and all."

"Were they close?" I asked in what I hoped was a casual voice. "Bert and Harper?"

Carrie shrugged. "I mean, they were friendly."

My suspicion was that they were *very* friendly, but now was not the time to lay that on my friend. "Did they spend a lot of time together?" I asked, trying to sound offhand about it. "I mean, just the two of them?"

A small frown marred Carrie's pretty face, but she just shrugged again. "Some. I mean, Bert said he was giving Harper some advice on some investments. But other than that, I don't think they had a lot in common. Except me."

"Did Bert give out advice to a lot of people...or just Harper?" I asked, feeling like I was treading in touchy territory.

"I-I'm not really sure. Bert's so good with money. I don't know what I would do without him. I mean, all those balance sheets and legal jargon could be Pig Latin for all I understand them." She paused. "But Harper seemed happy with what he was doing for her."

Hmmm. I'd bet she was. Bert was a good-looking guy. I could see lots of women being happy with what he could *do* for them.

I was about to ask more, when the man in question walked through the back door. He was dressed in a pair of casual jeans and a flannel shirt, but something about the attire felt as if he were playing the role of a rugged country man more than being one. His sandy hair was just a little too styled and his clean-shaven face a little too smooth. Though, as with Carrie, I could see the effects of a sleepless night in his eyes—puffy dark circles rimming them.

"It's crazy out there," Bert muttered. Then he paused, his gaze going to me. "Oh. Sorry. I didn't realize you weren't alone."

"I just wanted to stop by to check in on Carrie," I explained.

"Right." He gave me a dismissive nod before turning to his wife, pulling her in close for a hug and kissing the top of her head. "How are you, darling?"

"Much better after Emmy made me coffee."

She held up her cup, and Bert sniffed at it. "Scotch?"

"And plenty of it." Carrie lifted the cup in a salute.

"Sounds delightful. Uh, Emmy, you wouldn't mind making another, would you?"

I got the distinct feeling Bert saw me more as "the help" than the friend Carrie had introduced me as the previous night.

But instead of voicing those thoughts, I gave him a forced smile and the benefit of the doubt. A woman *had* died on his property the night before. A friend even. Grief didn't always allow the best version of ourselves to come forward.

"Happy to," I told him.

As I busied myself at the coffee machine, Bert sat at the island alongside Carrie.

"What are the police doing down there?" she asked him, her voice shaky, as if part of her didn't want to know.

"Last I saw, they were talking to Tripp."

"Tripp?" Carrie asked. "Why? Did he see something last night?"

"I don't know, babe," he told her on a sigh. "I think they're being thorough."

"Did they say anything about Dante?" she asked.

I glanced over my shoulder to catch Bert's response. Honestly, I was of the same mind as Carrie—I hated to see the creature put down over this. Sure, it was clear he was a dangerous wild animal. But it wasn't as if he'd gotten out and hurt someone. Harper had been in *his* pen.

"No," Bert answered. "Animal Control said they just had an order to secure the animal for now."

"Well, that's good," Carrie said, forced optimism in her voice. "I mean, maybe they just need to make sure he's okay, right?"

"I really don't know, sweetheart," Bert said again.

"Did you see how many reporters are out there now?" Carrie asked, changing the subject.

Bert nodded. "Vultures." He glanced my way. "How's the coffee coming?"

My forced smile was faltering. "Just about done," I managed, adding a generous helping of Scotch into his cup before I slid it toward him.

"It just doesn't seem real," Carrie said, shaking her head again. "I mean, what was Harper doing down there anyway?"

I'd been wondering the same thing. "Harper didn't say anything to either of you about going to see Dante last night, did she?"

Carrie shook her head. Bert did the same.

"And you didn't hear anything?" I asked.

Again Carrie shook in the negative.

"But we wouldn't have, then, would we?" Bert reasoned. "With the music and the party going."

Grant had said that Harper likely died around midnight—about an hour before I'd found her. I tried to think back to just how lively the party had still been at that time. "When did people start leaving the party?" I asked.

Carrie frowned. "Well, I guess it varied. I mean I think Eric, from the network, was the first to leave, right?" She turned to Bert for confirmation, who gave her a quick nod. "A few early birds trickled out after him. But I think it didn't really start to thin out until, maybe twelve-thirty or so?"

Bert nodded. "At least then." He paused, looking at me. "Why?"

I shrugged. "I guess I was just wondering if anyone might have seen Harper going outside."

"I didn't notice," Carrie admitted. "Then again, I was at the front door saying goodbye to a lot of people. And you"—she turned to Bert—"you were…"

"Around. Probably grabbing more wine." He gave her a wry smile.

Carrie shook her head. "Well, the police talked to everyone last night. I'm sure if someone saw something, they told that detective about it."

"I'm sure they did." Bert drained his cup and set it on the counter with a loud clink. "Well, if you ladies will excuse me, I have some transactions I need to attend to before the market opens in Tokyo."

"Of course," Carrie agreed, though the look in her eyes said she didn't relish the thought of being left alone.

Bert must have seen it too, as he added, "I'll be in the den if you need me."

She sent him a grateful smile, and he kissed her on the top of the head again before exiting the room.

Once he was gone, Carrie swished the dregs of her coffee in its cup, looking so sad and small that she kicked up maternal instincts in me that I didn't know I had.

"You sure you're going to be okay?" I asked.

She nodded into her cup. Then she sucked in a big fortifying breath of air before lifting her eyes to meet mine. "I have to go see Harper's family." She sent me a grimace. "Offering them my condolences is the least I can do."

"You sure you're up for that today?"

She shrugged. "Are any of us? I mean, her parents must be devastated."

"You said they lived in Napa?"

She nodded. "They have a place near the country club. I stayed there with Harper once when we did a wine tasting weekend." Her eyes took on a sad, faraway look as she relived the memory.

"I could go with you," I offered. While the last thing I wanted to do was face a grieving family I'd never met before, I couldn't stand how shattered Carrie looked. There was nothing any of us could do for Harper, but at least I could be there for my friend.

"Oh, would you?" she breathed.

I nodded. "I'd be happy to," I agreed, grabbing Bert's empty mug and placing it in the sink.

"I honestly don't even know them well," Carrie went on. "They were out of town when Harper and I were there last time, but I know their names are Alistair and Katherine, and Harper has an older sister who lives with them as well—"

Her thoughts were interrupted by a quick knock at the back door. It was followed a beat later by Detective Christopher Grant's frame appearing in the doorway.

Carrie tensed in her seat, both hands going around her mug in a subconscious embrace.

"'Morning," he said, nodding his head toward Carrie. His eyes flickered to me, but he didn't say anything.

"Uh, Emmy, this is Detective Grant," Carrie said, making unnecessary introductions.

"Emmy knows me," Grant said before I could answer.

"Oh. Right." If Carrie was surprised, she didn't indicate it. She probably thought all of us in Sonoma knew each other—after all, it was a considerably smaller town than Los Angeles.

"I don't mean to intrude, but I was hoping I could ask you a few questions," Grant said, directing the statement to Carrie.

She gripped her mug so tightly I feared it would shatter. "What kind of questions?"

He pulled the notepad from his back pocket, flipped to the relevant page, and looked up at Carrie. "I'd like to get a full list of everyone who was at the party last night. Including staff." His gaze momentarily flickered to mine.

"Uh…sure. I mean, I have the guest list somewhere, but there wasn't really any staff. I mean, Emmy and Ava were catering and serving. That's Ava Barnett."

Grant looked up, glancing my way again. "I know Ava too."

"Oh. Well, uh, we had a DJ. Up from LA. But that's it."

Grant noted that down. "DJ's name?"

"Um, Boomalot. DJ Boomalot."

Grant lifted one eyebrow at the comical name but didn't say anything. "And the guest list?"

"Right." Carrie slid off her stool and crossed to one of the large kitchen drawers. She withdrew a red leather day planner and placed it on the countertop, flipping the pages until she found what she was looking for. "It's all here detective. Everyone who RSVP'd is marked with a green highlighter."

Grant accepted the sheet of paper, his eyes skimming the list as he pulled out his phone and snapped a picture of it. "Can you tell me what time everyone left the party?"

"Emmy and I were just talking about that," she confessed. "I'm sorry…I'm not totally sure. I know Eric left first.

He's one of the producers of *Carefree Hearts*," Carrie explained. Then I listened to her rattle off a few more names of people she'd especially noticed leaving. Though, as she reiterated to Grant, she really didn't note the time of everyone's departure.

"What about Ms. Bishop?" Grant asked. "Did you see her leave?"

"Harper?" Carrie shook her head. "I told you yesterday I didn't even know she was gone until..." She trailed off, eyes going to me, and I could tell she was mentally reliving the scene—me in hysteria and her good friend dead.

"We're just being thorough," Grant told her. He paused, looking at his notes. "What about at the party? How did Ms. Bishop seem?"

Carrie frowned. "What do you mean?"

"What was her mood like? Was she upset about anything?"

"I-I don't think so." Carrie shot a gaze my way, as if looking for the right answer.

"Harper seemed to be enjoying herself," I filled in for her. "She had a few canapés and drank several glasses of wine."

"Did she argue with anyone?"

"W-what?" Carrie said. "No. I mean...no. Why would she?"

Instead of answering, Grant lobbed another question her way. "You mentioned Ms. Bishop had recently been fired, correct?"

"Did I?"

"Was she upset by that?" Grant asked.

Again Carrie turned to me. "I-I don't know. I mean, she said she was looking forward to a break. Didn't she say that, Emmy?"

I nodded. "She did. She seemed more amused than upset by it all, honestly." I paused. "Why?" I asked Grant, feeling there was something he was holding back.

His eyes flickered my way again, but he said nothing before turning back to Carrie again. "Did you notice anyone else missing from the party?"

"Missing?" Carrie asked.

"Around midnight. Anyone else unaccounted for?"

Carrie looked from me to Grant, again clearly not sure how to answer that question. "I don't know."

"It would be impossible to say where anyone was at any given time," I jumped in. "There were people coming in and out all night—on the patio, the lawn, at the fire pit." I paused. "Nobody you've talked to saw Harper?"

He shook his head. "It was dark though."

Especially at the back of the property, as I well knew. "This *was* an accident, wasn't it?" I hated to ask, but something felt intentional about Grant's line of questioning.

He pulled in a long breath, eyes going from me to Carrie, who still looked like a deer about to be shot down by whatever Grant said next. Finally, he answered. "We found scuff marks on the top rung of the corral's fence. They are consistent with premortem bruising found on the body."

"Meaning…" I'll admit, I felt like I was slow to catch on.

Grant turned his hazel flecks on me, something softening in their depths, if only for a moment. "Meaning, we have reason to believe Ms. Bishop did not enter the corral of her own accord."

I blinked at him, mental wheels turning. Harper hadn't walked into the corral by mistake. But the fence was higher than my waist. It wasn't as if you could trip and fall in over it. Possibly slip while climbing it, but bruising didn't feel like a slip. Bruising felt more like…

"I'm sorry, Ms. Cross," Grant said, addressing Carrie again. "But it appears as if this was not an accident. We believe Ms. Bishop was intentionally pushed into Dante's corral."

CHAPTER FOUR

———

I felt the words hit me like a punch. Carrie gasped beside me, likely experiencing much the same thing.

"Pushed?" she breathed out. "Who would do that?"

Grant glanced back down at his notebook before answering. "That's what I'm here to find out. I noticed a security camera near the front door. Do you have any at the back of the house?"

Carrie shook her head, though her features still looked as if she was in shock. "No. I mean, we're getting them. Bert's upgrading the whole system. Soon." She bit her lip. "Ohmigosh, is it my fault she's dead? Because we didn't have the new system up yet?"

"No, of course not," I assured her, crossing the room and putting an arm around her shoulders as she slumped over her empty coffee mug. I shot Grant a pleading look over her head.

He nodded and flipped his notebook closed. "I'll let you know if we have any more questions," he said, thankfully. "Is your husband around?"

"Bert's in the den," I answered for her, nodding my head to the right.

"Thanks." Grant gave me a quick smile before disappearing down the hall.

I thought about pouring Carrie more Irish coffee. But as soon as Grant left, she pulled it together and excused herself to go freshen up her makeup in order to face Harper's family. I'd kind of hoped she'd put that off in light of Grant's revelation. While the idea of someone pushing Harper into the wild animal's pen was horrific enough, as the implications of what Grant had said sunk in, I realized they were more chilling—one of Carrie's guests had intentionally killed Harper.

There had been a murderer at the party.

I tried not to think about that as I tidied up the kitchen with shaky hands.

Once Carrie was looking as fresh and presentable as possible under the circumstances, we jumped into my Jeep, and twenty minutes later we were pulling up to the address Carrie had fed my GPS for the Bishop estate in neighboring Napa county.

I slowed to a stop outside a pair of large wrought iron gates and rolled down my window to press a button on the intercom beside them. I gave Carrie's name to a woman with a Spanish accent, who admitted us, the gates slowly creaking open with an eerie whine in the still morning air. They just as slowly creaked shut behind us as I made my way down the meandering driveway toward the house.

Maybe *house* was an understatement. It was more like a French château planted in the middle of California, boasting manicured lawns, flaunting their lush greenery despite the ever-present threat of drought, blooming rose bushes, and carefully sculpted topiaries. I parked near a large stone fountain shooting water at least ten feet into the air, feeling distinctly out of place.

Carrie led the way to the front doors, where a woman in a crisp black and white uniform greeted us even before we'd had a chance to knock.

"It's a pleasure to see you again, Ms. Cross," the woman said in the same voice I'd chatted with over the intercom. "Please come in."

"Thank you, uh… I'm so sorry, I've forgotten your name," Carrie said.

"Sandra," the woman replied with a smile that said not many visitors to the faux château would have bothered to remember.

"Yes, of course. Sandra," Carrie repeated. "I had hoped to see Mr. and Mrs. Bishop to offer my condolences."

Sandra's pleasant smile immediately faded, a somber expression replacing it. "Yes. You were friends with Miss Harper."

Carrie nodded. "I was."

"I'm sorry," Sandra said, though who was consoling whom on their loss was a toss-up. "But I'm afraid Mr. and Mrs. Bishop are out of the country at present."

"Oh." Carrie's face showed a mixture of surprise and relief.

"But her sister is here. Mrs. Kellen. And her husband."

Carrie nodded and took in a steely breath. "Then I'd very much like to offer *them* my condolences, if I could."

"Of course." Sandra stepped back to allow us entry, closing the door quietly behind us as I stepped over the threshold. "Mrs. Kellen is in the great room. If you'd like to follow me."

We did, and by the time that we had made our way through the house, I'd almost given myself whiplash, my gaze going from one impressive item to another. Chandeliers, large oil paintings, marble floors, flocked wallpaper, and lots of antique furniture in impressively carved forms. While the style was a bit more old fashioned—and much more expensive—than my taste, the opulence was impressive. When Carrie had mentioned that Harper's family had been well off, she hadn't been kidding.

Sandra led us into the great room, which lived up to its name. The two-story high vaulted ceiling made the room feel vast, yet the wall of bookshelves filled with aged leather spines, coupled with the plush rugs, made the room feel cozy and inviting. Leather loungers filled the space, and impressionist paintings lined the rest of the walls.

"Mrs. Kellen?" Sandra said, addressing the sole occupant of the room. "Visitors to see you."

The woman dropped the newspaper she was reading and stood to greet us. She had the same high cheekbones that Harper had, as well as the same full lips, but that was where the similarities stopped. Kellen was shorter than her sister, and her figure was fuller. Her hair was the same chestnut color, though it too was shorter as well as wirier and shot with hints of gray. Overall, she felt like a faded version of her sister's beauty.

"Yes?" she asked us, eyes going from Carrie to me.

Carrie spoke first. "I don't know if you remember me, but I'm Carrie. Carrie Cross—Harper's friend?"

"Oh? Yes. Well, nice to see you again." Kellen blinked, as if she had no idea who the woman was.

"I'm so sorry for your loss," Carrie told her, and I could tell she was fighting back tears again.

But Kellen's expression was stoic. "Thank you." She nodded at Sandra, effectively dismissing her as the woman ducked her head and walked away. "Please sit." She directed Carrie to the settee beside her before her gaze fell to me.

"This is my friend Emmy Oak. You might know her," Carrie explained. "Well, at least know of her wines. She owns Oak Valley Vineyards."

Kellen's smile was tight. "Does she? Sorry. I suppose I'm not familiar."

Well, I wouldn't take that personally.

"Yes," Carrie went on. "Emmy was catering my party last night, where…" She trailed off. There really was no delicate way to say *where your sister was trampled to death.* Instead, Carrie clasped her hands in her lap awkwardly.

"You have a lovely home," I jumped in, trying to save Carrie as I took a seat in a stiff-backed chair opposite the pair.

Kellen turned her eyes my way, her smile slightly less strained at the compliment. "Thank you. It's been in our family for years. We take great pride in it."

"Hello, who is this?" a male voice called from the doorway. He was a few inches taller than Kellen, his frame filling out more like a football player's bulk than her stoutness. The gray at his temples was more pronounced than hers, but his eyes were rimmed in lines that crinkled with a welcoming smile in a way that felt a contrast to Kellen's cool demeanor.

"Friends of Harper's," Kellen supplied. "Come to pay their respects."

The smile died on his face at the mention of the dead woman. "That's very kind of you," he said in a somber voice.

"This is my husband," Kellen said, nodding toward the man. "Morgan Brice."

"Pleasure to meet you," he told us both.

"I can't imagine what you're going through," Carrie offered, turning her big brown eyes on Morgan. "I mean, I only worked with Harper, and I'm feeling such a void."

Recognition lit Morgan's face. "You're Carrie Cross, aren't you?" he questioned, his smile returning. "From *Carefree Hearts*. Stormy Winters, right?"

Carrie smiled back. "Yes, that's right. You're a soap fan?"

"I just catch the show every now and again," he confessed as he pulled another high-backed chair next to the settee and planted himself on it. "You know, to check in on Harper, so to speak."

Kellen made a sort of snorting sound but was ladylike enough to cover it quickly before turning to Carrie. "Was there something in particular we could do for you today, Carrie?" she asked, interest apparently already waning.

"I really just came to pass along my condolences." Carrie turned a sympathetic gaze Kellen's way. "And to see if there is anything I can do."

"Do?" Both of Kellen's dark eyebrow rose. "What could you possibly do?"

Carrie bit her lip. "Well, I'm sure you have a lot of announcements to make, and then there'll be the arrangements. Sandra mentioned that your parents are out of town. I can only imagine you must be feeling very overwhelmed."

"Hardly," Kellen replied, blinking her very well made up and very dry, I noticed, eyes at Carrie. "Lawyers, the staff—they'll see to everything. Sandra has arrangements well in hand, I'm sure."

I glanced to Morgan. At the talk of arrangements, his eyes had hit the floor, his hands fidgety.

"Well, if you need any help with anything, please let me know. Even if it's just fending off the press," Carrie insisted.

"Oh, yes. The press." Kellen rolled her eyes. "How vulgar they are. But then, that was Harper. Even in death, she has to drag the family through the mud."

I shifted in my seat, suddenly uncomfortable at her clear animosity toward the dead woman. Carrie frowned, seemingly mirroring my thoughts. "You must be dealing with so much," she offered.

Kellen shot her a look. "Bishops don't deal with things. We endure."

Carrie blinked, looking as unsure how to respond to that as I felt.

I cleared my throat. "Uh, were you and your sister close?"

Kellen turned her steely gaze on me. "No," she emphatically. "We were not."

Again tension hung in the room, neither Carrie nor I sure how to respond to it.

Morgan must have sensed our discomfort, as he spoke up. "Harper was something of the black sheep of the family," he said softly.

"That's putting it lightly," Kellen shot back. "She was a complete embarrassment. And before you think me calloused for saying so, Harper relished the fact, doing her best to get a rise out of all of us at all times."

"Kellen," Morgan said, averting his eyes. "She's dead."

"Oh, so we should paint her as a saint now, then?" Kellen scoffed.

"I'm sure it's all been something of a shock," Carrie said, finding her voice.

"Yes. Shock and sensationalism. What Harper did best," Kellen said.

Morgan turned his gaze away, fiddling with his wedding ring.

"It's been difficult for all of us," Carrie agreed. "I for one still can't believe that she's gone. I mean, the last time I saw her, she was so full of life, so full of promise, so full of—"

Kellen interrupted her with a bark of laughter. "Harper was certainly full of *it*, wasn't she?"

Carrie blinked at her in surprise. "That wasn't what I meant…"

"Look," Kellen said with a shake of her head. "The last time I saw Harper was at Christmas, when she came bustling through here with silly little Hollywood knickknacks for all of us like some cheap Santa Claus in a short skirt."

"Kellen," Morgan said again, his voice soft as he tried to silence her.

"Well, it's true. As if some souvenir store junk would change our parents' minds."

"Change their minds about what?" I asked, feeling like maybe there was a deeper reason for Kellen's animosity.

She turned her cold gaze on me. "The only thing that Mommy and Daddy wanted from Harper was for her to give up that ridiculous television show and start acting like an adult."

I saw Carrie frown beside me at the dig, her eyes going to the floor.

"They weren't fans?" I asked.

"No, they were most certainly not." Kellen released a deep-seated sigh. "Harper's head was always in the clouds instead of on the important things in life. When she packed up and moved to LA to pursue acting, of all things, Mommy and Daddy were mortified. As were we all."

"But she was very successful. *Carefree Hearts* is a big show," I pushed, feeling the need to defend Carrie, whose eyes were still on her shoes.

"Your definition of successful is obviously very different than ours. Last year Mommy raised over a million dollars for the children's hospital. Daddy started a foundation to help underprivileged children get a decent education, and I headed a program whereby we can get clean drinking water to villages in Africa. Do you really believe that what Harper was doing was worthy of using the Bishop name?"

Well...when she put it that way.

"Anyway, it's all beside the point now," Kellen said with a shake of her head. "Harper is gone, and I'm all Mommy and Daddy have left. Well, me and Morgan."

Morgan's gaze lifted from his clasped hands to meet his wife's, and there was something in his look that I couldn't quite read.

Carrie peeled her eyes from the floor even as her cheeks still held a pink tint. "Well, we'll leave you to grieve in private. But please do let me know if there's anything I can do."

"Yes," Kellen responded, her tone bored. "I'm sure you can see yourselves out," she said, before picking up her newspaper again.

* * *

I wasn't sure visiting with the Bishop-Brice family had done anything to calm Carrie's grief, but by the time I dropped her back off at her place, at least the CSI vans were gone and her eyes were dry. That was a step in the right direction. I left her at the front door with a hug and promise to call later, before pointing my Jeep back toward Oak Valley to get to work on those quarterlies before my accountant sent out a search team.

As my car bumped over the gravel and the winery came into view, I felt my shoulders relax, tension draining. Home had that effect on me. Every time the old winery buildings came into my view, contentment settled into my soul. I released a blissful sigh and pulled the car to a stop in the small parking lot.

While we weren't officially open for patrons until noon, as I walked through the main winery doors, I noticed two familiar faces at my tasting room bar already.

One, I was happy to see—Ava, looking fresh in an off the shoulder maxi dress that was just sheer enough to hint at her figure beneath it without giving away too much.

The other person, I had mixed feelings about—David Allen. He was tall, slim, and dressed in his usual uniform of worn jeans and a black T-shirt with the logo of some band I'd never heard of on it. His long dark hair hung in his eyes, a sardonic smile permanently fused on his face, and I knew the brooding bad boy vibe he was giving off was only half cultivated. David was a local artist, whose main occupations in life were card sharking the rich and clueless at the local golf club and living off a trust fund that kept him flush with marijuana and video games.

While David and I had very little in common, he had come to my rescue on a recent life and death occasion, which had prompted a tentative friendship between us. One he'd been exploiting lately, for the benefit of free wine whenever he could. Something he seemed to be doing now—a glass of red in one hand and the other slung not-so-casually on Ava's shoulder.

"Ems!" he called, spotting me first and removing his arm from around the back of Ava's chair, as if caught with his hand in the cookie jar.

Ava swiveled in her seat as I approach the pair. "Look who I found lurking around as I was pulling up," she said, shooting a glanced David's way.

"He does lurk, doesn't he?" I agreed, nodding toward David.

But he just grinned at my teasing. "I was worried about you, Ems. Heard all about your tragic catering gig in the *Sonoma Index-Tribune*."

I cringed. I had hoped the press would leave my name out of it, but the fact that David was here meant that clearly had not happened. "I'm fine," I said. Which was only partly true, but it was the short version.

"I never should have left you alone," Ava said, putting a hand over mine.

While I appreciated the gesture, I shook my head. "No, it's not your fault. There's no way you could have known what would happen. And nothing you could have done, anyway."

"Well, at least I could have been there!" she argued. "Tell me what happened."

While I was pretty sure Bradley Wu had done a bang-up job in his piece of summarizing, I gave them my version of the events of the previous night—including my visit to Carrie's house and Harper's family that morning.

When I was done, Ava gave my hand another fortifying squeeze of sympathy, and David was staring into his half-empty wineglass. "Sounds like the Bishops had some family friction," he said.

Which was saying a lot, coming from David. I'd first met him when his stepfather had been murdered in my wine cellar. No one put the fun in dysfunctional like David's family.

"Harper's sister wasn't exactly tearful," I confirmed.

"But people grieve in different ways," Ava added, always the optimist. "Maybe it just hasn't hit her yet."

"Maybe," I agreed. "But what really bothers me about it all is the idea that one of the guests at Carrie's party had to have killed Harper."

Ava's eyebrows drew together in a frown. "To think we might have served a killer."

"Not necessarily," David cut in, swirling his wine in his glass. "I mean, didn't you say that horse whisperer guy was at Carrie's house too?"

"Tripp," I supplied. "And, yes, he was. Carrie introduced me to him before the party started."

"*And,*" Ava added, "didn't she say it was Harper who recommended Tripp? Maybe they had a history."

I pictured the gruff cowboy and the high-maintenance actress I'd met at Carrie's party. I had a hard time seeing the two run in the same circles. "I don't know…" I hedged. "Plus, there's something else," I said, my mind going to the way Harper and Bert had snuck off together just moments before her death.

One of David's dark eyebrows rose into his hair, a wicked smile snaking across his features. "Oh, do tell."

I hesitated, suddenly feeling like a gossip. "Don't repeat this to Carrie," I warned. "But I saw Harper just before she died. With Bert. Alone."

"No!" Ava slapped the bar with both hands for emphasis.

"Wow. This is better than an actual episode of *Carefree Hearts*, huh, Ava?" David said, still grinning.

She ignored his ribbing, riveted to the new revelation. "What were they doing?"

"Well, nothing really," I admitted, relaying the scene I'd witnessed.

"So, you think Bert was giving Harper a little more than just financial advice?" David asked when I'd finished.

"Honestly? I don't know what to think," I told him. "But I'm torn about if I should tell Carrie. I mean, the last thing I want to do is upset her over nothing. Especially now."

"But if Bert *was* having an affair…" Ava said, giving me a pointed look.

I sighed. "Then Carrie deserves to know. I'd want to."

"Well, I know one person who might be able to give us some insight into what their relationship was like," Ava said.

David and I both turned questioning looks to her.

"Nolan Becker," she offered. "He and Carrie and Harper all worked together, and I know he was friends with Bert. I'm sure he spent tons of time with Bert and Harper together."

"I'd hate to bother him at a time like this," I said.

Ava bit her lip, her cheeks flushing. "Actually," she said, "I was on my way to see him now."

For the first time since I'd walked in the room, I saw David's sardonic smile falter. "Oh?" he asked. "Do we have a date?"

Ava's blush deepened. "Kind of." She turned to me. "He asked me to lunch last night as I was leaving the party. I was going to tell you about it but, well…everything kinda happened, and it didn't feel like the right time."

I waved her BFF sin off. "No worries. It's been a rough morning."

"Anyway," Ava said, clearing her throat, that confession clearly taking a weight off her shoulders. "I called Nolan to cancel, you know, in light of everything, but he said it would actually be good to take his mind off things for a bit."

"Take his mind off things? Is that a Hollywood euphemism?" David teased.

Ava ignored it, adding, "I could certainly ask Nolan what he thought of Harper and Bert's relationship."

"Well, I guess if you're seeing him anyway. And you know, if the conversation takes that sort of turn," I said, still not sure I wanted to come out and accuse Bert of anything, especially to someone close to the couple.

"You think he'd be honest about it?" David asked. "He is a professional liar, after all." He gave Ava a look that was hard to read, and I suddenly wondered if I detected a hint of jealousy.

"Why wouldn't he be?" Ava countered.

David shrugged. "Alright, then, why don't we make it a double date?" He turned to me. "What do you say, Ems? Care to be my lunch companion?"

I frowned. "Oh, I don't know. I don't want to impose…"

"No, actually it's a great idea," Ava said, nodding.

David shot me triumphant smile.

"It is?" I asked her. "You want us tagging along on your lunch date?"

"Honestly?" Ava said. "I could use a wingwoman. Nolan makes me kind of nervous."

"Really?" I'd never known Ava to be nervous around a man in her life. Usually she had them eating out of the palm of her hand. Case in point: David's little green monster peeking out from behind his shaggy hair.

"I know. I shouldn't be," Ava said. "But he's just a little intimidating. Did you see how blue his eyes are? And that smile? And that hair? And—"

"We get it. He's perfect." David rolled his eyes.

Ava stuck her tongue out at him.

"You know, I wouldn't have pegged a soap actor as your type, Ava," David said.

"Dr. Drake Dubois is every woman's type, David," Ava countered.

I thought I heard David snicker, but he quickly covered it, grabbing his jacket off the back of his chair. "Then it's settled," he said. "Lunch with the rich and handsome *doctor*. My treat. Shall we, Emmy, my dear?" He held out his crooked arm to take mine.

What could I say? I was outnumbered. Besides, I had a strict policy never to turn down a free lunch.

CHAPTER FIVE

———

Verdant was one of the more upmarket restaurants in downtown Sonoma. The décor was all very industrial chic, with its cement counters, vertical gardens, and iron lanterns, though the menu was filled with small plates, luscious sauces, and lots of exotic ingredients. I self-consciously smoothed down my hair, suddenly very aware I was in jeans and a T-shirt. Granted, I'd at least thought to put a light scarf overtop the tee before we left the winery, which livened it up a bit from couch surfer to casual diner, but as I took in the rest of the patrons, I still felt a bit unprepared. Especially since my "date" was in a shirt with a guy in dreadlocks touting *Ganja for All.*

Ava spotted Nolan already seated and waiting for her, and as she raised her hand in a wave, her bevy of silver bracelets tinkled with her movements. I grinned at her enthusiasm and followed her as she wound her way through the tables toward him.

"Ava, you look lovely," Nolan gushed, standing to kiss her on the cheek.

For the second time that day, I was surprised as Ava blushed.

"So do you," she replied, running her hand down his arm.

He nodded knowingly, then moved his gaze to David and me. I thought I glimpsed a flick of irritation behind his eyes, but he hurriedly blinked it away.

"Nolan, you remember Emmy, don't you?"

"Of course. The lady with the wines." He gave me a wink that had me wondering if I'd imagined that irritation.

"And this is David Allen," Ava said, finishing the introductions.

David slung an arm over my shoulder. "Emmy's date," he said, matching Nolan's wink.

Oh brother.

"I hope you don't mind that I invited them along to lunch?" Ava said, turning her eyes Nolan's way.

If he did, he covered it well, flashing her a genuine smile. "Not at all. The more the merrier, right?" He stood to shake hands with David.

"You look familiar," David told Nolan as he returned the man's greeting. "Are you from the area?"

"No," Nolan said, pulling out a chair for Ava. "But you've probably just seen my face on TV."

"Sorry. I'm not the soap fan that Ava is." David shrugged.

If Nolan was offended, he didn't show it, waving David's comment off. "It's true that most of my fans are women. Though, I'd doubt if they're all as lovely as our Ava."

Ava giggled. An actual giggle, like a tween pining after a boy band.

I tried to ignore it and moved to sit, but David made a big show of pulling my chair out for me and bowing toward it. "My lady."

My eyes twitched to roll, but I behaved. We were, after all, in a nice restaurant.

A server appeared and handed us all menus, which I perused as Nolan asked for Ava's input on local cuisines. I only half listened, realizing as I read the mouthwatering descriptions that I hadn't eaten yet that day. I debated whether to go for the King Salmon or the seared Wagyu—after all, David was paying.

"So, Nolan," I heard David pipe up beside me, interrupting my deliberations about where to spend his ill-gotten gains. "How long have you and Carrie been friends?"

Nolan set his menu down on the white oak tabletop in front of him and leaned the elbows of his linen dress shirt on it. "Oh, a few years now, I suppose. Ever since the network hired her on to the show."

"And Harper?" David asked, shooting me a sidelong glance.

At the mention of her name, Nolan's charming countenance faltered. "Harper actually came on a year before Carrie, so I guess it's been what…three or four years now we've all worked together."

"I'm so sorry for your loss," Ava said, putting a hand on Nolan's arm.

He sent her a sad smile. "Thank you. It's honestly hard to believe she's really gone."

"I can't imagine," I added. "You were close?"

"I suppose. I mean, we all spent time together. Shooting days are long."

"What about Bert?" David shot me that glance again.

"Bert?" Nolan asked, prying his eyes way from Ava (with difficulty) to give David his attention.

"Did he spend time with you all as well?" David clarified.

Nolan shrugged. "Sure. I mean, he's devoted to Carrie. The two seemed practically joined at the hip some days." He grinned, sending a meaningful look Ava's way.

I thought David was about to ask more, when the server appeared again to take our orders. Nolan went for the salmon, Ava the sea bass, and I ordered the Seared Wagyu Steak—mostly because it was the most expensive thing on the menu. David gave me a knowing grin, as if reading my mind, before ordering the same, along with a bottle of Cabernet Sauvignon for the table.

As the server left, Nolan turned his attention once again to Ava. "That's a very beautiful bangle you're wearing, Ava. Tell me, did you make it yourself?"

Her smile intensified to the point I nearly needed my sunglasses.

"Yes. I have my own store not far from here. I make most of the jewelry I sell, including all of these."

"I'd love to visit your shop sometime," he told her, his gaze intent on hers.

I thought I heard Ava sigh.

Oh geez.

I cleared my throat to remind them David and I were still there. "I hope you got away from the press okay?" I said. "I noticed a whole mess of them sitting outside Carrie's this morning."

Nolan's reluctance to pull his gaze back to me was evident. "Yes. They've dispersed a bit since then. But I managed to sneak away with a *no comment* and a quick escape, James Bond style." He chuckled, eyes back to Ava, who giggled encouragingly on cue.

"Carrie mentioned Bert had to threaten the press with trespassing charges to get them off the property," I noted.

Nolan shrugged. "I guess I'm used to it. You know, paparazzi just become part of the scenery if they follow you around enough." He flashed Ava a self-deprecating smile. "It's an actor's burden."

Ava gave him a sympathetic nod.

It was going to be hard not to gag on my Wagyu if these two didn't cut it out.

"Bert sounds very protective of Carrie," David said, sipping slowly from his wineglass. "Wouldn't you say, Nolan?"

Nolan pried his eyes from Ava's cleavage. "Hmm?"

"Bert and Carrie," David repeated. "You mentioned their relationship was very close."

Nolan cleared his throat. "Uh, yes. Very. I mean"—he turned to me—"you saw them at the party. Bert barely left Carrie's side."

I licked my lips, carefully taking the opening. "Except to talk to Harper."

"Harper?" Nolan frowned. "What do you mean?"

"Well." I did more lip licking, trying to come up with a way to word this that didn't outright accuse his friend of adultery. "I, uh, saw Bert and Harper chatting at the party. Alone. Away from the rest of the crowd."

I watched his reaction carefully. But if Nolan had any inkling about their relationship being anything but innocent, he didn't show it, just shrugging. "I think Bert was helping her with some investments."

"You think that's *all* he was helping her with?" David asked.

Nolan's eyes went to him, irritation clear now. "What are you trying to say?"

"Harper did seem awfully flirty," Ava added.

But Nolan just laughed. "Well, that was Harper. Look, Harper loved men. All of them. If she flirted a little with Bert, that was just her way." He paused, turning to me. "Carrie knows that. She knew Harper as well as anyone."

I bit my lip, not sure if I should mention said flirting had been done upstairs...near the bedrooms. And from the snippet of conversation I'd overheard, it hadn't sounded like any financial advice Gene Schultz had ever given me.

"Did Harper bring a date to the party?" David asked.

I frowned. I honestly hadn't thought to ask Carrie that. I turned to Nolan, letting him field this one.

"I don't think so," he answered. "None I was introduced to."

"Any idea if she was seeing anyone?" David pressed, again giving me the side-eye that said he was digging for dirt.

"Knowing Harper? Probably several someones." Nolan's smile faltered at the end of that sentence, his eyes going sad again. "Poor thing. All she ever wanted was to be loved."

I suddenly felt bad for interrogating him about his friends' lives when he'd just lost someone so close. Ava put her hand on his arm again, sending him a sympathetic smile.

Luckily, I was saved feeling much more guilt as our entrees arrived, and I dug into my free meal, courtesy of David, with gusto, savoring every expensive bite.

* * *

Once I had fully gorged myself on imported steak, David and I left to give the new couple some alone time, and I let David drive me home. Where I fully intended to get some work done.

We had a small party booked in our outdoor venue for the following week, and I had to finalize the menu so Conchita could start putting in the food orders. And I'd also promised Hector that I would walk the south fields with him that afternoon to take a look at a couple of dead vines that he thought might have been victims of a hungry deer. And, of course, there were the ever looming quarterly tax returns awaiting my attention.

However, as I entered the main building, the sound of Jean Luc's accent rising in both volume and agitation drew me away from my mental to-do list and toward the tasting room.

Only a couple of small tables held patrons, but being early, that was to be expected. My eyes scanned over them, homing in on the bar, where I spotted Carrie. Her face was in her hands, her shoulders bobbing up and down with sobs.

My sommelier, Jean Luc, stood beside her, his tall, thin frame stooped as he patted her back awkwardly with one hand.

As I entered, my eyes connected with Jean Luc's, and his gratitude at my arrival was evident in his smile. "Emmy!" he called. "Zo glad you are 'ere." His Hercule Poirot worthy mustache twitched above his mouth as his thick French accent greeted me. While Jean Luc had been living in the states for years, his French accent remained as thick as ever. Sometimes, I wondered if it was on purpose. Jean Luc's sense of French pride sometimes bordered on stereotypically comical. However, the weekend wine lovers seemed to eat it up, so I was hard pressed to complain.

"'Ze Mademoiselle Cross eez a bit upset," he explained unnecessarily, sidling away from her as I approached. Clearly handling that much female emotion was beyond his pay grade.

Though, truthfully, almost anything was beyond his pay grade.

Carrie looked up, her wet eyes turning toward me and away from my poor sommelier. "Oh, Emmy!" she cried, leaping up from her barstool.

"What happened?" I asked, catching her in a hug. "Are you okay?"

She pursed her lips together and shook her head, the tears streaking down her cheeks as clear evidence of her state. "I'm sorry, but I didn't know what else to do. I don't really know anyone else here."

"It's fine," I said, not sure exactly what she was talking about. "What happened?"

"It was awful. They took him, Emmy. They took Bert."

"Who took him?" I asked, trying to get her to calm down enough to give me a straight story.

Carrie took a deep breath in then let it out on shaky sigh. "The p-police," she stammered. "The police took Bert!"

CHAPTER SIX

———

Before I could even instruct him, Jean Luc had a glass of wine poured for Carrie, setting it on the bar in front of her stool before he faded away, likely in fear of more female emotions. I guided Carrie back to her seat and sat beside her, waiting until she'd gotten the hiccupping sobs under control before pressing for more details.

"What happened?" I asked her. "Did the police say where they were taking Bert?"

"Not really. Just to the station for questioning."

Well, questioning was better than being under arrest. "What sort of questions?"

She shook her head, sniffling into a cocktail napkin. "I don't know. I-I'm afraid they think Bert had something to do with Harper's death." She barely got out that last thought before another loud hiccup/sob thing came out. "How can they think that, Emmy?"

I had a guess, but I didn't think that was helpful right now. "What exactly did the police say?"

"They said they had some things they needed to clear up."

I bit the inside of my cheek. I had a few questions about Bert I'd like cleared up too, but I wondered if they were the same set as the police's.

"Well, maybe they just need him to answer a few questions about the party," I reasoned. "You know, who was there, what they were doing?"

"Maybe." She blew her nose and looked up at me. "But that detective seemed so forceful that Bert asked if he needed a lawyer."

I knew firsthand how Forceful Grant could make a person sweat. "What did Gran—uh, the detective say to that?"

"He said Bert was entitled to have representation present." Her eyes brimmed with fresh tears. "That sounds bad, doesn't it?"

Well, it didn't sound good. But instead of voicing that thought, I patted Carrie's hand. "Detective Grant is good at his job."

Carrie took a deep breath, then an equally deep drag from the glass of Chardonnay in front of her. "Do you know him well?" she finally asked.

"Well enough," I hedged. I wasn't sure how she'd take the news that I'd been to second base with the guy currently interrogating her husband.

"Well, can you talk to him?" she implored. "Tell him that there's no way Bert had anything to do with Harper's death?"

As much as I wanted to make Carrie feel better, that was a negative. For one, chances of Grant listening to my direction in his murder investigation were slim to nonexistent. And for another, I wasn't sure how convincing I could be that Bert was innocent when I wasn't entirely convinced myself.

"Carrie, did Grant say why he wanted to question Bert?"

She turned a blank look my way. "Well, about Harper's death."

"Right." I nodded. "But...why *Bert* specifically?"

Carrie took in another shaky breath before answering. "I don't know. I overheard him asking about the investments Bert had been helping Harper with. Like maybe something went wrong with one?" She turned a questioning look my way. "But that's not Bert's fault! I mean, he's usually amazing with money, but the markets turn, right?"

"Of course," I consoled her, doing more hand patting. "Had Bert been consulting with Harper a lot lately?"

Carrie reached the end of the cocktail napkin's usefulness and began digging in her purse for a tissue. "What do you mean?"

"Well, I mean, did Harper and Bert spend a lot of time together. Like...alone?"

Her head snapped up, her wet lashes blinking rapidly at me. "Emmy, what are you trying to say?"

Oh boy. Here went nothing… "I saw Harper and Bert together. At the party. Before she died."

"So?" Carrie finally pulled a tissue from her purse, blowing her nose loudly. "Everyone saw Harper and Bert at the party."

"I mean…they were alone. Upstairs." I didn't mention that Harper had seemed awful keen at the time to keep that info from Carrie.

Carrie paused, her tissue halfway to her nose again. For a moment, I thought she was going to come to the same conclusion I—and apparently Grant—had about Bert. But instead, she shook her head, as if shaking that unpleasant thought out of it. "Bert and Harper were friends." She paused. "Harper was friendly with all of us."

Some more than others. But I didn't press the issue. Clearly Carrie was under enough stress right now. Whether or not Bert and Harper had really been having an affair behind her back, it was over now.

"I'm sure Grant will get to the bottom of this," I told her. I just hoped for her sake that Bert wasn't there when he did.

Carrie nodded, though she looked about as unsure as I was. She twisted her tissue around her fingers, frowning as she stared at it. "There's something else," she said quietly. She took a deep breath again and lifted her eyes to meet mine. "Something I haven't told the police."

Now she had my full attention. "What is it?" I asked softly.

She pursed her lips together, as if trying to decide if she could trust me. "I saw something," she finally said.

"When?"

"At the party." She paused, and I could feel her still mentally deliberating. "I-I didn't want to say anything before. You know, when we thought it was just an accident. I mean, it would only have made Harper look bad, which isn't fair now that she's gone."

"Understandable," I said, hoping to calm her into getting to the point.

"But then when Detective Grant said it was intentional—I mean, that someone meant to hurt Harper. Well…" She trailed off, looking at her tissue, which was rapidly disintegrating as well now. "Well, I think maybe Harper was in trouble."

"What kind of trouble?"

Carrie shook her head. "I don't know. I only saw it for a second."

"Carrie, what did you see?" I asked her pointedly.

"Her phone," she finally confessed. "I didn't mean to! I mean, it wasn't like I was spying. I just…well, my agent was talking about this new streaming show that was casting, and I wanted to introduce Harper to him. You know, because she was out of work. I thought maybe he could get her an audition or something."

"And?"

"And when I tracked Harper down, she was out on the front porch getting some air, and she had her phone out. I accidentally saw part of a message on it before she noticed me."

"What did it say?"

Carrie licked her lips. "Blackmail."

I blinked at her, letting that punch line sink in. "Blackmail?" I asked. "Are you sure?"

She nodded. "I didn't really think anything of it at the time. I dunno. I guess it could have meant anything, right?" She shook her head. "But then when the police said her death wasn't an accident, well, I just sort of started thinking…maybe it does mean something."

I nodded. "Did the message say anything else?"

She shrugged. "I don't know. I only got a quick glimpse at it before Harper saw me and covered up her phone." She bit her lip. "That seems bad, right? I mean, like she was trying to hide it?"

I glanced at Carrie's glass of wine, thinking I could really use one of those right then. "Honestly? I don't know." I paused. "You think Harper was being blackmailed?"

But Carrie just shrugged again. "I don't know. She never said anything. But if she was in trouble…if someone *was* blackmailing her…maybe that person was the one who hurt her?"

That put a whole new spin on things. Mental images of Harper's friends who'd been at the party flickered through my brain, but none had seemed particularly hard up for cash. Not hard up enough to resort to extortion. Not that I'd quizzed everyone in attendance on their net worth, but nothing in Harper's actions had seemed even the least bit uncomfortable or nervous around anyone.

However, there had been one person at Carrie's house that day who, by self-admission, hadn't fit in with that crowd.

"Carrie, how well do you know Tripp Jones?" I asked, thinking back to the rough-around-the-edges cowboy who'd been with Dante that fateful afternoon.

"Tripp?" she asked, confusion on her face at my seeming change of subject. "Not that well, I guess. I mean, I only just met him a couple weeks ago. When we bought Dante."

"And you said Harper was the one who recommended him to you, right?"

She nodded.

"How well did *Harper* know him?"

Her eyelashes fluttered up and down as she blinked at me. "I-I don't know. She said she hired him. A few months ago. She said he was excellent with horses, but I didn't really ask beyond that." She paused. "Why? You don't think Tripp had anything to do with her death, do you?"

I didn't know what to think. Harper had died at the hands of the horse Tripp had been training. And she had known him prior to the party. If someone had been blackmailing Harper—and she'd refused to pay, possibly even threatened to expose the blackmailer publicly—maybe that someone had seen the drunk actress and the wild horse as an opportunity to get rid of a problem.

The only question was, whose problem had Harper been?

* * *

Thanks to the combination of tears and Chardonnay, I offered to drive Carrie home and get her car to her later. The sun was sitting low in the sky by the time I pulled up to Carrie's vacation retreat. The police cars were noticeably absent, and the paparazzi had trickled down to just two dented cars filled with diehards toting cell phones and paper cups of coffee. We drove past them, thankfully uneventfully, and I dropped Carrie at her front door, telling her to call me day or night if she needed a friend. I almost hesitated to leave her alone, until she reminded me that Nolan was still staying the weekend at their house. Satisfied she had someone to watch over her if need be, I gave her a hug and a promise to call tomorrow before trekking back down her driveway in the waning sunlight.

As much as I was still waffling on Bert's innocence—at least as far as his involvement with Harper was concerned—the idea that someone had been blackmailing the beautiful actress was an interesting development. Hadn't Harper's sister, Kellen, said something about Harper being all about sensationalism and scandal? Maybe she'd had something in particular in mind— some secret Harper was keeping that might have *really* dragged the family name through the mud. I tried to think of what it could be but came up blank. Honestly? There was little the Hollywood world didn't tolerate these days. I mean, stars often *faked* scandals just to keep themselves in the news.

Then again, maybe the blackmailer hadn't been threatening to go to the press with Harper's scandalous secret but to Mommy and Daddy. I could well see Harper paying to keep in the family's good graces—especially if there was a sizeable trust fund involved or inheritance in her future.

So who had known Harper's dirty little secrets?

While anyone in Harper's inner circle could have had the access to her personal life to dig up dirt, I kept going back to the fact that none of them seemed that hard up for money. Nolan's suave GQ look, Bert's investments, Carrie's growing portfolio yielding enough to purchase a vacation home—none felt desperate enough to stoop that low. My mind again honed in on the odd man out in the equation. Tripp Jones.

While I hadn't seen him at the party, he had been on the property that day. I wondered if he'd been there when Harper had died. Had he left when the party started, or had he, as Carrie had suggested, stuck around to entertain the guests with his real life cowboy routine? Maybe David was right—maybe Tripp and

Harper did have a past of some sort. Maybe just enough for Tripp to have stumbled onto something about Harper that she'd wanted to keep quiet.

On a whim, I pulled to the curb at the next light, grabbing my phone from my purse. I punched Tripp Jones's name into a search engine, and after a few quick clicks, came up with an address just outside of town, conveniently on the way to Oak Valley. It was located on Rosebay Meadows, which sounded like a nice place.

I keyed it into my GPS and pulled back into traffic.

Fifteen minutes later I turned onto the street in question…and realized the irony in the name. There were neither roses nor meadows on the dirt lane that wound into the hills above town. There was, however, dry grass, hard packed dirt, and a smattering of single wide trailers and rusted mobile homes—some looking inhabited and overflowing, and others long abandoned. I drove slowly, feeling more depressed with each inch of barren scenery, until my navigation system told me I'd reached my destination.

It was a small trailer, set back a few feet from the road. And it certainly wasn't one of those adorable tiny homes I'd seen on television. This was a clunker. I thought that once upon a time it may have been white with a brown stripe around its middle. However, now the white was more gray, the stripe was faded, and the tires weren't just flat—they were missing, leaving the bare hubs to be half buried in the dirt. At one point it looked like someone had tried to fancy the place up with a white picket fence surrounding the lot, but most of the slats were now gone or broken, the gate was hanging by a single hinge, and the grass had long given up on life. Not that I blamed it. I wouldn't want to live there either.

I parked on the dead grass to the right of the road and got out of my Jeep, locking the door behind me. Pushing my keys and phone into my pockets (because you just never knew when you'd need them in a hurry), I walked toward a pair of cement blocks masquerading as a step. I knocked on the screen door and jumped back as it rattled, groaned, and threatened to fall from its hinges.

Footsteps pounded within the trailer, causing the entire thing to tremble, and I feared the rust might win its battle and the whole thing could collapse before my eyes. Luckily, it was a tiny trailer, and it only took a couple of footsteps before the door opened, and a half-naked cowboy stood in front of me.

Tripp may not have been living on easy street, but his toned torso was a bright spot in the dreary scenery. I tried not to stare at his abs, but somehow my gaze couldn't help wandering toward his belt buckle riding so low on his hips I could almost see the top of his...

"Can I help you?" he demanded.

I snapped my eyes up to meet his. In my defense, if he didn't want people staring, he should probably put a shirt on before answering the door.

"Uh, yes. Yeah, I'm Emmy Oak. We, um, we met yesterday. At Carrie Cross's house."

His eyes narrowed, and if he recognized me, he didn't let on. "And?"

"And...I was wondering if I could ask you a couple of questions."

His dark eyes narrowed further, until they were mere slits beneath his cowboy hat. "What are you, a reporter? Cuz I seen enough of them already today."

He moved to close the door.

"Wait! Uh, no. I, uh, wanted to ask you about horses."

He paused. "Horses?"

"Uh, yeah. That's right. I am...thinking of buying one. And Carrie said you were the best trainer in the area." I could almost feel my nose growing with the lie, but it must have done the trick, as he opened the door wider again, leaning against the frame.

"What kinda horse you buyin'?" he asked.

"Uh, what kind would you suggest?"

He snorted. Clearly that was not the right answer. "Look, lady, I know all 'a Carrie's rich friends thought that a wild horse was a real novelty, but that animal deserves better than what she did to it."

"*She* did to it?" I asked.

His face puckered into a sneer. "Animal like that needs someone who knows how to handle it. Mrs. Cross didn't know its mane from its tail. And look what happened. Poor creature will probably be destroyed now."

"And a woman is dead," I reminded him.

His eyes went dark, something flitting across them before he ducked his head down from my view. "That too."

"Did you know her well?"

His head snapped back up. "Excuse me?"

"Harper Bishop. The woman Dante trampled to death." I almost felt bad for being so blunt, but I was fishing for any reaction to break through his hard exterior.

He worked his jaw back and forth a couple of times. Then he turned his head, spitting on the patch of weeds to my right before answering. "I knew her."

"Did you know her *well*?" I repeated.

"Well enough."

Well enough for what, was the question. I tried a different tactic. "Carrie said Harper recommended you to her. Did you train a horse for Harper too?"

He leaned back on his heels and hooked his thumbs into his belt loops, his gaze assessing. "Aren't you Carrie's cook or somethin'?" he asked. "You sure you can afford a horse?"

I cleared my throat, trying not to take offense to that. "I catered her event. I own a winery." I purposely left out the fact we were barely keeping our heads above water. "And ten acres of vineyards. I thought horseback riding might draw in some customers."

His eyes did the assessing thing again, scanning my jeans and T-shirt, and I made a mental note to dress it up tomorrow—clearly one never knew where the day would take her and how posh she might have to pretend to be.

I wasn't sure what kind of conclusion Tripp came to about my ability to afford a horse, but he turned and walked back inside the trailer. He could have just been tired of talking to me, but he left the door open, so I chose to take it as an invitation to follow him.

A decision I regretted the moment I stepped inside. The mobile home was as small and cramped as it had appeared on the outside. Possibly even more so, the feeling exacerbated by clutter littering every surface. Worn cowboy boots had been discarded by the door, shirts and jackets slung over the backs of the two wooden chairs propped up beside a scarred Formica table. The small kitchenette was filled with dirty dishes and a couple dumbbells on the floor that looked heavy enough to have been responsible for some of Tripp's impressive physique. Through a doorway, I could see an unmade bed and more piles of clothing, boots, and who-knew-what-else beside it. Faded floral bedsheets had been tacked over the windows as makeshift curtains, and the stench of stale cigarettes and unwashed gym clothes almost choked me.

Tripp slouched down into a chair, and I slowly lowered myself into the other. I heard the distinct crack of timber as my backside hit the seat, and I cringed, hoping it would hold me.

Tripp pulled a pack of cigarettes from his pocket, slipping an unlit one into his mouth, which bobbed up and down as he talked. "So," he said, crossing his long legs at the ankles in the space between us. "What kinda questions you want to ask me about horses?"

Considering I knew zilch about them, I started with the questions I really wanted answers to. "Did you train a horse for Harper?"

He snorted out a laugh. "You really got a thing for her, huh?"

"I want to make sure you have the right experience," I lied. "I'm checking your references."

I wasn't sure he totally bought that, but he nodded. "Alright. No, I didn't train a horse for Harper. I taught her to ride."

"A horse?"

He shot me a look. "No, a dinosaur."

I resisted the urge to roll my eyes. "When was this?"

He took the cigarette out of his mouth, rolling it over in his fingers as he answered. "I dunno. Maybe three or four months ago?"

"So she was just taking horseback riding lessons from you?"

"For a short time."

"Why only a short time?"

"That was all she needed."

"She was that good?"

Tripp barked out a sardonic laugh. "No, she was that *bad*."

"I'm not following," I told him, for once being honest.

He sniffed loudly, leaning his head back so far the cowboy hat shadowed his eyes. "Look, her character on that TV show she did was supposed to ride a horse in some scene. She didn't want to end up flat on her face, so she hired me to give her a couple lessons."

"Just a couple of lessons?" I clarified.

"Yep."

"Three months ago?"

"Yep."

"And you hadn't seen her since?"

"Nope."

He was a man of few words. None of which were proving particularly insightful into their relationship or whether or not Tripp had dirt on Harper.

"Did you get to know Harper well during the lessons?" I pressed.

"Well enough to know she didn't belong on a horse." He tipped the brim of the hat up and gave me a grin that held more taunting than humor.

"Harper must have been impressed with you if she recommended you to Carrie after just a couple of lessons."

He shrugged. "What can I say? I'm impressive."

"So you never trained a horse for Harper?"

"Didn't I say that?"

"But she recommended you train Dante."

"She did. She knew I'm good with animals."

Which was great, because he was terrible with humans. And while I felt like his answers had been truthful, I also felt there was something he was holding back.

"Do you think you could have tamed him? Dante?" I asked, honestly curious.

"No doubt in my mind," he said, not even hesitating. "They don't take kindly to being captured, but he'd 'a calmed down."

"Did you spend a lot of time with him?"

He shook his head. "Not nearly enough. Yesterday was the first full day I'd had with him."

"What time did you leave?"

His eyes twitched, a frown hitting his face before he could prevent it. "Why?"

I shrugged, aiming for nonchalant. "Just curious. You know, if you were there when it happened."

He leaned his head back again, scanning my face for anything I might give away. Being that I was a terrible liar, I feared that was a lot. I looked down at a nonexistent smudge on my shoe to avoid eye contact.

Which must have worked, because he finally answered, "Yeah. I was there. All the noise from the party had Dante agitated. Figured I should stay on a bit till he calmed."

I felt my heart speed up at the insinuation of his words. "Did you see Harper go into his pen, then?"

For the first time since he'd opened the door, I saw a flicker of actual emotion behind his hard façade. "No." He shook his head. "I, uh, I'd gone into the barn. Dante seemed like he was settling down, so I was putting away the tack and getting ready to leave."

My hope deflated. "So you didn't see what happened?"

He shook his head. "Poor thing." For a moment I thought he meant Harper, until he opened his mouth again. "I shoulda never left him alone. None of this is his fault, you know."

While that was debatable, I agreed that Dante wasn't entirely to blame. He'd been the murder weapon, but the intention to put Harper in his path had been purely on the part of a human.

"I don't suppose Harper ever mentioned any problems with anyone?" I asked, going for one final fishing expedition before I lost him.

But Tripp shook his head. "If she had 'em, she didn't confide in me. But I hardly measured up to her social status, then, did I?" He gave a condescending sneer. "Heck, she didn't even acknowledge I existed when I saw her and her sister downtown couple days ago."

My head snapped up. "What did you say?"

"I said, their kind just looks down their pretty little noses at hardworking folk like me."

I shook my head. "No, I mean about seeing Harper and her sister. You mean Kellen Bishop-Brice?"

He blinked at me, as if not understanding the question. "Well, I didn't ask her name, but Harper called her 'my sister.' And she looked like Harper, 'cept older and kinda shorter. And had a look on her face, like her stick was even farther up her backside, if you know what I mean."

I did. I knew exactly the look he was talking about, because I'd seen it just that morning. When Kellen had sworn the last time she'd seen her sister was months ago.

So why had she lied?

* * *

I left Tripp's trailer with more questions than answers, and I felt the weight of the emotional day catching up with me as I drove back down the dusty road to the main highway. Fatigue settled in as I watched the sun melting into the patchwork of vineyards along the hills, fantasies of a hot shower and a glass of wine running through my head as I approached our tree lined drive.

Oak Valley Vineyard had been in my family for generations. My great-grandparents had planted the first vine, and for years it had been a part of the flourishing Sonoma Valley. Then the corporate giants had moved onto the scene, and the little wineries like ours had to compete for retail space with the mass produced wines sold at bargain prices. My parents had tried to keep up in the digital age—first my father, until he'd died of a heart attack when I'd still been in my teens, then my mother, who'd bravely taken over the reins as I'd left in a rebellious blur of grief to go to culinary school. She'd done her very best to keep us afloat, but the changing times and the changes in her own mind had been more than she could push back against.

Early onset dementia, the doctors had told us. I'd dropped everything and moved back home, but my mother had insisted that I focus on the winery—not her. She'd gone into a home where, as she put it, she could enjoy her "forced retirement" without being a burden to anyone else. Of course a burden was the last thing I'd thought of her as, but my mother had a stubborn streak as deep as my own. She'd won that particular battle, and I'd vowed to do my best to keep Oak Valley going.

Along with Conchita, Hector, Jean Luc, and even Eddie, that was exactly what I was doing—my best to ensure the Oak Valley legacy didn't end with me. While I loved the land, the vines, and of course the wine, I couldn't profess to enjoy the business side of the equation or the stress that went along with it. Had I ever considered selling to one of those giants? Only in the depths of the night when no one could possibly hear my thoughts. Truthfully though, it would break me if it ever came to that.

I tried to block those dreary thoughts out as I made the last curve of our driveway, into the small gravel parking lot now bathed in the last lingering purple hues of daylight.

Only as I spotted another vehicle parked in the lot beneath a low hanging branch of an oak tree, my thoughts turned from dreary to downright anxious.

Detective Grant's black SUV.

CHAPTER SEVEN

———

I found Grant sitting at the counter island in the big kitchen, sipping a glass of Sauvignon Blanc with Conchita hovering around him like a mother hen. The scent of spicy tomatoes and roasted garlic mingled with warm fresh bread instantly made me feel at home. I discreetly swiped under my eyes for any rogue eyeliner that may have smudged throughout the afternoon and tried to smooth my hair in my reflection in the window before facing my visitor.

Tried being the key word. The spring breeze had not been kind to my now extremely messy bun. I finally gave up, and both Conchita and Grant looked up as I walked into the room and set my purse down on the counter.

"Emmy." Grant's eyes crinkled as he smiled at me, their soft hazel flecks twinkling despite a tiredness I saw in their depths and the thick five o'clock shadow dusting his jaw.

"Grant," I countered.

He was still wearing the same faded jeans and button-up shirt that he had been earlier that morning at Carrie's house, but now they looked a lot more rumpled, and I could tell his day had been at least as long as mine. Possibly longer, since his had included processing a crime scene.

"I wasn't expecting to see you here," I commented, trying not to get lost in his dark eyes.

"I was in the area. Thought I'd stop by and see how you were holding up."

While the words were comforting, I could hear the hard professional edge lingering in his voice and wondered if this was purely a social call.

"I'm fine," I told him. Which, with some time and distance since finding Harper, was mostly true.

He nodded.

"Emmy," interrupted Conchita, "I was just about to feed this wonderful man some Prawn, Garlic & Chili Linguini. Would you like some?"

She gestured to the stove, where I could smell it cooking, the steam highlighting the zesty aroma and causing my stomach to growl in response.

"I'd be a fool to say no," I told her.

"I didn't aim for a dinner invite," Grant explained. "Conchita insisted."

Mrs. Matchmaker sent me a wink behind his back. I had to admit, this was one time I didn't mind her meddling. There were worse ways to spend an evening than eating linguini and staring into Grant's eyes.

"She's convincing like that," I said, playfully winking back at her.

Grant smiled, and some of the edge eased out of his posture, allowing relaxation to settle into his shoulders.

As Conchita pulled a loaf of French bread from the oven, I grabbed a wineglass and filled it from the open bottle on the island.

"So, I heard you talked to Bert this afternoon?" I said, eyeing Grant.

He sipped his wine before answering. "I did."

"And I'm assuming the result of that conversation was not him in a cell?"

One corner of Grant's mouth tilted upward. "No, he's at home with his wife."

I could almost hear the "for now" at the end of that sentence. "So what did you ask Bert?"

"Questions." Grant gave me a sly smile.

I rolled my eyes in response.

"Here," Conchita said, setting a wooden cutting board holding the sliced loaf of bread and a mound of butter on the counter in front of us. "Eat while it's hot."

While I was itching to ask Grant more, I did not need to be told twice when it came to food.

"This smells amazing," Grant said, mirroring my thoughts. I watched him pick up a warm slice of bread and slather it with enough butter to make Paula Dean cringe.

I couldn't help the small grin that pulled at my mouth. I had to say, I liked a man with a healthy appetite. Though as I silently studied him, I noticed the dark circles shadowing his eyes that made me think maybe he hadn't just had a long day but a long previous night as well.

"How late were you at Carrie's last night?" I asked softly, feeling that weird maternal instinct kick in again.

"Late," he answered around a bite of fresh bread. "Or early this morning," he amended. "Depending on your point of view."

"I'm sorry." I put a hand on his arm, not hating the feel of the taut muscles beneath his shirtsleeve. "You look like you could use some sleep."

He let out a short laugh. "Words every man longs to hear from a pretty girl."

"I didn't mean it like that," I told him, pulling my hand back and reaching for a slice of bread to cover my grin at having just been called pretty by the hot guy. "I just meant that you should probably get some rest tonight."

He turned his dark eyes my way, the hazel flecks glinting mischievously at me. "That doesn't sound like any fun."

I felt heat immediately flood my body, overrunning my mind with fantasies and making my mouth go dumb.

Luckily, I was saved answering him as Conchita placed two large bowls filled with linguini on the counter in front of us.

"Aren't you joining us?" I asked her, regaining my voice.

"No, no. I ate earlier. Hector's waiting on me to watch *Jeopardy!*." She turned to Grant. "We always watch it together. It's kind of our thing,"

I smiled. I knew Conchita and Hector had several "things," and each one served to keep their spark alive.

Grant nodded, sipping from his glass again. "Well, we better not keep you then."

She shrugged. "Eh, serves him right to wait a little. I swear I caught him cheating at Final Jeopardy last night. He had his phone out. He said he was just checking the baseball scores, but I think he was googling the answer." She shook her head at the indecency of it, and I could see Grant stifling laughter.

"Anyway," she went on, untying her apron, "there's ice cream in the freezer once you're finished with this. It's your favorite, Emmy. Mint Chip."

"Thank you," I told her, feeling my night look up. Grant, linguini, and ice cream? Be still my beating heart.

We dug into our bowls of food as Conchita put on her jacket and grabbed her purse. Once she'd said her goodbyes and left us alone, the room felt smaller and a lot more intimate.

I cleared my throat, trying to ignore the feeling.

"So what *did* you question Bert about?" I asked him. "You had Carrie really worried, you know?"

He glanced up from his plate. "How is she?"

It warmed my heart that he cared. While I knew he was human beneath his badge, it wasn't often he allowed that part of himself to peek through. "She's okay," I reassured him. "Worried, but she'll be okay." I paused. "Unless you plan to arrest Bert?"

Grant shook his head. "You know I can't discuss an ongoing investigation."

I knew. I'd heard the line a million times from him.

But it didn't stop me from trying.

"So you do think he had something to do with Harper's death?" I asked, taking a bite of prawn.

He shot me a look. "I didn't say that."

"You told Carrie that her husband was entitled to representation. That doesn't sound like you guys were chatting about the weather," I pointed out.

He grinned, shaking his head at me. "You are relentless."

"Okay," I said, twirling pasta around my fork, "so just tell me this—what made you take Bert downtown today? I mean, did you find something, or did someone say something, or…" I trailed off, hoping he'd fill in the blank for me.

He shoved a bite of food into his mouth and left me hanging as he chewed thoroughly before giving me an answer. "Someone said something."

"Oh?" I prompted. "Go on."

He narrowed his eyes as he turned to look at me, seemingly debating how much to share. "We found a witness who contradicted Bert's original statement. So we called him in to clear it up."

I felt my eyebrows drawing down into a frown. "What kind of contradiction?"

But that was apparently as far as he as willing to go, as he shook his head. "Sorry, Emmy. I really can't discuss it."

A standard line that I totally ignored. "You're saying Bert lied? And it has to do with Harper?"

He sighed, taking a sip from his wineglass. "I'm not going to be able to just enjoy this meal, am I?"

"Nope." I shot him a grin. "You should know by now, Detective. Everything comes with a price. Even linguini and Sauvignon Blanc."

He chuckled. "Alright, fine." He set his wineglass down carefully on the counter. "Bert originally told us that the first time he saw Harper in Wine Country was when she arrived at his housewarming party. But a witness came forward who saw the two of them together the night before." He paused, eyes cutting meaningfully to me. "*Alone* together."

I grabbed my wineglass to cover any reaction I might have been having. While part of me wanted to tell Grant my suspicions about Bert and Harper and what I'd seen at the party, the image of Carrie bawling her eyes out in my tasting room that afternoon kept coming back to me. If she was that upset at Bert being brought in for questioning, how would she feel if he was arrested? And, worse yet, because I'd been the one to push Grant in his direction?

"Bert was giving Harper some financial advice," I said as I set my wineglass back down. "Maybe they were discussing that?"

"Maybe." Grant's face was all hard angles and assessing eyes that gave nothing away as to what he was thinking.

"Where were they seen together?"

"Tyler's Place. They had a back booth. The hostess said Bert specifically requested it for privacy."

Yeesh. That didn't look good.

"Maybe he just didn't want the paparazzi bothering them?"

"Sure." Grant chewed a bite of linguini. "Because we have a real paparazzi problem in Sonoma."

"Did anyone ever tell you that sarcasm is not attractive?"

He just chuckled again, the deep rumble causing parts of my body to go warm that had no right warming at the dinner table.

"Look, there are lots of reasons Bert and Harper might have been meeting secretly," I said, doing a bang-up job of playing devil's advocate. Though who I was trying to convince of Bert's innocence at this point—Grant or myself—I wasn't sure. "I mean, Carrie's birthday is coming up. Maybe they were planning a surprise party."

"Maybe." Grant stabbed a prawn with his fork.

"So, what did Bert say when you confronted him today?"

Grant gave me a sidelong glance. "What could he say? We have a witness."

"Right." I nodded. "But did he say why they were meeting?"

"Something about some investments."

"See!" I stabbed my fork in the air to make my point. "Bert *was* just giving Harper some financial advice."

Grant shot me a look that had me immediately second guessing my conclusion.

"He *was* investing money for her, right?" I asked.

Again I could feel him debate how much to share. But he must have realized I was going to pull it out of him sooner or later anyway, as he set his fork down on his plate and turned to face me. "We looked into Harper's finances."

"And?"

"And we haven't found any evidence of investments."

My heart sunk right down to my stomach, which knotted around the linguini. "You haven't?" Poor Carrie. This did not look good.

Grant shook his head. "We did, however, notice some discrepancies."

"Discrepancies? Like what?"

"We have a forensic accountant going over her things right now, but the pattern of deposits and withdrawals seem inconsistent with what we'd expect."

I narrowed my eyes, trying to read between the lines. "You mean, they're bigger than they should be?"

"We'll know more when the accountants are finished," he hedged, turning back to his plate and picking up his fork.

I watched him as I idly twirled pasta, my mind going to the word Carrie had seen on Harper's phone. *Blackmail.* If someone had been shaking Harper down for cash, that could explain the discrepancies in her accounts. Large withdrawals to pay the blackmailer, and possibly even large deposits as she shuffled money to different accounts in order to raise the funds.

"You guys have Harper's phone, right?" I asked in what I hoped was a nonchalant tone.

He nodded into his bowl of pasta. "We do. Tech guys are processing it now. Why?"

"No reason." I shrugged, keeping my eyes on my plate to avoid giving away any sign I was holding something back. "Just, you know, thinking it might give you some insight into Harper's life."

"People's phones usually do." He paused. "Anything specific you think we'll find?"

"Nope," I lied, quickly picking up the bottle of wine as a diversion. I moved to fill his glass, but he stopped me with a hand over the rim before I could pour.

"Uh, I'm good," he said. "Thanks. Gotta drive home."

"You could always sleep here." The words were out of my mouth before my brain had a chance to tell my lips what a horrible idea they were. I cringed, wishing I could magically pull them back out of the air before he heard them.

Instead, they hung there—with me feeling like I'd just invited the wolf into the sheep's den for a snuggle, and Grant's dark eyes going all warm and dangerous, like he might enjoy playing the wolf for an evening.

Before I knew what was happening, Grant stood, taking the bottle from me and placing it back on the counter. Then his hand reached out, and our fingers intertwined, his thumb gently tracing circles on my skin.

My mouth went dry as he leaned in closer, his lips hovering just above mine. The musky scent of his aftershave was subtle and spicy, making my thoughts go fuzzy and my hormones rise to the surface to take over. I heard his breathing quicken, his gaze dropping to my mouth. Seconds later, his lips followed, skimming mine so softly that I let out a small sigh. At least I think that sound was me. I was having a hard time focusing my thoughts, all of my body putting its attention on the very hot, very enticing man currently nibbling on my lower lip.

I only got to revel in the sensation a moment though, as a chirp from his phone broke the silence, the sound jarring and intrusive.

Grant pulled away, and no one could judge me for whimpering just a little.

He retrieved his phone from his pocket, scrolling through a message.

"Work?" My voice was husky, and I barely trusted myself to talk.

He nodded. "They've moved Harper's autopsy up to first thing tomorrow morning."

The dark rings under his eyes looked even darker as he checked his watch, and I knew that no matter how much I wanted the evening to end differently, he needed to get some sleep.

And if he stayed here, sleep was the last thing we'd be doing.

"But I have ice cream?" I offered lamely.

He looked up and smiled. "Tempting."

"Rain check?" I asked, hating the hint of desperation my hormones were adding to my voice.

He nodded. "Definitely. Tell you what? Tomorrow night, I'll cook."

"Is that a threat or a promise?" I asked with a laugh. While Grant had many skills, culinary prowess was not at the top of that list.

He joined in my laughter, tucking his phone back into his pocket. "Okay, I'll bring the groceries, and you can play chef and be spared the wrath of my cooking."

"Now *that* is an offer I can't refuse."

* * *

Morning came much too quickly, and while my clock said it was time to rise, my body fought the notion with a vengeance. I'd never been much of an early bird—keeping more of chef's hours, working late and sleeping in—but running a winery had put those habits to rest, forcing me up at dawn most days. It was something I'd become used to, even if I'd never be a chipper morning person, but after the emotional roller coaster the last two days had been, it was taking all the effort I had to force my eyes open.

As a consideration to my protesting body, I decided to get the day started from bed, grabbing my phone from my bedside table and opening my email app. I allowed the incoming new mail to load as I propped myself up on my pillows. I scrolled through messages asking me if certain parts of my anatomy needed enlarging, wondering if I wanted to play roulette, and telling me that I'd inherited $900 million from a Nigerian uncle I'd never met. All I had to do to collect it was to give them my passport and bank account details. If only life were that easy.

Sending all the ticked emails to my trash folder left me with four that needed my attention. I was tempted to send the email from my accountant, Gene Schultz, to trash as well, pretending I had never seen it, but I knew it would come back to bite me in the long run. Instead, I hurriedly sent him a response saying I was working on my quarterlies. Which wasn't a lie. I had been working on them. For the entire quarter. I just still didn't have enough money to pay them.

Emails read, I finally dragged myself out of bed and into the shower. As I let the hot water rush over me, my mind wandered to the events of the previous day. While Carrie's revelation that Harper might have been being blackmailed was a big one, it was Bert lying about meeting Harper in a "private" booth at Tyler's Place that weighed on me. Carrie had poo-pooed the idea of an affair when I'd brought it up to her, but how would she feel if faced with real evidence? Not, I supposed, that a meeting with Harper in a public place was clear evidence she'd been sleeping with Carrie's husband. But if it had been all in innocence, why would Bert lie about it?

And what about the investments he'd supposedly been making for her? If Grant hadn't found any evidence of them, did that mean the story had just been a cover? A reason to spend time with Harper that he'd manufactured for Carrie's sake?

I shut off the water, toweling myself dry as I thought of how devastated Carrie was over the death of her friend—a friend so close that she'd called her a sister. How devastated would she be to find out that her *sister* had been seeing her husband behind her back? As much as I knew Carrie didn't deserve that, she also deserved the truth.

And I was suddenly determined to get that for her.

Remembering my mental note from the day before to dress it up a bit, I grabbed some flat-front white capris, pairing them today with a flowy pale blue blouse and silver teardrop earrings that had been a gift from Ava. I slipped on a pair of low heeled sandals and did a quick makeup routine before deeming myself ready to be seen in public.

I stopped in at the kitchen just long enough to grab a chocolate chip muffin and a cup of coffee to go, then hopped into my Jeep and pointed it toward Carrie's place.

Despite the fact that it was still early, the commuter traffic slowed me some, and it was a good twenty minutes later before I reached Carrie's driveway. No police officer was on guard today and no paparazzi in attendance. Apparently the dead soap star was old news already. I thanked goodness for small favors as I pulled up the drive and wound toward the house.

It felt more quiet than on my previous visits as I parked near the front door—no CSI, no Dante, and no sign of life other than the nature around me as I got out of the car. A black Jaguar was parked in the drive, a fine sheen of morning dew still covering it. Despite the call of the birds, the rustle of leaves, and the distant sound of Barkley doing what dogs did best, the surroundings felt eerily still. It was almost as if the air itself knew a tragedy had occurred here and was being still in deference to the dead.

I locked the car behind me and crossed to the large double doors, giving a sharp rap as I realized I should have called ahead. Not everyone was forced to be the early riser I was.

Luckily, I only had to wait a beat before footsteps pounded against the marble floors on the other side, and the door opened to reveal the man of the house.

"Oh! Good morning, Emmy." Bert had a gym bag in his hand and a look of surprise on his face.

"'Morning, Bert," I replied. "You look like I've just caught you going out."

"You did. I'm on my way to the club. The Links. I'm meeting Nolan there for a round of golf this morning." His white polo shirt and pressed slacks would fit in well at the exclusive golf club.

"I see," I responded. If Bert was grieving Harper's death, it didn't show. Apparently, the golf game must go on.

"I'm sorry—did Carrie know you were coming?" he asked, half turning back toward the house. "Because she's not here."

"She's not?" I asked, suddenly curious where she might have gone at barely nine in the morning.

"No, she went to see someone about Harper's memorial."

"Kellen?"

Bert squinted as if trying to remember. "No, I think she mentioned a Sally or Sandy or something like that."

"Sandra," I supplied, remembering the name of the Bishops' housekeeper. "Harper's sister did say she was making the arrangements."

"Yes, well, anyway. Carrie said she felt she had to be a part of it." He shook his head, as if not understanding why.

"Maybe it will be cathartic for her. To help lay Harper to rest," I offered.

"Hmm. Yes." He glanced at his watch.

"But, I, uh, actually didn't come to see Carrie," I told him, feeling his impatience. "I came to see you."

"Me?" Bert's eyebrows lifted in surprise.

"Yes. I was hoping you could clear up a couple of things for me. About the party."

He frowned. "I don't know what I could possibly clear up about the catering... Carrie didn't forget to pay you, did she?"

"No, nothing like that," I assured him. "I just wanted to talk to you about Harper."

He sighed loudly, as if that was the last thing he wanted to discuss with anyone. "Look, if you want to know about Harper, ask Carrie. She knew her best." He stepped out onto the front porch, pulling the door closed behind him as a signal he was done chatting.

"But you knew Harper well, too, didn't you?" I asked as he turned his back to me to lock up the house.

"I suppose," he mumbled, not meeting my eyes as he shoved the key into his pocket and motioned to leave.

"I mean, the two of you met each other often, didn't you?" I pressed. "Without Carrie?"

Bert paused, his gaze slowly lifting to meet mine. "What are you getting at, Emmy?"

I had a feeling he knew exactly what I was getting at. But I took a deep breath and went all in. "I know about you and Harper, Bert," I said, a lot more boldly than I felt.

His expression remained a perfectly neutral poker face. The man didn't even blink. "And exactly what is it that you think you know?"

"I know you were seeing her. Behind Carrie's back."

Anger flashed behind his eyes, so briefly I almost thought I imagined it. "That's ridiculous." He gave a laugh that was more scoff than humor.

"I don't think it is," I said, pushing with bravado I didn't feel. "You did see Harper at Tyler's Place the night before the party, right?"

"How did you find..." Bert sucked in a breath, his nostrils flaring with the effort. "Yes, I had a meal with Harper. So what?"

"Did Carrie know about it?"

"No." His tone was clipped, and the anger was definitely not imagined now. His eyes were intent on me, his hand clenching and unclenching around the gym bag's handle.

"So you *were* seeing Harper behind Carrie's back," I reiterated.

"Look, this is silly. I met Harper for dinner. That's it. It was perfectly innocent."

"Then why hide it from your wife?"

"I didn't hide it. I just… Carrie had a lot going on that day. Planning the party and everything. I…it just slipped my mind to mention it."

An excuse flimsier than tissue paper.

"And did it slip your mind when the police first questioned you too?"

His eyes narrowed. "I don't know what you're trying to do here, Emmy, but I'm late for tee off. Nolan is waiting for me."

"Come on, Bert," I said, trying for a softer tone to inspire his confidence. "I *saw* you with Harper."

He frowned. "At the restaurant?"

I shook my head. "No, here. At the party. I saw you and Harper going upstairs…" I let the sentence trail off, leaving the exact scene I'd witnessed to replay in his mind.

No attempt at poker face could conceal the emotion rising in him then. His jaw tensed, his eyes narrowed, and his breath came harder, so loudly I could hear it in the small space between us. "You were *spying* on us?"

"I *happened* to walk by," I corrected. "And don't turn this around on me. You and Harper were sneaking upstairs together while Carrie entertained your guests."

He shook his head. "It's not what you think."

"I know what I saw, Bert," I told him.

"It's not like that!" he said, his voice rising to a shout.

"What is it then?"

His eyes flashed with rage, and he took a menacing step toward me, shoving one long finger in my face. "It's none of your business, *caterer*."

I swallowed hard, suddenly realizing just how many pounds Bert had on me—all of them gym-honed muscle. Carrie wasn't home. Nolan was miles away. No police officers lingering on premises. We were alone here.

Quite possibly at the site where he'd killed the last woman who'd crossed him.

Sudden fear pounded in my ears as I watched Bert's face contort with anger.

But as he took another step forward, instead of coming at me, he moved around me, stalking purposefully to his car.

I took a slow, shallow breath to calm my nerves as I watched him beep the flashy Jaguar open, throw his duffel bag into the back with a force I wasn't sure it deserved, and slip into the driver's seat, slamming the door after him. Then he peeled out of the driveway so quickly that his back tires squealed against the pavement in protest.

Well, that went well.

I took a couple more deep breaths, watching the dust settle back on the drive as Bert's taillights disappeared, before I approached my Jeep again. I'd mostly gotten my shaking hands under control as I beeped the doors open. I was about to get in and follow Bert's hasty retreat.

But then I caught the scent of something on the light morning breeze. I paused, hand on my door handle.

Smoke.

While it was still chilly enough that someone in the area might have stoked up their fireplace to have a cozy morning by the hearth, we'd had enough wildfires in California in recent years that the scent immediately inspired concern. Along with a need to find the source. I shut my driver's side door and beeped the car locked again, doing a quick visual scan of Carrie's house. No sign of smoke coming from the two chimneys I could see. Luckily, none billowing from any windows or doors either.

I circled around the back of the house, coming close to the stables, now empty, with Dante still in Animal Control's custody. While there was plenty of dry grass and hay that would go up like tinder, thankfully nothing looked to be ablaze there either.

But the scent was getting stronger.

I continued around the back of the property to the far side of the home and felt relief flood my stomach as I finally spied the source of the smoke—Carrie's stylish fire pit. Orange flames rose from the center of the massive pit, surrounded by a sturdy stone rim that would keep the blaze contained to an ambient warmth and not a hazard to the landscape. Though, while I was relieved to see it was man-made and contained, I glanced around for who might have set it. Carrie was at the

Bishops', and Nolan and Bert were golfing—and while Bert had been in an emotional state as he'd peeled out of there, I doubted he would have been irresponsible enough to have left this burning.

I was about to approach and see what I could use to douse the flames, when someone beat me to the spot.

I watched a figure approach the stone surround, and immediately recognized his tight fitting jeans, cowboy hat, and worn boots. Tripp Jones. I felt a frown form between my eyebrows, wondering what he was doing there. With Dante in custody, there was little call for a horse whisperer on the property at present.

Tripp picked up a log from a pile near the pit and tossed it onto the fire. While my instinct had been to douse it, clearly he was interested in keeping it going. I wondered if he'd been the one to start it while I'd been arguing with Bert. I was about to approach him and let him know no one else was at home to keep the fire contained, when I saw Tripp throw something else into the pit.

A black plastic bag.

I watched the orange and gold flames crawl across it, growing in strength momentarily before they devoured the bag from view.

I felt my breath come hard, a million possible scenarios for why Tripp might be on Carrie's property throwing things into her fire pit racing through my head until one practically jumped to the forefront.

Was Tripp Jones destroying evidence?

CHAPTER EIGHT

As much as I itched to see what was in the bag before the fire turned it to ashes, I kept my distance, ducking back behind the side of the building to stay out of view. I didn't know what Tripp was doing, but with the way he kept glancing up nervously and shifting from foot to foot, I got the feeling it was something he didn't want anyone else to know about. And I wasn't sure what he'd do if someone—say, a nosey blonde winery owner, for example—did know. I'd already had enough of facing off with intimidating men for one morning. So I stayed put, keeping out of sight.

The flames and the smoke made it difficult to see anything burning beneath the rim of the stones, but Tripp stoked the fire with a metal rod, eyeing whatever it was he'd tossed into the pit as the flames continued to burn. Finally, seemingly satisfied the fire was doing its job, he threw the metal rod onto the ground beside one of Carrie's Adirondack chairs and grabbed the large metal cover for the pit, placing it atop the stones. Then he turned on his bootheels, making his way toward a blue pickup truck parked a few feet away.

I heard the engine turn over and saw dust kick up beneath his moving tires, waiting just until he'd cleared the ridge back down to the main road, before I bolted from my hidden position and dashed across the lawn to the fire pit.

I grabbed the metal cover, throwing it off the fire and to the ground. While Tripp had made sure his plastic bag had caught, I could still make out the bundle nestled beside wood logs at the bottom of the pit. I picked up the metal rod from the ground, digging in the fire until I pulled Tripp's bundle to the side—away from the flames. The acrid scent of burning plastic mixed with the smoke stung my eyes as I lifted the remnants out of the pit and threw them to the ground beside me. I stomped on them to put out the red embers, and I realized it was clothing. Or, what had been clothing.

I crouched down to get a better look, seeing I had what seemed to be half of a silky jacket and the skirt of a sparkly little red dress. Both were singed at the edges and matted with burned plastic in places, but the outlines were unmistakable. And they hardly looked like Tripp's style. For one thing, as I checked the blackened tag of the jacket, I could still make out it was as size 2. Even if Tripp had been inclined to dress in more feminine styles from time to time, there was no way his broad chest would fit a petite 2.

I flipped the tag over, seeing the label bore the mark of a trendy boutique in Napa that Ava and I had window-shopped at a couple of times. Only window-shopped because neither of us could actually afford the clothing there. Whoever had owned this shirt had us both beat in the fashionista department.

My mind immediately went to Harper.

I fingered the fabric of the garment, still warm beneath my touch. If I had to guess, it was silk charmeuse. Not exactly cheap. And not something I'd be throwing away—let along burning to a crisp.

So why was Tripp destroying it?

While my initial thought had been that Tripp was destroying evidence, even if these had belonged to Harper, what were they evidence of? Harper had been found dead in the same clothes that she'd had on at the party…if there had been any evidence of her killer on them, they were in police custody, now being processed. Burning the rest of her wardrobe would do nothing to negate that. Maybe the clothes had something to do with the blackmail…but what, I couldn't imagine.

I was still trying to figure out what Tripp's game was when my cell buzzed from my purse. I pulled it out, looking down at the readout, but it was a number I didn't recognize. I swiped to take the call.

"Hello?" I asked, putting the receiver to my ear as I replaced the cover of the pit with my other hand.

"Uh, hi," came a male voice. "Um, I'm looking for Emmy Oak?"

"This is she," I answered, trying to place the caller.

"Oh. Well, I hope you don't mind me calling you. I found your number on your website."

"Not at all," I said, hoping I was talking to a potential customer. "May I ask who is calling?"

"Oh. Right. Sorry. Uh, this is Morgan Brice. Harper Bishop's brother-in-law."

I cocked an eyebrow at the phone. "I remember you," I said.

"I hope I haven't interrupted anything," he fussed.

"No. No, I was just..." Spying on a murder suspect? Interrogating an adulterer? Sticking my nose all sorts of places I was sure Grant would say it didn't belong? "...heading to my car," I finished lamely as I dropped the singed garments and did just that, walking back across the lawn toward the house. "Was there something I could do for you?"

He cleared his throat. "Uh, yes. Well, I mean...your friend Carrie was just here."

"Is she alright?" I asked, concern jumping to the forefront of my thoughts.

"Oh, yes. Yes, she's fine. She wanted to help with the memorial arrangements. Very kind of her, really."

"That's Carrie," I told him.

"Yes, well, she did mention that the police had been asking her and her husband lots of questions lately. That they're investigating Harper's death as a murder, not an accident?"

"They are," I confirmed.

"I-it's hard to believe."

"Morgan, was there something I could help you with?" I asked, getting the impression he was dancing around something. He'd gone through some trouble to get my number, and I had a feeling it wasn't just to make small talk.

He cleared his throat again. "Uh, yes. Actually. Look, I...if the police are involved, I thought it best to set the record straight about something. I mean, I wouldn't want anyone to get the wrong impression. You know, about...anything."

"I see," I said, not really seeing at all.

"I was going to talk to Carrie," he continued, "but…well, she's obviously very upset right now. I know actors are emotional creatures, and I'd hate to cause her any more undue stress. But I remembered you'd come with her yesterday, and you seemed close to her, and I thought, well, maybe I could talk to you and *you* could set the record straight for me. So to speak."

The more he talked, the more confused I was about what he wanted to talk about. "What is it you wanted to set the record straight about?"

"Uh…" He paused, and I could hear sounds like a phone being shuffled from ear to ear. "Would it be possible to discuss this in person?"

"Does this have to do with Harper?" I asked, thinking of the shreds of designer clothing in Carrie's fire pit.

"I-uh, would really much rather meet in person. I can meet you in Sonoma."

"Do you know the Half Calf on Main?" I asked.

"I can find it."

"I'll meet you there in half an hour."

* * *

The Half Calf was a small mom-and-pop coffeehouse in downtown Sonoma, whose humorous logo featured a baby cow enjoying a latte while lounging on a crescent moon. It had become a favorite haunt of Ava's and mine not only because it was located next door to her jewelry boutique, but also because they served the best caramel flan lattes on the planet.

Late morning was busy, and there was a nice line forming as I pushed through the glass front doors to the tune of a jingling bell. I took a spot in line behind a half dozen other caffeine starved patrons, watching the barista quickly take orders, hearing the sound of a coffee machine grinding beans, and inhaling the heavenly aroma a moment later. God bless the first man who had found coffee beans growing in his garden and decided to smash them and blend with hot milk. I owed him a debt of gratitude even larger than my tax bill.

The line moved quickly, and it was only a few minutes later that I'd given my order to the barista behind the counter and had a steaming caramel flan latte and a slice of fresh Blueberry Lemon Bread with Lemon Icing sitting in front of me.

I took them both to a table near the back of the restaurant, where I could see the front door and watch for signs of Morgan Brice. As I nibbled, sipped, and waited, I shot a quick text off to Ava, filling her in on my morning thus far.

She responded with a lot of *ohmigosh*es (at Bert's anger), a surprised emoji (at Tripp burning what appeared to be Harper's clothes), and *a stop by with deets after* (at my impending meeting with Morgan). I was sending off a promise to do just that, when the bell over the front door jingled again, and I glanced up to spot Morgan Brice entering the coffeehouse.

He was wearing dark slacks and a sport coat that felt almost too heavy for spring, and his brows were drawn together in an expression of concern. His eyes darted around the room, and it wasn't until they found me that the frown ironed out some. He skipped the coffee line, quickly navigating the sea of tables to reach me.

"Thanks for meeting me," he said by way of greeting as he approached my table.

"Of course," I told him, watching him pull out a chair to sit opposite me.

"I, uh, just wanted to set the record straight," he said, laying his hands on the table and clasping them together in a possibly subconscious pleading motion.

"So you said." About a hundred times. I was beginning to think maybe it was a rehearsed line. "Did you want something to drink?" I asked, gesturing to the counter.

But Morgan shook his head. "No, no. I'm fine. I...just wanted to talk." His eyes darted to the side, as if making sure none of the other patrons were listening in to his enthralling conversation. Clearly he was nervous.

"Are you okay?" I asked, trying my best comforting voice to put him at ease. "Are you and the family holding up alright?"

"Fine." He looked down at his hands. "I mean, we'll be fine. Eventually. It's been...difficult, to say the least."

"I'm so sorry. How's Kellen?"

He fidgeted with his wedding ring. "I know Kellen probably didn't seem very sympathetic to you."

That was an understatement.

"But the thing about Kellen," he went on, "is that she's a strong woman. She feels emotion deeply, but she's never been one to show much. It's the way she was brought up."

I nodded, thinking her parents sounded like an interesting pair, what with the "way she was brought up" and the disdain for Harper's acting career that would make many other parents proud. "Are they coming home for the memorial?"

"Yes. They should arrive in the next few days."

A sadness settled in my stomach. I had yet to think about children of my own, but I could imagine the pain losing one would cause.

"I'm so sorry, Morgan. Really, if there is anything I can do, please don't hesitate to reach out."

"Thank you." Morgan gave me a small smile, and I could see genuine tears misting his eyes. While Kellen might have been raised to keep emotion at bay, I could see Morgan was clearly grieving.

"Were you close with Harper?" I asked.

He sucked in a long breath. "I was. Once upon a time. Actually, it was through Harper that I met Kellen."

"Oh?" I asked.

He nodded and looked distantly over my shoulder, his eyes drifting into a memory. "Harper and I were actually high school sweethearts, if you can believe it." He gave me a rueful smile. "How I got that lucky back then, I'll never know."

"But you ended up marrying Kellen?"

He nodded again, this time his eyes going back down to his hands, his finger twisting his gold wedding band. "Those two sisters…always so competitive. I'll bet you thought Kellen was the older one, right?"

I'll admit, I had. "She's not?"

He shook his head. "No. Two years younger. Harper just had this glow about her—this natural beauty that was almost unreal."

One could argue that Harper's beauty wasn't *all* natural—her lips had undergone some clear enhancing, and her double Ds had been man made. But I didn't interrupt.

"She had a grace about her," he went on. "Almost ethereal. Like she was too beautiful to last here on earth." His voice trailed off, again stuck in another time, and I wondered if maybe Morgan hadn't still had some feelings for his sister-in-law. I didn't get a chance to ask more, though, as he cleared his throat. "Poor Kellen. I think maybe she's always struggled to get out of Harper's shadow."

"Sibling rivalry can be hard," I noted. Not that I had any firsthand knowledge of that.

"It can," he agreed. "But I have to take some of the blame for the animosity between Harper and Kellen. At least, after Harper left for LA."

"How so?" I asked, sipping my latte.

"Harper always dreamed big. And if I'm being honest, she liked to shock and bait her parents. I think it was a game for her—the more Kellen strove for their approval, the more Harper tried to get their attention by doing just the opposite. Anything for shock value. Getting a tattoo, drinking, running off to Hollywood. That last one probably hit them the hardest. Shattered their dreams of their daughter devoting herself to philanthropy and bridge." He did that rueful grin, and again I had a feeling maybe Morgan hadn't been raised with the same silver spoon in his mouth that the Bishop sisters had.

"And that's when you started seeing Kellen," I guessed. "After Harper moved to LA?"

He nodded. "I didn't take her leaving me well. As you can imagine any young man would not. Kellen was…comforting."

That was the last thing I could imagine Kellen Bishop-Brice being, but I stayed silent as he continued.

"Anyway, Kellen and I were married soon after that."

"And have you lived in the family home ever since?" I asked, thinking nothing put a strain on a marriage like living under the in-laws' thumbs.

But if Morgan minded, he didn't show it. "The Bishops are very generous. They support Kellen's work. She's on the board of several charities in the area."

"Yes, she mentioned that," I mused, reading between the lines of what he was saying: apparently Mommy and Daddy funded the Bishop-Brice's way of life. I didn't imagine being on a board of a charity paid more than warm fuzzy feelings, and I noticed Morgan had yet to mention any sort of job he held. I wondered if he'd settled for the second sister less out of love and more out of the type of comfort her parents' money could provide him.

"The Bishops seem to be quite well off," I said, watching his reaction.

He nodded. "Oh, they are. But like I said, they've been very generous to Kellen and me. And of course, one day it will all go to their daughters." He paused. "Or I guess, just Kellen now."

I felt my eyebrows rise at that admission. While Kellen had clearly not been her sister's biggest fan, the end of her sibling rivalry had apparently just doubled Kellen's inheritance. And with the amount of money it appeared the Bishops had, I could only imagine how many zeroes that added. Women had killed for a lot less.

My thoughts must have been plain on my face, as Morgan quickly backtracked. "I mean not to make it out as if Kellen is just waiting around for an inheritance." He gave a strained laugh. "Not at all. She dotes on her parents. Adores them."

"I'm sure she does," I reassured him. Though, I was beginning to wonder just how deep her animosity toward her sister was. "Did Harper visit the family often?" I asked, trying to steer the conversation back around to what I assumed was his reason for meeting me here.

"Hmm? Oh, well, some. But no, not often. After Kellen and I married…well, let's just say, holiday dinners were a bit awkward. Harper would do everything in her power to make Kellen feel like she was a second choice. Which was not the case," he defended hotly.

Maybe a little too hotly. Doth he protest too much? But I stayed silent as he went on.

"I halfway think Harper was doing it to punish me as much as her family. I don't think Harper ever forgave me for marrying Kellen." His breath was long and deep.

"Morgan, what was it you wanted to clear up?" I asked.

He leaned across the table, lowering his voice to barely a whisper. "Look, if the police are asking questions, I know this will come out. And I don't want it to look like we're hiding anything. We're not. I mean, Kellen's not. I'm sure she just misspoke. Like I said, she feels things quite deeply."

"What did she misspeak about?" I asked.

"Well, I know she told you she hadn't seen Harper since Christmas."

I nodded. "But that isn't true, is it?" I said, remembering how Tripp had told me he'd seen the two sisters together.

Morgan blinked at me, surprise clear on his face that I'd somehow seen through her lie. "No. I mean, not really. We did see her at Christmas—that much was true. But…well, I believe Kellen also saw Harper more recently."

"How recently?"

Morgan did more lip licking. "The day before she died."

My feelings on that coincidental timing must have shown on my face, as Morgan plowed on. "You see why I wanted to make sure that we cleared this up? I mean, I'm sure Kellen just forgot about it in her grief. It does funny things to people, you know. But…well, it could look bad. If anyone thought she was being purposely deceitful. Which she was not."

I wasn't quite as certain about that as he was, but I nodded anyway. "Did you see Harper as well?"

He shook his head. "No. In fact, Kellen didn't even mention it to me. Not really. I, uh, overheard her talking on the phone. To Harper. She was arranging to meet with her."

"And I'm assuming they did follow through with that plan to meet?"

He nodded. "Kellen left the house shortly afterward. I imagined it was to see Harper."

"But she didn't discuss it with you?"

Morgan's eyes darted from side to side again, as if he expected his wife to pop up and accuse him of ratting her out at any minute. "No. No, she, uh, didn't talk about it. But I could tell something had upset her. As soon as she came home, she poured herself a double martini. At *three* in the afternoon." He shot me a look like we all knew what that meant.

"Any idea what could have upset her so much?" I asked.

But again he shook his head. "No, but like I said they had quite a—"

"Sibling rivalry," I finished for him.

He gave me a shaky smile. "Uh, yes. Exactly."

Sibling rivalry was one thing…but I could imagine what a lifetime in Harper's beautiful shadow could do to a woman. That, added to feeling like second best even to her husband, an upsetting private visit the day before Harper's death, *and* half of a sizeable inheritance at stake? Suddenly I could see several reasons Kellen might have for making sure that Carrie's housewarming party was her sister's last.

CHAPTER NINE

———

Having unburdened his conscience, Morgan quickly left the Half Calf, and we parted ways—him to drive back to Napa and me to hop back in line to grab a latte for Ava before making good on my promise of deets.

"Good morning," I called as I entered Silver Girl a few minutes later, setting a steaming paper cup on a glass counter holding several of Ava's handmade creations on sparkling display.

Ava appeared from the back a moment later, a smile hitting her face when she caught sight of me. One that grew as her eyes landed on the paper cup.

"You're a gem. I overslept and haven't had the time to get a coffee yet," Ava said, gratefully grabbing the offering. "I was seriously about to die of caffeine deprivation." The bangles on Ava's arm jingled as she lifted the drink to her lips.

Today she was wearing a teal blouse in a soft billowing fabric that on some might look bulky, but on Ava it somehow just accentuated her slim build. She'd paired it with skinny jeans, bringing the bohemian fabric into the modern era, and an eclectic mix of silver jewelry that instead of looking mismatched felt like a collection that had comfortably come together over time.

"It's not like you to oversleep," I said, leaning on the counter to get a closer look at a new pair of earrings in the case. Hoops with silver and gold intertwined in a basket-weave pattern, which would look awesome with my go-to little black dress.

"I know. I blame it on the delicious dreams I was having all night."

I raised an eyebrow her way. "Oh? They wouldn't happen to have starred one tall, dark, and handsome soap star, would they?"

She nodded, then scrunched up her nose. "It's bad, isn't it? I'm, like, crushing in the worst way."

I couldn't help returning her smile. "I take it you two had a good time at lunch yesterday after David and I left?"

"Ohmigosh, Emmy, we talked forever. Did you know he's a Virgo? And he's buying a beach house in Malibu? And he wants a puppy?" She did a squeal at the end of the last thought, the idea of cute puppies on beaches too much for her to contain.

"You're right. This is bad," I teased.

She swatted me playfully on the arm, though I was quick enough to duck away from the brunt of it.

"Anyway, he asked me out again tonight," she added.

"That sounds serious."

Ava gave a blissful sigh, her hip resting against the cabinet as she sipped her coffee. "We're going to Silvio's."

"That sounds *very* serious." Silvio's had a waiting list six weeks long and prices high enough that I'd have been paying off the meal for another six. I had to admit at being a little impressed with Nolan's game.

"So," Ava went on, visibly shaking herself back to reality. "How was your chat with Morgan Brice?"

"Interesting," I told her. I quickly filled her in on everything he'd told me, as well as my visit to Tripp's trailer the day before, my confrontation with Bert that morning, and the clothes I'd seen Tripp disposing of afterward.

When I finished, Ava's forehead was puckered in thought. "So Kellen lied about having seen her sister?"

"Looks that way," I agreed.

"And you think maybe she killed her for the other half of the inheritance?"

I shrugged. "Or maybe she'd just had enough of living in Harper's shadow and feeling like her husband's second choice."

Ava nodded. "I can see how that would wear on someone." She paused. "But how does the blackmail fit into that?"

I shook my head. "I have no idea. I don't know, maybe Kellen didn't want whatever Harper was being blackmailed about to get out? She did mention Harper always being an embarrassment to the family."

"But Kellen wasn't at the party," Ava pointed out.

"Napa's only twenty minutes away. It's possible Harper mentioned the party when she saw her sister the day before and Kellen figured it would be a great place to get rid of her problem."

Ava shrugged. "Maybe. But, honestly? Tripp burning those clothes has guilty written all over it. I could totally see him having something on Harper and shaking her down for money over it."

"She refused, and he killed her?" While it was possible, it didn't seem like the smart move on his part. I mean, he didn't have much chance of getting money out of a dead woman.

"Maybe," Ava said. "Or maybe they fought and he lost his temper. Or maybe this wasn't the first time he'd asked her for money—maybe Tripp had been blackmailing her for a while, and she finally got sick of it and refused."

That scenario I could see happening. "So what do you think he was blackmailing her over?" I asked.

"Maybe Tripp found out that Harper was sleeping with Bert?"

I nodded, thinking that, too, felt likely. Bert and Harper had been indiscreet enough that I'd caught them together. So had the hostesses from Tyler's Place. It was possible Tripp had seen something as well, especially if Bert and Harper had been seeing each other for a while.

"Maybe," Ava went on, "Tripp sees something that hints at an affair or Harper lets something slip while he's giving her horseback riding lessons. Then, when Carrie calls him to come train Dante, he realizes he could make some money off of this knowledge. He blackmails Harper, saying he'll tell Carrie everything if she doesn't pay up. Maybe she does the first time. Maybe Tripp gets greedy and comes back for more. Either way, something goes wrong at the party, and he shoves her into Dante's corral, knowing full well the animal will do his dirty work for him."

I did an internal shudder, picturing Harper after the effects of said dirty work. "Okay, I can see it going down that way," I agreed. "But then what was Tripp doing with Harper's clothes?"

Ava pondered that for a beat, sipping at her drink before she answered. "Maybe the clothes were some sort of evidence of the affair that Tripp was using as leverage?" she suggested. "Like…maybe he found them in a compromising place. Or maybe there was even some biological evidence of the affair on them. You know, Monica Lewinsky style."

"Eww," I said, really not wanting to picture that.

Ava shrugged. "I guess you'd have to ask Tripp to know for sure."

"Yeah, he didn't seem like the real forthcoming type," I told her.

She sipped again, and I could see her mental wheels turning "You said you were at his place yesterday, right?"

I nodded. "A trailer a few miles north of town."

"I don't suppose you happened to see anything there that pointed to him blackmailing Harper?"

"Like what?" I asked. "A shoebox labeled *blackmail proceeds*?"

"Ha. Ha. Very funny." Ava shook her head at me. "But if he was extorting money from Harper, there has to be some trail. I mean, you said there was a message. What if we could find a record of it?"

"Grant said the police have Harper's phone," I pointed out. "If Tripp sent the message, they'll know about it."

"*If* he sent it from his phone," Ava countered.

"Where else would he send it from?"

"Well, if I were going to do something illegal, I'd buy a burner phone. One of those cheap disposable ones. Wouldn't you?"

"Right." She had a good point. "They would be untraceable."

"Unlesssssss," she said, drawing the word out, "someone was to find that burner phone in Tripp's possession."

I frowned. "I have a bad feeling which *someone* you might be referring to."

Ava shot me a look. "You know that the more time that goes by, the more opportunity Tripp has to dump it."

"Maybe he already has," I pointed out. "He did get rid of Harper's clothes."

"But maybe he *hasn't*," she argued. "And maybe this is *someone's* only opportunity to find it."

I sighed, hating that she was right. Even if Grant had a whiff of the blackmail already, by the time he could get a warrant for Tripp's trailer, it could be too late. "Fine," I said. "Let's go talk to Tripp."

Ava's eyes shone with a dangerous Charlie's Angels light. Like she was picturing the two of us as crime fighting PIs with feathered bangs and bell-bottoms.

"But," I said, hoping to bring her back down to reality a little, "we're just going to talk."

Some of the light dimmed. "Sure. Okay. Just talk."

Why did I have the feeling those were famous last words?

* * *

"The name Rosebay Meadows held such promise," Ava commented as I slowly wound my Jeep up the dirt road toward Tripp's place. "I see neither roses nor meadows."

"I think I saw a lovely rusted toilet in that last yard," I said as I moved the car farther up the road. I pulled to a stop outside Tripp's sagging picket fence, and we both stared at his not-so-mobile home.

"Geez, I guess horse whispering doesn't pay," Ava commented.

"Or maybe he's not as good as he says he is."

"It does look like the home of someone desperate for a little cash though," Ava pointed out, ever the optimist.

We got out of my Jeep, and I beeped it locked before following Ava to the trailer, carefully avoiding a broken beer bottle and a pile of cigarette butts on the hard cracked dirt. She rapped her knuckles on the metal door, and we listened to it echo on the other side, though I didn't hear any answering footsteps.

"Maybe he's not home?" I suggested.

"You said you saw him leave Bert and Carrie's this morning?" Ava asked, glancing around the side of the trailer.

I nodded. "Early. Like, around nine."

"What was he driving?"

"Blue pickup. Why?"

Ava took a few steps to our left. "I don't see one parked anywhere."

"You're right." I followed her, walking around the side of the trailer to peek behind it. More dirt, more weeds, more dead grass. No pickup truck. "I guess he's not home." I didn't think it made me a chicken to be just the slightest bit relieved at that thought.

Though, while I took a step back toward my Jeep, Ava took one closer to the trailer.

"I guess we should probably go…" I trailed off, hoping she'd get the hint.

But she ignored me, using the cinderblock holding up the back of the trailer as a step up to peer into a window. "Hard to see anything with the sheets on the windows."

"Yeah. Well, I guess we should just…"

"Looks dark inside though," Ava said. "There's definitely no one in there."

"Yep, no one home. So we should probably just…"

"Keep an eye on the road, will you?"

"Wait—what?"

I watched as Ava tugged at the window frame. "It's rusted shut."

"What are you doing?!" I hissed, instinctively looking over my shoulder for anyone watching even though we were clearly alone.

"Trying…to…open…the…window," she huffed under her breath, her muscles straining against the rusted frame.

"Ava, this is a very bad idea—"

But I didn't get to finish that thought, as she finally won the battle of the sill, and the window slid free with a grating of metal on metal.

"There!" She gave me a triumphant look. "Now, we can go in and look around."

"What are you *doing*?! That's breaking and entering, Ava."

"I didn't break anything," Ava protested. "In fact, I just fixed his sticky window. He should thank me."

"Yeah, I'm sure he'll do that. Right after he's done calling the cops."

"Relax, Emmy. He's not home."

"But he could come home at any minute," I protested, my eyes cutting to the road. Which, thankfully was free of blue pickup trucks. For now.

"Then we better hurry," Ava countered. "Give me a hoist up. I'll get inside and then open the front door for you."

"Do I look strong enough to lift you?" I asked.

Ava gave me an assessing glance, possibly not having understood the question was rhetorical. Because there was no way I was going to lift her through the window.

"You're right," she finally said.

I gave an internal sigh of relief.

"I'll have to lift you through the window."

Relief retracted.

"Oh no. No, no, no, no!" I backed away, both hands in front of me as if to ward her off. "You are not roping me into this."

"Come on, Emmy," she pleaded. "You know you want to see what's in there."

"Not that badly!"

"I'll just give you a little boost."

"I don't even think that will work. I weigh more than you!"

"But I go to the gym more often than you do."

She had me there.

"No. I'm putting my foot down," I said, actually stomping the ground. "Hard no."

Ava stepped down from the trailer. She shook her head at me. And she opened her mouth, using very calm, controlled language, like one might to a toddler throwing a tantrum. "Emmy, you are already an accessory after the fact to my not-breaking-and-entering. So you might as well get in there and at least make this crime worth it."

If I were a cartoon character, my jaw would have been on the ground. "Accessory after the…" I shook my head. "Fine," I huffed. What else could l do? She was right. I was already in too deep. "But let's make this quick."

"That's the spirit!" She was such a good friend, she didn't even take a moment to gloat. Instead, she leaned down and laced her fingers together to create a foothold for me. Ignoring every fiber of my conscience, I grabbed hold of the windowsill with my fingers and put my left foot in Ava's hands, hoisting myself up so that my top half was even with the window. Then Ava used all of her Pilates muscles to lift, tipping me headfirst through the small, grimy window.

The thing about the windows in mobile homes from the seventies was they were not that large. Well, not as large as my hips, for example. And before I knew it, I was stuck.

Fortunately, with Ava pushing and me wriggling, I finally managed to free myself, crash landing onto Tripp's bed.

Unfortunately, I landed face first onto a mound of clothing that had been tossed on top of it, and the stench of stale cigarettes and sweaty man filled my nostrils. I stifled a gag reflex as I wriggled off of them. I pulled my phone from my pocket and used the flashlight to illuminate the dim room.

And gagged again as I saw the pile of crumpled boxer shorts I'd fallen into.

I yelled, jumping back to distance myself from the undergarments as fast as I could.

"What's wrong?" Ava's face appeared in the open window. "Are you okay?"

"No!" I yelled again.

"Shhhh!" she admonished. "Someone might hear you."

"That's easy for you to say! You're not the one who had Tripp's underwear on her face."

I could see Ava covering a laugh as she disappeared back below the windowsill. "I'm going around to the front door," she called. "Let me in."

I might or might not have said a few choice swear words under my breath as I navigated around several piles of dirty clothes, discarded takeout containers, and the generally sticky and unwashed feel of the place.

Maybe now I understood why Tripp burned clothing. When I got home, I was lighting a fire, and everything I was currently wearing was going in it.

Sidestepping a pair of dumbbells and a pile of empty beer cans, I made my way to the front of the trailer, ready to let Ava in. Only by the time that I got there, she was smiling at me from the open door.

"What the..."

"It was unlocked," she commented matter-of-factly.

"What do you mean, *unlocked*?" I asked.

"I mean, I turned the handle and it opened. Tripp must have forgotten to lock it when he left."

I thought a few more swear words—really good ones this time!—and vowed that next time I committed B&E, I would try the door first. Scratch that—there wasn't going to be a next time. Nope, this was going to be my last break and enter ever!

Ava stood with one hand on her hip, the other swiping her flashlight app across the dim interior of the trailer. While it was still just early afternoon, with the sheets tacked up on every window and general clutter packed in front of them blocking out the light, it was dark enough inside that I had to squint.

"Well, where should we start?" she asked.

I shook my head. "*If* he has a burner phone, it could be anywhere."

Ava moved to a cupboard above the sink, opening it to find a stack of papers, a couple of old DVDs, and a box of Pop-Tarts. After checking in the box with no luck, she moved on to the next cupboard.

I reluctantly made my way back toward the bedroom. Discarded mounds of laundry mingled with wet towels and old boots. An open *Playboy* magazine sat on his bedside table, his bong sitting on top of it. Charming. A metal horse bit and stirrups were lying on the floor next to a bank of built-in storage drawers, and an empty bottle of Jack Daniel's peeked out from beneath the bed.

I ignored it all, held my breath, and opened the drawer closest to me. Relieved that it held nothing but socks, I moved on to the next. That one held several pairs of Wranglers, and the rest of his *Playboy* stash.

"Have you found anything?" Ava called.

"Not yet. You?"

"Nothing. Well, nothing other than a lot of junk food and a dead roach."

"Gross." I dropped to my knees to search under the bed. "Hang on…" My light fell on a navy blue gym bag with a logo of the Links club on it. I pushed the empty bottle of Jack aside and tugged the bag toward me.

"What is it?" Ava asked, coming into the room behind me.

"Duffel bag." I showed it to her. "But Tripp doesn't strike me as one of the Links set," I said, pointing to the logo.

"Definitely not," Ava said. She crouched down beside me.

"It's heavy," I noted. I unzipped it, and Ava turned her light toward the contents.

A stack of twenty-dollar bills shone back at us.

Make that lots of stacks, all bundled together with rubber bands.

Ava gave a low whistle. "Whoa."

Whoa was right. I moved the top couple of stacks to reveal more beneath.

"How much do you think is in there?" Ava asked.

"A lot," I decided.

Ava grabbed a couple of bundles and started counting. "There's got to be thousands here. I'm guessing at least ten grand."

"What is Tripp doing with ten grand in cash under his bed?" I mused out loud.

"Blackmail payment?" Ava offered.

I nodded. "Could be."

"Which means Harper *did* pay him before she died."

I glanced down at the Links logo on the side of the bag again. If Tripp wasn't a member, that meant the bag belonged to whomever had paid him off. Harper lived in LA full time—if she belonged to any exclusive clubs, I would imagine they'd be in Beverly Hills, not Sonoma. And while I could well see the Bishops being wealthy enough to afford the membership fees to the Links, I also knew Napa had several equally exclusive golf courses, including the Links' sister club, the Napa Greens, so I had a hard time seeing them driving all the way to Sonoma to play a round and pick up a Links duffel.

However, there was one person I knew who *did* play at the Links. In fact, he'd supposedly been on his way there today, carrying a bag very much like the one I was staring at now.

"Ava, I'm not sure this money came from Harper," I said, an alternate theory forming.

Ava put down the stack of cash in her hand. "What do you mean?"

"I mean, I saw Bert today with a bag just like this. What if it *was* this bag?"

Ava blinked at me. "Why would Bert be giving Tripp ten grand in cash?"

"Well, if Tripp was blackmailing Harper about the affair…maybe he blackmailed Bert too?"

Ava sucked in a breath. "Dang. What a naughty horse whisperer." Her eyes cut to the pile of cash again.

"It's possible Tripp tried to blackmail Harper first, it backfired, and he killed her, and then he went after Bert."

"Emmy," Ava said, her voice suddenly dropping to a whisper.

"Or maybe this is a blackmail payment for something totally different," I said, another idea coming to me. "Maybe the police are right that Bert was the one who pushed Harper into Dante's pen, and Tripp saw it and decided to blackmail Bert over it."

"Emmy…"

"Or, worse yet, maybe Bert paid Tripp to kill Harper for him, and this is the blood money."

"Emmy!" Ava grabbed my arm and started to shake.

I blinked at her, jarred out of my thoughts. "What?"

"I just heard a vehicle."

My heart leapt into my throat. "A what?!"

"A truck. Outside. I think Tripp is home."

CHAPTER TEN

My heart missed a whole series of beats as I listened in the darkness. Sure enough, I heard an engine nearby, wheels crunching over the dirt road. Ava killed her flashlight and moved to the front window. She lifted the faded floral sheet just enough to see outside. "Uh-oh."

"Uh-oh?" I squeaked out.

"Blue pickup."

Uh-oh.

My fingers fumbled as I quickly zipped the bag back up and pushed it under the bed where I'd found it.

"Turn your light out!" Ava warned, her voice barely above a whisper.

I did as she asked, only my hand shook so badly that my phone slipped from my hands, dropping to the floor with a clatter as it landed under the bed next to the duffel bag.

Crap.

Ava leapt onto the mattress and stopped near the open window, ready to hoist herself out.

"Hurry up, Emmy," she warned, pulling herself up on the sill.

"I dropped my phone."

"What?"

"It's under the bed!"

I heard the truck motor die, followed by the sound of a vehicle door opening. It slammed shut, and footsteps crunched on the gravel.

"Emmy, let's go," Ava begged.

"You go." I shoved my car keys at her. "Go to the Jeep. I'll be right behind you." I had no idea if I would be right behind her, but there was no point in both of us getting caught.

In the dim light I could see her bite her lip. "I can't leave you."

"I'll catch up," I promised. "Now go!"

Reluctantly, she did. I didn't wait to watch her shimmy out the window, instead diving under the bed and reaching for my phone.

My fingers curled around it just as the sound of the door handle turning rattled the silence. I heard it open, the screen smacking against the side of the mobile home, then boots smashed against the vinyl flooring.

I pushed myself under the mattress as far as I could get and prayed that Tripp wouldn't see me.

"Sorry," Tripp said, presumably into his phone, as I could only see one set of boots. "I have no idea what they plan to do with Dante." There was a pause, then, "I told you, Mrs. Cross, it's up to Animal Control."

Mrs. Cross. He was talking to Carrie.

"No, I don't know if they'll release him." Tripp sounded irritated as he flipped on a light.

From my position I watched him kick off his dusty boots before moving to the refrigerator. A can cracked, the hissing of gas escaping the open lid muffling his voice as he said something else into the phone. I heard gulping as he listened to Carrie's answer, then he told her, "Look, I'll call them tomorrow, but there's no promises they'll even talk to me. That's the best I can do." I could only guess what she said on the other end, but a beat later he mumbled a goodbye and then threw the phone onto the table.

Then there was silence.

My stomach cramped with fear as I wondered how the heck I was getting out of this. I watched Tripp's boots walk toward me. Then he dropped himself onto the bed, the mattress squashing above my head. I willed myself not to move, not to breathe, not to make any sound. My heart hammered in my chest so hard, I was sure he could hear it.

From the tinkering of metal and the rustle of clothing, I figured Tripp was undoing his belt. He stood, and his jeans dropped to his ankles.

Oh no. I closed my eyes, praying the next thing I saw was not little Mr. Tripp au naturel.

Thankfully, a heavy pounding on the trailer's front door came to my rescue before he could go the full Monty on me. His jeans went back up, and he stood, padding on bare feet to answer it.

"Hi, there," I heard a voice say.

Not just any voice.

Ava's.

I could have cried with relief as I listened to her bust out her flirtiest self. "Gosh, I hope I'm not bothering you?"

Tripp obviously hadn't been expecting to see a blonde bohemian bombshell on his front steps, as he stumbled over his first words.

"Uh, n-no," he managed.

I shimmied forward, the dust bunnies under the bed begging me to sneeze.

"I'm in a bit of a jam, and I was hoping you might be able to help me?" Ava asked.

"Help you with what?"

"I'm having a little car trouble. Silly, really, but I just don't know the first thing about these machines." She was laying the Damsel in Distress on thick—Ava owned a vintage 1970s Pontiac GTO that she kept in mint condition, and I'd venture to say knew more about cars than many mechanics.

But Tripp was eating it up. I heard him ask, "Sure. What kinda trouble?"

"I'm not really sure. See, I was going to visit my uncle down the road a bit, and it just sort of started sounding funny. Turns out my uncle's not home, but I saw you drive by in that pickup, and thought, well, now there must be a cowboy who knows about cars."

"Uh-huh," came his answer.

"Would you mind terribly taking a look for me? You know, if I wouldn't be imposing too much?"

I couldn't see what she was doing, but I could guess that she was batting her baby blues, because Tripp responded almost immediately.

"Yeah, I guess I could take a look." I heard more footsteps, then the slam of the front door.

I took that as my cue, and I slid out from under the bed. I quickly shoved myself through the window feet first, this time gravity helping my hips make it past the frame as I hit the dirt with a thud.

I picked myself up and carefully peeked around the side of the trailer.

At the road, Ava had the hood to my Jeep popped open, leaning over to peer at the engine as she chatted to Tripp. While Tripp peered at her backside in her tight skinny jeans.

I said a silent thank-you to my bestie and quickly dashed around the other side of the trailer, moving as quietly and quickly as I could to the right, into a grove of spindly trees. Using the foliage as cover, I moved parallel to the dirt road, practically running through the brush until I rounded a bend and could no longer see the trailer, Ava, or Tripp.

I crossed back to the road and continued walking as I pulled my phone out to text Ava.

I'm out. Down the road.

I planted myself on a tree stump a few yards farther down and waited for my ride. I almost felt bad leaving Ava up there with Tripp, but I decided if I didn't see her in five minutes, I'd go back and rescue my rescuer.

Luckily, four minutes later, my red Jeep came bumping down the road, Ava at the wheel. She pulled over in a cloud of dust, and I quickly let myself into the passenger seat.

"That was a close one, huh?" she asked, her eyes shining again with her Charlie's Angels look. If I didn't know better, I'd say she was enjoying this.

"Too close," I agreed. "But thank you for the distraction. That was brilliant."

"Hey, what are sidekicks for?" She grinned at me. "Though, with the way that guy was looking at my booty, I feel like I need a shower."

I looked down at my "dressed up" dust covered blouse and used-to-be-white capris. She wasn't the only one.

* * *

I dropped Ava back off at Silver Girl, and while I was eager for that shower, I was more eager for something else: to find out exactly why Bert's duffel bag was filled with at least ten grand in cash in Tripp Jones's trailer. Bert had eluded my questions once today, but this time I wasn't going to let him get away with that. Either he came clean to me, or I'd be coming clean to Grant. As much as I didn't want to see Bert in custody for Carrie's sake, it was looking more and more like he was mixed up in something bad. Maybe even something that had led to Harper's death. And if he wanted me to keep protecting him, I wanted the truth.

I wound up the driveway to Carrie's vacation getaway and pulled to a stop in the same spot near the front door that I'd occupied earlier that morning. Before I could talk myself out of it, I killed the motor of my Jeep, and paused only a moment to dust some of the earth off my clothes before I made my way toward the door.

I rapped sharply on the wood and nervously tapped my foot on the porch as I took a series of shallow breaths, waiting to confront Bert. Again.

Only as the door opened, it wasn't the man of the house who answered this time, but Nolan Becker.

"Emmy. Nice to see you again," he said, showing off a row of white teeth in a welcoming smile.

"Hi, Nolan." He was dressed in a pressed shirt in a deep blue that brought out his eyes, paired with black pants and Italian leather shoes that I could almost see my reflection in. He was freshly shaven and smelled divine.

I felt like Pig-Pen standing next to him and involuntarily took a step back in case I smelled like it too.

"Are you looking for Carrie?" he asked. To his credit, his eyes only flickered momentarily to my dirty clothes.

"Actually, I was hoping to have a quick chat with Bert."

"Oh." Surprise showed in his eyes, but he quickly covered it. "Uh, well, he's not home, I'm afraid."

While I'd gone there determined for answers, I'd be lying if I didn't say some relief relaxed into my shoulders at not having to deal with that confrontation. "Did he say where he was going?" I asked.

Nolan leaned on the doorframe. "He and Carrie drove into town to talk to a lawyer."

I felt my stomach clench. "Why? Did anything happen? Have the police been back?"

But Nolan shook his head. "No, nothing like that. Carrie said it was just in case. I think she's…well, she's worried the police might come back to question Bert again."

So was I. Then again, they might have ample reason to.

"Nolan, Bert said he was meeting you at the Links this morning," I said, watching his reaction carefully.

He nodded. "Yeah. We played a round. Had a couple of drinks. Why?"

Well, at least that much of Bert's story had been true. "What time was this?"

A small frown marred Nolan's face. "Tee off was a little after nine, I guess. Bert was a couple minutes late, but they still fit us in."

"Did he have a duffel bag with him? One with the Links logo on it?"

The frown deepened, proof Nolan's forehead was Botox free. "Well, not on the green, of course. But I think maybe I saw one in the locker room." He paused, crossing his arms over his chest, his biceps straining the fabric of his shirt. "Why? What's this about, Emmy?"

I pursed my lips, hesitant to share my theory with Bert's friend. It seemed that however the gym bag of cash had ended up in Tripp's trailer, at least Bert hadn't delivered it that morning. But that didn't mean he hadn't handed off another logo duffel to the cowboy at some earlier date.

"Just curious," I finally settled on.

But the frown didn't leave Nolan's face. "Does this have something to do with Harper's death?"

"Maybe," I hedged. "Did Harper ever talk to you about being in some sort of trouble?"

Nolan shook his head, eyes going to a spot over my head, as if thinking back. "No. What sort of trouble?"

"Maybe financial trouble?" I said, dancing around the subject the best I could without tipping my hand.

But Nolan laughed. "Well, if Harper was hard up for cash, she hardly dressed the part. I think she had an open account at every boutique on Rodeo Drive." He shifted, gaze coming back to meet mine. "You're asking an awful lot of odd questions, Emmy."

I let out a breath. "I know. I...I have reason to believe Harper was being threatened." I watched his reaction. "That she was possibly even being blackmailed by someone."

"Blackmail?" Nolan's eyebrows went up toward his hair.

I nodded.

"Over what?"

"Honestly? I'm not 100% certain yet." Which was the truth. Granted, I had a pretty good guess it had something to do with Bert.

But if Nolan had any knowledge of it or if Harper had confided in him, he didn't show it, instead just shaking his head, as if subconsciously denying such a thing could be true. "Are you sure about this?" he asked.

I nodded. "Pretty sure. She never mentioned anything to you?"

"This is the first I'm hearing of it."

"She never said she was in trouble?" I pressed. "Or...mentioned anything about Bert?"

"Bert?" He shook his head harder. "You don't think Bert had anything to do with this, do you?"

I blew out a breath. "I don't know. I hope not, for Carrie's sake." Again, true, if not a full disclosure.

"Look, Bert's a good guy," Nolan said, conviction behind his voice. "He loves Carrie, and I don't know what kind of mess Harper might have gotten herself into, but I'm sure it had nothing to do with Bert."

While I wasn't quite as sure, I nodded anyway, feeling like I'd pushed the bounds of their friendships far enough. "Right," I agreed. "I'm sure Bert is a great guy."

Having established that, the frown on Nolan's face finally smoothed some, his usually charming countenance returning.

"Anyway, I'll let Bert and Carrie know you stopped by, but I've actually got to get ready."

"Ready for what?" If you asked me, he already looked ready for a magazine shoot.

He shot me a grin. "I'm taking your friend Ava to Silvio's tonight."

I felt some of my own tension ease at his charming smile. "That's right. She told me about that. It sounds like fun," I said, meaning it. And possibly feeling just the slightest bit envious—at least of the meal Ava was about to have. "I won't keep you. Enjoy your dinner with Ava," I called as I walked back to my car.

Nolan sent me a smile and waved before disappearing back inside the house.

As I got into my Jeep, I sent off a quick text to Carrie. *Heard you were talking to a lawyer. Hope you're okay. Call if you need anything.*

Part of me felt guilty that I was practically helping Grant build a case against her husband rather than helping point the finger away. The least I could do was be supportive as a friend. Especially if things started to look worse for Bert.

CHAPTER ELEVEN

As soon as I got home, I indulged in the longest shower known to womankind, washing off not only the physical dirt from my body, but the icky internal feeling at having been in Tripp's trailer. I also tried to wash off the guilt of seemingly digging Bert a deeper hole rather than throwing a lifeline to get him out, but that was a little hard to shake.

As much as I wanted to believe Bert, I couldn't come up with a scenario where he was the innocent doting husband everyone thought he was. For one, he'd clearly lied to Carrie about making investments for Harper. Grant had found no trace of those. But while he wasn't investing for her, he *had* been close to her. I'd witnessed that myself. What was it Harper had said as she'd led Bert away upstairs? *You wouldn't want your darling wife to come looking for us.* As much as Bert had protested that what I'd seen "wasn't what I thought," I was having a hard time picturing it as anything other than an affair.

Of course, then there was the cash in Tripp's trailer. Blackmail payoff? Payment for murder? I wasn't sure what a horse whisperer charged, but I had a feeling it wasn't usually payable in a duffel bag of bundled twenties. Whatever he was doing with that much money—in what looked to be Bert's duffel bag, no less—it didn't feel above board. Innocent people usually used banks.

As I shut off the water and toweled dry, I sincerely hoped Carrie and Bert were visiting a really good lawyer. The more I thought about it, the more it seemed Bert was going to need one.

I tried to put thoughts of Harper to the side as I dressed in a pair of jeans, a comfy sweatshirt, and slippers in the shape of bear paws. Then I padded down the stone walkway between my cottage and the main building to my office, determined to get some real work done. Not because I wanted to. But because if I didn't get those quarterlies turned in soon, Gene Schultz might show up on my doorstep. And an antsy accountant was almost as scary as Dante.

I spent the better part of the next two hours filling in various forms, uploading payroll spreadsheets, and staring at balances due that were larger than the balances in my bank account. While the paperwork portion of the task was painful, the actual paying of the taxes was downright agonizing. Mostly because I knew I couldn't. There was no way around it—I was going to have to file for an extension while my balances accrued interest. As I sent the whole mess off to Schultz, I only prayed that this year's bottling brought in extra profits faster than the extra interest piled on.

I was just contemplating that cheery thought when a familiar male voice called from down the hallway.

"Hello? Anyone home?"

I walked around my desk and peeked my head out of my office to find Grant standing just inside the main entrance, a paper grocery bag in one hand.

"Uh, hi," I said, suddenly very aware that I'd let my hair air dry in lieu of my usual multi-product blow dryer routine. I ran a hand through it, attempting to smooth out any frizz that might have resulted.

"Hi, yourself." Grant's white linen shirt hung over the band of his dark jeans and was rolled at the sleeves, showing off his tanned forearms. His hair was damp, face clean shaven, and the hazel flecks in his eyes danced with his smile as he gave me a quick head-to-toe look. "Nice slippers."

"Thanks. They're my bear feet." I paused. "Get it? *Bare* feet?"

He let out a small chuckle. "I get it. I guess I didn't realize how casual dinner was tonight."

Dinner tonight. I did a mental forehead smack. With all that had gone on that day, I'd completely forgotten about Grant's promise to come over for dinner.

"Yeah, well, um, I was in a casual mood," I mumbled, hoping my cheeks weren't actually flushing as red as they felt.

Grant shrugged. "I like it. You look cozy."

While I might have preferred *sexy*, at least he hadn't gone with *frumpy*.

"You brought food?" I asked, trying to divert his attention from my wardrobe choices.

"I did." He held up the brown grocery bag. "Everything you need to make Chicken Piccata. At least according to the recipe app I downloaded at the store." He gave me a sheepish grin, and I couldn't help a chuckle in response.

"I'm sure whatever you have will work," I said, leading the way down the hall, past my office, and toward the big kitchen.

Grant followed behind me, setting the bag down on the kitchen counter island as I washed my hands and pulled a couple of wineglasses down.

"I have a Chardonnay and a Pinot Blanc opened. Both pair delightfully with chicken piccata."

"I'll try the Pinot Blanc," he said, leaning casually against the counter as I grabbed the bottle from the chiller and poured two glasses.

"So," I said as I slid one toward him. "Any news on Harper's case today?"

He shot me a look over the rim of his glass as he took his first sip. "We're leading with that, huh?"

"Felt like a good opener." I shrugged and sipped from my own glass.

He shook his head, though his smile was playful. "You're like a broken record, Oak. What is it that fascinates you about murder cases so much?"

I almost choked on my wine. "Fascinates?" I shook my head. "No, you've got me all wrong. I just want this cleared up. Trust me, if I never got close to another dead body again, I'd be a happy woman."

"Hmmm." He gave me a narrow-eyed thing, like he didn't totally believe that.

I avoided the look by turning my back to him to unpack his grocery bag. I pulled out chicken breast cutlets, capers, and fresh lemons. The app he'd downloaded hadn't failed him. As I pulled out fresh vegetables that looked intended for an accompaniment salad, I could feel my stomach grumbling already, reminding me I'd missed lunch.

"You mind cooking the chicken while I prep the rest of this?" I asked.

"Not at all," he said, setting his glass down on the counter. "If you trust me with it."

"I'll take a chance," I teased, pulling out a cast iron skillet and placing it on the stove top.

He came up beside me, his hip brushing mine. I tried to ignore the sudden flush of heat the slight touch sent through me.

Grant accepted the pan and got to work heating it up with olive oil and butter as I prepared a flour dredge for the chicken.

"So how was your day?" Grant asked, making casual conversation.

"My day?" I asked, my voice going up a pitch higher than I might have meant it to as I tried not to think about the felonious parts of it.

He gave me a funny look, but nodded.

"Oh, uh, well…fine. It was fine."

He grinned. "Sounds enthralling. Do tell me more."

I couldn't help laughing at myself. "Okay, I…" I paused, mentally going through all I'd done and editing it for cop ears. "…stopped by Carrie's house and saw Bert. Then I had coffee with a…friend…at the Half Calf. Then I popped into Silver Girl to see Ava. And we…took a drive into the hills to visit another friend's place."

I looked up to find him still giving me that funny look. "Sounds like you saw a lot of friends."

I nodded, averting my eyes again as I dropped the chicken into the pan. "Yep. I'm a friendly gal." I cleared my throat. "How about you? How was your day?"

He shrugged. "Uneventful."

Darn. Good evasive answer. I should have gone with that one.

"Didn't you have Harper's autopsy this morning?" I asked, remembering his early departure the previous evening that had prompted this rain-check meal.

Grant nodded, adjusting the heat on his burner.

"How did that go?"

"Fine." He shrugged then sent me a lopsided grin. "Not really great dinner conversation, though."

"Good thing we're not eating yet," I shot back.

"Touché," he said, pointing a spatula at me.

I was about to ask more, when I felt my phone buzz in my back pocket. I pulled it out to see a text from Ava.

Did you know Silvio's charges $50 for crab cakes?

I stifled a laugh. *Eat extra for me!*

A moment later, her answer came in. *I'll see if I can smuggle some out in a doggy bag.*

While I appreciated the sentiment, I doubted Silvio's was a doggy bag kind of place.

"Business?" Grant asked, nodding toward my phone.

"Sorry." I shoved it back into my pocket. "No, actually Ava. She's on a date tonight with Nolan Becker. The actor," I clarified.

Grant cocked an eyebrow my way. "Really?"

I nodded. "Why?"

He shrugged. "Nothing. I just wouldn't have pegged a Hollywood actor as her type."

"That's where you're wrong. As Ava says, Dr. Drake Dubois is every woman's type."

Grant shot me a questioning look.

"Well, *almost* every woman's type," I amended, feeling heat start to fill my cheeks. I sipped my wine to cover it. "Anyway, it's new. This is their first real date. I mean, she met him for lunch yesterday, but David and I were there, so that doesn't really count."

"Is that how it works?" he asked, eyes cutting playfully to me. "Real dates have to be solo?"

I nodded. "And preferably dinner. And preferably at an expensive restaurant like Silvio's."

"So does that mean this doesn't count as a date?" he asked, the same teasing glint in his eyes as he nodded toward the pan of chicken he was cooking.

The question caught me off guard, and I felt that heat filling my cheeks again. "It's close," I mumbled.

"Hmm. Guess I'll have to try harder next time."

I ducked my head to cover the blush coursing through me.

Luckily, if he noticed, he didn't mention it, instead turning back to his cutlets and flipping them over to brown on the other side. I snuck a glance at him through my hair. He was freshly showered and shaven, and his shirt looked too clean and pressed to have been the one he'd worked in all day. He'd taken the time to shop for groceries. Even downloading an app to find a recipe. It occurred to me that it was possible Grant *had* thought of this as a date.

I suddenly felt twice as dowdy for forgetting all about dinner and showing up in an old sweatshirt and novelty slippers. I resisted the urge to go throw on a little makeup.

I cleared my throat, trying to steer the conversation back to more neutral territory. "Carrie's really worried about Dante. Do you know if Animal Control is going to let him go?"

Grant shook his head. "I'm honestly not sure. It's usually policy to put down an animal in the case of a death. But, there are extenuating circumstances in this one."

"Like the fact someone purposely pushed Harper into his pen."

Grant nodded.

I grabbed a head of romaine and started chopping to busy my hands while I attempted to sound casual with my next question. "Have you guys talked to Tripp yet?"

"Tripp?"

"Tripp Jones. The horse trainer Carrie had at the house to tame Dante."

Grant stopped flipping his chicken and turned his full attention toward me. "What do you know about Tripp Jones?"

I licked my lips. "Not much." Other than firsthand knowledge that he was a boxers guy and not briefs. "I just…wondered. You know. What he might know. About…things."

Oh boy. That sounded so weak it was practically in muscle atrophy.

I could tell Grant had much the same reaction—his spatula abandoned, arms crossed over his chest, hazel flecks in his eyes homing in on me with an assessing stare.

"Emmy, Tripp Jones is not the kind of guy you want to get involved with."

That was interesting wording. "What do you mean?"

"I mean he has a record."

I felt my eyebrows heading north. "Like a police record?"

Grant nodded.

"For what? Blackmail?"

Grant's face contorted into a frown. "Blackmail? Where did you hear that?"

"Uh, nowhere. Just…guessing."

He shook his head. "No. He has an arrest record, though charges were eventually dropped due to lack of evidence."

"What sort of charges?"

Grant took a moment to answer, turning his attention back to the sizzling skillet in front of him. "Homicide."

I froze, the hairs on the back of my neck suddenly zinging to attention. "Wait—Tripp Jones was arrested for murder?"

He nodded.

"Who did he kill?"

"I didn't say he killed anyone. I said he was arrested and charges were dropped."

"Po-tay-toe. Po-taw-toe."

He shot me an amused grin.

"Who was it?" I asked.

"An ex-girlfriend. Apparently the two had broken up the week before she was found dead."

"Don't tell me she was trampled by a horse?"

"No," he said emphatically. "Fell down a flight of stairs."

"Or was pushed," I floated.

"Or was pushed," he agreed as he pulled the perfectly browned cutlets from the heat. "But like I said, not enough evidence to go to trial. Charges were dropped."

"Which doesn't mean he didn't do it," I pointed out. "Just that there wasn't any evidence." My mind immediately went to how Tripp had been burning Harper's clothes earlier that day. Had he again been getting rid of evidence that tied him to a homicide?

"I think there's something I should tell you," I confessed.

Grants eyes flickered up to meet mine. "That doesn't sound good."

"Yeah, it's not." I let out a breath. "I, uh, kind of saw something at Carrie's house today."

He turned toward me, crossing his arms over his chest again, leaning his hip against the counter. "What kind of something."

"Tripp Jones. Possibly getting rid of evidence."

If he had any emotion about the fact I'd waited this long to tell him, he hid it, his expression totally unreadable. "Go on."

I did, regaling him with the entire scene I'd witnessed at the fire pit, including the fact that I'd rescued a couple pieces from the embers and recognized them as high end. "They were definitely the type of thing Harper would have worn," I finished.

"But you don't know for certain that they were Harper's," he clarified.

I shook my head. "But why else would he be burning them?"

Instead of answering, he asked, "Where are they now?"

"Still at Carrie's, I guess." I paused. "Unless someone cleared out the fire pit."

Grant closed his eyes, and I could tell he was thinking a bad word. "So they could be gone now?"

Oops. Guess I hadn't thought of it that way. "Kinda, yeah."

He shook his head. "I'll stop by Carrie's tomorrow."

"You think there was something on them that Tripp was trying to hide? Something that points to him as her killer?"

"I think," Grant said, his face still unreadable, "that you should leave this alone."

I rolled my eyes. "I'm just asking a question."

"And disturbing a crime scene—"

"The fire pit was on the opposite side of the house from the crime scene."

"—and spying on a guy with a police record—"

"I just *happened* to see him!"

"—and trying to get details of Harper's autopsy from me."

Well, he had me there.

"Look, Carrie is my friend," I told him. "She's upset about this. All I'm trying to do is be there for her."

Some of the cop softened from his face, and he took a step forward, his hand going to my arm. "I know," he said. "You're a good friend. Just, be there for her a little farther away from Tripp Jones, okay?"

I nodded. "Okay." That was one promise I intended to keep. I'd had my fill of being near Tripp while trapped under his bed. "But are you going to tell me?"

He frowned. "Tell you what?"

"What you found at the autopsy?"

He let out a breath, eyes going to the ceiling. Possibly praying for patience, but I figured that was between him and the Big Guy.

"Emmy, you're killing me."

"Just spill it, and I promise I will not bring up a single dead body at dinner."

"This is an ongoing investigation. You know I can't discuss it."

"So there *is* something about it to discuss, then?"

"I never said that."

"You didn't have to. I can see it in your eyes." A bluff, but I was out of real arguments.

He shook his head. "You're not going to let this go, are you?"

"You know I'm going to find out sooner or later anyway," I reasoned.

He narrowed his eyes. He sucked in his cheeks. He took a couple of deep breaths, possibly angling for patience again. "Fine. But then can I enjoy my meal in peace?"

"Scout's honor," I said, holding up three fingers.

The look on his face said he wasn't quite convinced I was ever a Girl Scout, but he relented anyway. "The ME's report showed Harper's blood alcohol level was normal."

I felt a frown form. "What do you mean by normal?"

"She hadn't been drinking that night."

"No, that's not right." I shook my head. "No, Ava said she poured Harper several glasses of Zinfandel. Harper even posted about it on social media."

"That may be, but I can assure you Harper did not ingest any alcohol that night. Stomach contents showed no sign of wine."

I frowned. "Then what was she doing with the wine we were pouring her? Just dumping it?"

"Maybe."

"But why?"

Grant drew in another long breath, as if still not sure he should be talking to me. "It's possible she was trying to keep up appearances."

"The appearance of being drunk?" I asked, still confused.

"Probably more likely the appearance of being her usual self." He paused. "The ME found that Harper Bishop was three months pregnant when she died."

CHAPTER TWELVE

———

I blinked at him, trying to process this new bit of information. "You're kidding?"

"Trust me—I wouldn't kid about something like that."

"But she didn't look pregnant," I mused, more to myself than Grant as I conjured up the mental image of her in the slinky emerald dress. There'd been no hint of a baby bump.

"I guess she wasn't showing yet, but the ME was pretty clear about his findings."

I nodded, thinking that wasn't the sort of thing he'd be likely to mistake. And, now that Grant had mentioned it, I realized I hadn't actually seen Harper *drink* from the wineglass I'd witnessed her holding. But who had she been trying to keep the pregnancy from?

And maybe more importantly, who was the father?

"Can the ME tell whose baby she was pregnant with?" I asked as I took the skillet from him and finished the recipe on autopilot, creating a zesty pan sauce to cover the chicken. "Like, with the baby's DNA or something?"

"Possibly," Grant said, moving to one of the barstools at the counter. "But he'd need something to compare it to."

"So you'd need, like, a hair sample or something from the guy?" My mind immediately went to Bert.

Grant nodded. "Cheek swab is usually preferred, but I supposed they could use a hair. Forensics isn't my department, so I leave that to the scientists."

I pursed my lips, hesitant to voice the unspoken thought I could feel floating in the air between us. "But you think it might be Bert's?"

Grant paused, and I could tell he was choosing his words carefully. "I think that's one theory."

I plated our meal and took a seat beside Grant, but my appetite from earlier had suddenly disappeared. The problem with Grant's theory was that it was a good one. I was almost sure Bert and Harper had been having an affair. Was the pregnancy a result of that liaison?

"Do you think Bert knew that Harper was pregnant?" I asked, hating the idea.

"That's something I'd certainly like to ask him," Grant said, carefully evading the question.

I glanced up at him. His gaze was on his meal, not making eye contact.

"You think Bert found out, and he killed Harper to cover it up before Carrie discovered it," I said, finishing off his theory for him.

Grant glanced up only long enough for his eyes to flicker to mine before they were once again enthralled with his chicken piccata. But the fact he didn't deny it spoke volumes.

I picked up my fork and stabbed a piece of meat, forcing myself to chew it. Normally the contrast of the briny caper, tangy lemon, and rich but delicate sauce was something I'd savor. But right then I barely tasted it, forcing the bites down. If Harper had been pregnant with Bert's baby, was that what Harper had been blackmailed over? Maybe Tripp had somehow found out and decided to make a buck off that knowledge.

"Your guys find anything on Harper's phone yet?" I asked, trying to sound casual.

"Not that I'm aware of." His gaze rose to meet mine. "Why? Got something in mind yet?"

I shrugged. "No. Just…you know…wondering if maybe she texted anyone or said anything. You know, that might point to the father." Or blackmailer. But if Grant had yet to find evidence of that, it was one nail I wasn't hammering into Bert's coffin.

At least not yet.

"Emmy, I know Carrie is your friend," Grant said, suddenly looking softer. "But that doesn't mean Bert is a great guy."

I pursed my lips together. "This does make him look guilty, doesn't it?"

Grant paused. Then slowly nodded.

Which was a terrible sign. Grant didn't make guesses. If he was admitting that Bert was his main suspect, that didn't bode well at all for the former child actor.

"Carrie doesn't deserve this," I told him, feeling tears back up in my throat. For Carrie, and for me being such a lousy friend that I agreed with Grant on this one.

The unshed tears must have seeped into my voice a little, as Grant stood and in a moment was at my side, arms pulling me toward him. "I'm sorry," he mumbled into my hair.

I closed my eyes as I leaned my head against his solid chest, letting his arms encircle me, hugging me close with a warmth that went well beyond the heat radiating from his body. I inhaled the subtle musky scent of his aftershave, the strong male aura of it wrapping around me in a comforting embrace.

Part of me never wanted to move, but after a beat, he pulled back, tilting his head down toward me. "You okay?" he asked, his voice deep and low between us.

I nodded. "I'm good."

He reached out and tucked a stray strand of hair behind my ear. "Good." His finger lingered at my ear, slowly tracing down my jawline to tip my chin up ever so slightly toward him. My breathing stilled as he dipped his head toward me, closing the gap between us as his lips brushed against mine.

I melted on the spot, all thoughts chased from my head as my entire body focused on the soft touch of his lips on mine, his arms around my waist, and his strong, broad chest pressing against mine. Someone moaned, and it could have been me. But a more masculine groan followed, and Grant's breathing deepened, his heart beating quickly against my body.

My hands made their way into his hair, and my hips may have even tried to move closer to his. All on their own, I swear. Nothing about the way my body was moving was under my control, and I had a feeling in about two seconds my hormones would take over completely, and I'd be useless to resist them.

Unfortunately, that would be two seconds too long.

Something vibrated against my thigh, making me jump.

He groaned again, though this one was all disappointment as he pulled away. "Sorry," he mumbled, extracting his phone from his pocket.

I licked my lips, still tasting him there. "It's okay," I lied, trying to get my breathing under control as I made plans to destroy that phone.

He glanced at the screen. "The station," he said, swiping to read the message.

"Everything okay?" I asked, still trying to pull my head back down to earth and out of the delightful fantasyland it had been about to take a detour into.

He frowned as he read the screen. "Yeah. There's an incident downtown." He scrolled a beat before turning the phone off and shoving it back into his pocket. "I have to go. Sorry."

"Already?" I really hadn't meant that word to come out on a whine, but suddenly the only mode my voice could do was unhappy teenager.

He must have noticed, as his mouth curved into a half smile. "Trust me. I'm *very* sorry."

I might have whimpered a little before I got my hormones under control again. "It's okay," I said, clearing them from my throat. "I understand."

"Another rain check?"

"Sure," I agreed. Even though I was pretty sure I'd need an umbrella for all of the rain checks I'd been racking up this week.

He leaned in and pressed his lips against mine one last time before he turned and walked out the door.

Taking all my fantasies with him.

* * *

I picked at my dinner alone in the kitchen for a few minutes, but my appetite was gone. I boxed up the rest of the food and stuffed it into the refrigerator, hoping at least it would make a good lunch tomorrow.

As much as Grant's kiss had momentarily chased all thoughts of Harper, Bert, and Carrie from my head, with him gone, they came back just as quickly. The news of Harper's pregnancy only served to make Bert look more like a suspect. My heart went out to Carrie. And my guilt. She'd come to me for support and help when the police had called Bert in for questioning. And everything I'd done since then had just served to further push Bert toward a cell. Not that I wasn't questioning if that was where he belonged, but I'd certainly been the opposite of helpful.

I closed my eyes, imagining how Carrie would react when she found out Harper had been pregnant. I couldn't imagine that playing out well for anyone.

Assuming of course, the baby was Bert's.

A ray of hope occurred to me. Hadn't Nolan said that Harper liked men—plural. Maybe the baby was someone else's altogether. Maybe one of the other guests at the party, even. Carrie *had* said that she'd invited lots of people from *Carefree Hearts*. Cast, crew, producers. Maybe Harper had been seeing one of them, and they hadn't taken the news of her bun in the oven well.

I hadn't particularly noticed her with any other men, but the truth was I hadn't really been looking. I'd been busy pouring wine, serving platters, keeping the guests happy, and later cleaning up the aftermath in the kitchen. It was only chance that I'd run into Bert and Harper. But maybe Harper had snuck off with more than one man that night.

I wondered if Carrie would know if Harper had been seeing anyone. Nolan hadn't seemed to think there was anyone special in Harper's life, but maybe Harper wouldn't have confided in him. Would she have confided in Carrie? Possibly. Carrie had made it seem like the two were close.

I picked up my phone and dialed Carrie's number. Unfortunately, it went straight to voicemail. She must have it turned off. I glanced at the time. Just past nine. Too early for her to be asleep, but if the press were still bothering her, I could see her turning her phone off to avoiding being hounded for interviews all evening.

On a whim, I grabbed my purse and a pair of shoes and headed for my Jeep to make one last trip to Carrie's house that day.

*   *   *

The grounds were shadowed in darkness as I pulled up the driveway—sparse landscape lighting strategically placed to uplight the majestic oak trees was the only relief to the inky blackness. As I pulled up to the house, it too looked dark, only a few windows on the ground floor dimly lit. A gray sedan was in the driveway, and I parked beside it—noting the Jaguar I'd seen Bert get into earlier that day was still absent. Nolan's sports car was absent too. Lucky Ava—her date was lasting a lot longer than mine had.

My feet crunched on the gravel as I made my way to the front door. While the place had an air of abandonment, I still knocked, hoping Carrie and Bert were just having a quiet evening in. I waited, hearing nothing in return but rustling trees and the insects singing their evening song. I tried again, ringing the bell, then wrapping my arms around me for warmth as I waited on the porch. The heat of the day had long since dispersed, bringing with it a cool breeze that would feel almost peaceful under other circumstances.

After waiting long enough that I was beginning to shiver, I gave up, deciding no one was home. I headed back to my Jeep, plonking my tush on the driver's seat, and I was about to turn the key in the ignition and head home, when something caught my eye.

A light.

I watched it flash briefly in an upstairs window.

I frowned. If someone was home, why hadn't they answered the door?

I watched it flash again, and realized it wasn't a lamp or a flicker of television I was seeing. This light was a sweeping beam. Like a flashlight.

And there was only one reason I could think of for someone to use a flashlight in a house that clearly had working electricity—they didn't want their presence known.

Someone was sneaking around in Carrie's house.

I felt my heart rate pick up as I tried to decide what to do. I could call Grant, but I knew he was downtown—that was a good twenty minutes away at least. Whoever was snooping around Carrie's house could be long gone by then. Even if I called 9-1-1, it would take the police some time to arrive. Then again, if my imagination was getting away from me and this was just some electrical issue Bert was trying to fix, I'd really have been a crappy friend.

I swallowed, watching the light flicker again, and grabbed my phone, calling Carrie's number.

Again it went straight to voicemail.

I bit my lip.

What if the intruder was Tripp, destroying more evidence? I'd already messed that one up once by not grabbing the burned clothes. I couldn't let him do it again.

I didn't let my brain go anything further than that—for fear it might talk me out of it. I jumped back out of the car and ran toward the house.

I bypassed the front door this time, walking around the back of the house. Luckily, the back door was unlocked, the knob turning easily in my hand, and I slipped inside. The kitchen was eerie in the darkness, the moonlight filtering through the windows the only thing I had to guide my way. I thought about switching on my flashlight app, but I quickly nixed that idea, not wanting the intruder to notice it the way I had his light. Instead, I felt my way through the kitchen, blinking my eyes in the dark as I moved down the hallway toward the staircase.

The light I'd seen from my car had either moved on or been extinguished, as only darkness was visible above me. I wasn't sure if that was a good sign or a bad one. I took a shallow breath and gingerly climbed the first steps. Luckily, the stairs didn't creak under my weight as I slowly ascended.

My eyes were quickly adjusting to the low light, and the moonlight flooding the landing gave me a glimpse into the open room at the top of the stairs. Unable to see if anyone was inside, I kept to the shadows as I moved closer. My breath felt shaky, but I forced one foot in front of the other until I stopped at the open door.

Discarded clothing was littered across the floor. A Louis Vuitton suitcase was open on the bed, and several articles of clothing were sprawled alongside it. I guessed that it was

Harper's room. After all, I didn't think Nolan would wear the lace negligee draped over a nearby chair.

I paused, straining to hear any sign of who might have been roaming around with a flashlight.

Nothing but the muted sound of crickets outside the window came back to me.

I was starting to think maybe I'd imagined the whole thing. Maybe it had been some trick of light from a passing car or some robot vacuum come to life on the upper floor.

I took a step inside the room, feeling a little sad at seeing Harper's beautiful things. I couldn't tell if the haphazard state they were in was from someone rummaging around by flashlight, the police having gone through the room, or from Harper having hastily gotten ready for the housewarming party. Two pairs of heels lay on the floor at the end of the bed, as if she'd been vacillating about which to wear with her emerald dress. A jewelry bag was open on the dresser, the contents splayed out across its top, and a small collection of clutches and handbags sat in an armchair by the window.

One thing was for sure—Harper had expensive taste in clothing. Gucci, Prada, Burberry—the gang was all there. A hot pink leather Hermes handbag was particularly cute. I hoped it went to a good home now. I supposed they all belonged to Harper's next of kin—maybe her sister, Kellen? Though, I could hardly picture her sister enjoying the hand-me-downs.

I moved toward the chair, not able to stop myself from getting a closer look at the handbag that probably cost more than my Jeep. I unzipped the main compartment and peeked inside, though there was nothing there to suggest it had been in daily use. It was largely empty, apart from a bottle of hand sanitizer and some old receipts. I could tell from the label it was real though. No knockoffs for this diva.

I was trying to shake the niggle of envy, my mind so busy lamenting the fate of such a lovely accessory in the absence of its owner that I almost didn't even register it.

A faint sound.

Like footsteps on thick pile carpeting.

On instinct I spun around in the darkness to see the source.

But it was too late.

All I saw in the faint moonlight was a large shadow, before something hard connected with the side of my head, and pain exploded at my temple. I felt weightless for a split second as the floor rushed up to meet me.

And then everything went black.

CHAPTER THIRTEEN

———

I was somewhere soft and cool, like a fluffy cloud. The tendrils of moisture tickled my cheeks. In fact, the fog felt like it was all around me—rushing through my brain and making it hard to focus, filling my ears so that noises seemed far away, creating a dark shroud over my eyes so I couldn't see. Or—wait. Maybe my eyes were just closed.

I tried blinking, the act harder than I could ever remember it being.

"Emmy!"

A voice made it through the fog in my ears. Female. It still sounded far away, but I could faintly make it out now.

"That's it, Emmy. Open your eyes."

I was trying. I almost yelled back to the voice that I was stuck in a cloud, but I realized my voice wasn't quite working properly either. I let out a sort of croaking sound that sounded more animal than human.

"Shhh," the female voice said. "It's okay. I'm here."

I finally managed to pry my eyes open enough to make out a shape and found the source of the voice. Ava. She was peering down at me at an odd angle.

"A-Ava?" I asked.

"Oh thank God you're okay," she said, her blonde brows drawn together in concern. "Nolan's calling for help." She gestured over her shoulder, where I saw another figure standing off to the side. "An ambulance is on its way."

I shook my head in the negative, knowing what kind of bill the poor uninsured like myself would incur from a simple ambulance ride to the hospital. I could barely afford an Uber.

"I'm fine. I don't need an ambulance." I felt carpet fibers tickling my cheeks, and realized I wasn't lying in a cloud but on the floor.

"Don't move," Ava instructed. "You could have a concussion."

"I don't have a concussion." At least, I didn't think so. I took a deep breath and tried to sit up.

Bad idea. The room spun, nausea instantly taking hold in my belly. I plopped unceremoniously back down onto the carpet.

I heard footsteps, and a moment later Nolan appeared in my field of vision. "The police are on their way," he assured Ava. Then his eyes went to me. "Good. She's conscious."

"She can hear you," I told him.

A smile flickered on his face. "Right. You okay?" Nolan knelt in front of me. "Emmy, can you tell us what happened?"

"I-I'm not really sure," I confessed, looking from one concerned face to the other. I tried pulling myself up into a sitting position again, and this time the nausea only slightly derailed me, causing me to lean against the side of Harper's bed.

Harper's room.

The handbags. The flashlight.

"I think someone hit me," I finally said.

"Hit you!" Ava gasped.

"Who?" Nolan asked. "Did you get a good look at them?"

I shook my head. Slowly, in deference to the headache that was blooming at my temple. "No. I didn't see anyone. But I did see a light. Like a flashlight. Like someone was looking for something." I quickly gave them the shortened version of events, from me arriving to seeing someone sneaking around the empty house.

"Emmy, you could have been seriously hurt." While Ava's words were admonishing, her tone was soft in a way that went straight to my heart.

"I-I wasn't thinking," I admitted. "I just wanted to see who was here. I thought you were out," I said, turning to Nolan.

He nodded. "Ava and I came home to find the back door open. We thought someone had broken in."

"Nolan told me to wait outside while he went in to check it out," Ava added. "Only then he came running out saying he found you unconscious."

I swallowed hard, realizing how lucky I was that they'd gotten home when they had.

"I guess you didn't see anyone else leaving?" I asked them.

Ava's eyes went to Nolan.

But he shook his head. "No. We must have scared them away."

Thank goodness for small favors.

I let Ava and Nolan help me up, and while Harper's bed was closer, I convinced them I was strong enough to go downstairs and wait on a sofa in the living room for the police to arrive. Mostly because the idea of lying in the bed surrounded by the dead woman's clothes was more than my frazzled nerves could take. Especially if I'd just been attacked at the hands of her killer.

Nolan made us tea, and Ava held my hand and tutted at me like a mother hen while we waited for the cavalry to arrive. First on the scene was a uniformed officer who looked familiar—like he might have already been to Carrie's house at least once that week. I went through my version of events for him and was just getting to the part where I blacked out, when the ambulance pulled up. I cringed at how much of a hit my already battered bank account was going to get as the EMT gave me a once-over. After what I feared was several hundred dollars worth of his time, he finally diagnosed me with a "bump on the head" and told me to ice it, take an over-the-counter painkiller, and get some rest.

I was about to ask Ava to drive me home and do all three of the prescribed items, as well as maybe have a glass of calming Pinot to go with it, when a familiar face walked in the open front door.

Grant.

I closed my eyes and said a silent curse to the gods of police radios.

I watched him have a brief word with the EMT who met him at the door. Then he quickly crossed the room to my side.

"You okay?" he asked. While the lines of his jaw were tense, the softness in his voice was tender and warm enough to make the tentative grip on my composure slip.

I nodded, sniffing back tears that begged to be shed. "I'm fine. Just a bump on the head. Official diagnosis," I said, trying at humor to keep those tears at bay.

Though, it was lost on him, his face not even hinting at a smile. "What happened?" he demanded.

"I, uh, hit the floor."

"After someone hit *her*!" Ava piped up, still sitting on the sofa beside me.

Grant's eyes cut to Ava for just a moment, before homing in on me again. "Is that true?"

"Uh…sorta." Something about the intensity in his eyes had me feeling like I was on trial here instead of being the victim.

He sucked in a breath, his nostrils flaring with the effort, before he turned to Ava again. "Would you mind waiting in the kitchen?"

Ava gave me questioning look. I sent her a nod. I was pretty sure I could handle Bad Cop alone.

Maybe.

Ava gave my hand a quick squeeze before swishing her long, elegant skirt back toward the kitchen, where Nolan was chatting with the uniformed officer.

Grant took her place, though even seated he towered over me enough to be intimidating. "So who hit you?" he asked, his voice tight.

I shrugged. "I wish I knew," I said. Then I launched into my narrative for the third time that evening, covering the high points of having seen someone in Harper's room, gone inside to investigate, and been knocked unconscious.

Grant kept a perfect poker face the entire time, any emotion he might have felt carefully hidden, save for the hazel flecks in his eyes that seemed to pick up their frenzied pace the more I talked. They were practically flashing with fire by the time I ended with waking to find Ava and Nolan hovering over me.

"And you didn't see anyone?" he asked again.

I shook my head. "No. I only caught a glimpse of a shadow when I turned around. And it was dark."

"How did you get in the house?"

I paused, that question catching me off guard. "I…I just came in the back door."

"It was unlocked?"

"Yeah. I suppose it was. You think the intruder got in that way too?"

Grant drew in a long breath, clearly more comfortable asking the questions than answering them. "The responding officer on the scene said it looked like the lock had been tampered with."

"So someone *did* break in," I said, more to myself than Grant.

He nodded. "Unfortunately, the security system here leaves something to be desired."

"Carrie is going to upgrade it," I said automatically, remembering our first conversation. Which seemed like eons ago now, not the scant 48 hours it had actually been.

"She should. What with the publicity she's gotten lately, this place was a burglary waiting to happen."

That pulled me out of my own thoughts. "Burglary? Wait—you don't think this was a random break-in, do you?"

"Can you give me any reason to believe it wasn't?" The tone in his voice was almost a challenge.

I could give him several, but all felt like they begged an explanation that I feared could veer into self-incrimination territory.

"I think someone was going through Harper's things," I finally said.

His eyes flickered to the stairs. "We're waiting on CSI to go through the guest room again."

Which was some comfort. If whoever had been looking through her room had left any fingerprints behind, I knew Grant's team would find them.

"It would be too coincidental for this to be random," I continued.

Grant's eyes gave nothing away as to if he believed that or was chalking this up to a local cat burglar. "Coincidences happen."

"Her jewelry was out on her dresser," I said. "And her Hermes bag is still there."

His blank look told me the designer label was lost on him.

"It's worth forty grand, even used," I informed him. "If someone was burglarizing the place, don't you think they would have taken it?"

"Maybe you scared him off."

"Maybe he was trying to scare *me* off by whacking me on the head," I countered.

Which, in hindsight, might not have been the smartest argument, as at the mention of head whacking, his jaw tensed, his eyes narrowed, and I could see his breath coming faster. "And *that* scares *me*," he said, his voice tight again.

Emotion backed up in my throat at the admission of fear from Bad Cop. I sniffled it back, trying to be strong. "I'm fine," I managed to get out.

He nodded, though his eyes said he didn't believe that much more than I did. Finally he scrubbed a hand over his face and rose from the sofa. "Let's get you home," he said.

I let him grab my hand and help me up, feeling almost steady on my feet, even if the sudden change in elevation cause my stomach to go queasy again. "Ava said she could drive me home," I told him.

But he shook his head. "Sorry. Tonight, you're all mine."

My stomach flipped for a whole new reason, making me lightheaded.

Oh boy.

* * *

I blamed it on the bump on the head that the entire ride back to Oak Valley Vineyards I was picturing visions of Grant's firm chest and soft lips keeping me company all night. If I'd been thinking clearly, I'd have realized that Grant's offer had less to do with heat and more to do with a possible concussion. And Grant was way too much of a gentleman to take advantage of an injured woman.

Much to my dismay.

As soon as he'd walked me to my cottage, he'd insisted on sleeping in my guest room. I wasn't sure who he trusted the least—me or him. In the end, I hadn't protested when he'd settled me into my own bedroom with a couple painkillers and left me alone.

To be honest, I probably wouldn't have known what to do with him that night anyway. Okay, that was a total lie. I had a feeling no woman would ever be at a loss for what to do with a body like Grant's. But the circumstances were less than ideal, and a soft pillow and a good night's sleep were all my brain was cut out for that evening.

The soft pillow came as soon as I shut off the lights and lay my head down. The good night's sleep was more elusive, unfortunately. I wasn't sure if it was Grant's nearness, the thousands of questions buzzing through my head surrounding Harper's death, or the fog of the goose egg coupled with painkillers, but I spent the better part of the night tossing and turning.

Just before dawn, I gave up and silently padded down the stairs, hoping a cup of hot tea would help.

I didn't need a light as moonlight flooded in through the open windows. The sounds of the early morning rustled the trees as an owl hooted his hello, and my bare feet quietly tapped the floorboards. I paused at the bottom of the stairs and found Grant curled up on my worn leather sofa, an empty water glass on the coffee table in front of him. I couldn't help a grin. Apparently he'd had trouble sleeping as well.

Though, he was in perfect repose now, his features relaxed, the usual creases in his brow gone as he dozed upright beneath the afghan my grandmother had crocheted for me. The stubble dusting his face was pronounced, his hair was messed, and he was snoring lightly. He'd discarded his linen shirt, a thin cotton tee alone covering his chest, which rose and fell at a peaceful rate. His gun glinted in the moonlight as it sat on the side table next to the sofa.

It felt good to have him in my house, and watching him sleep felt intimate. Like I was getting a glimpse into the man that he rarely showed the world. I didn't want to leave.

Instead, I curled up into the large chair opposite him and lay my head on the armrest. I smiled in the early morning light and allowed sleep to finally consume me.

* * *

I woke with the sun streaming in. The blanket that had covered Grant was now tucked around me, and his gun was gone from the table.

I sat up and listened for him, but the house was quiet. I did, however, detect an aroma of coffee coming from the small adjacent kitchen. Tossing the blanket off, I walked the few feet from my "cozy" living room to my "cozy" kitchen to find my one appliance—a stainless steel coffee machine—percolating with liquid heaven. A novelty mug that read *Too early for wine?* sat on the counter beside the machine, and next to it was a sticky note.

I thought you might need this.
PS: It's creepy to watch someone sleep.

I grinned to myself before sticking the note on my fridge.

CHAPTER FOURTEEN

———

As an attempt to distract from the lump on the side of my head, I dressed in a cheery yellow sundress, hoping the color would rub off on my mood. I paired it with some silver Grecian sandals and upped my usual makeup routine, going heavy on the eyeliner. After carefully blow-drying my hair, I felt almost human again. I was just adding a spritz of my favorite perfume as a finishing touch, when my phone buzzed with a text from Ava.

In the big kitchen with Eddie. I have croissants from the Chocolate Bar.

My mouth watered. The Chocolate Bar was a shop owned by my friend Leah, who had a flair for baked goods and a love of chocolate that rivaled my own emotional attachment to bacon. I was about to shoot back a text asking if there was coffee too, when another one buzzed in from her.

And lattes from the Half Calf.

I chuckled out loud. She knew me so well.

Locking the door to my cottage behind me, I made my way down the short stone walkway to the main winery buildings and entered the kitchen through the back door.

Ava stood at the counter, her back to me, in a pair of jeans with flower embroidery up the legs and a loose blouse in a pale blue color. Her head was bowed, deep in conversation with Eddie—who in contrast to Ava's subtle chic look was wearing the world's loudest Hawaiian shirt I'd ever seen in shades of fuchsia and orange that suddenly made my head start to hurt again. Beside him, Conchita nibbled on a croissant, eyes pinging from Eddie to Ava as they whispered amongst themselves.

"Good morning," I said, breaking the three apart.

Eddie looked up first, his eyes narrowing as he took me in. "Oh, honey, you look horrible."

I rolled my eyes. "Gee, thanks." I looked down. "I thought this dress was nice."

"It is," he assured me. "But you've got steamer trunks under those eyes. Girl, were you up all night?"

"One can only hope," Conchita added. "Her detective spent the night."

Eddie gasped, hands going to his mouth in a dramatic gesture.

"He's not *my* detective." At least, not yet. "And he spent the night in the guest room," I informed them.

"Well, that sucks," Ava said, sipping from a paper cup with the Half Calf's logo on it. She stepped forward and handed me another one.

"It's fine," I assured her. "In fact, it was kind of nice." I felt warmth rushing through me at the memory of watching Grant sleep.

"You're blushing." Eddie grinned at me. "You sure he spent the *whole* night in the guest room?"

"Yes!" I answered. Well, mostly.

"Bummer." Eddie shrugged.

"Come sit," Conchita insisted, leading me over to an empty barstool. "Ava told us everything. How's your head?"

"Better," I said. Which was the truth. The pain had subsided to a dull ache.

"Good," Eddie said, nodding. "Then we want the deets."

I hesitated. Between Eddie's flair for the dramatic and Conchita's mother hen complex, I wasn't sure how many details were wise. On the other hand, if I left those details to their imaginations, I feared how far they'd run. Since Ava had already filled in the broad strokes, I went with the lesser of two evils, and I told the entire story once again, relaying everything that had happened the night before—from Grant's revelation about Harper being pregnant, to my trip to Carrie's house, to the attack from the intruder.

"Oh, girl, you are so lucky Ava and Nolan came home when they did!" Eddie exclaimed

"That's what I said," Ava chimed in. "If Nolan hadn't invited me back to the house for a glass of wine, who knows what might have happened."

I shuddered, not wanting to think about that. "Sorry I ruined your nightcap with Nolan."

She waved me off. "Don't be silly. It's not your fault. Besides, Nolan said he's making it up to me tonight. He's taking me dancing downtown." She waggled her eyebrows up and down, as if *dancing* was a code word for something much more intimate.

"You know," Conchita said, her face puckered in thought, "if Bert was with Carrie last night, he couldn't have been the one to hit you over the head, *mija*."

"That's right!" Eddie agreed. He turned to me. "Which means Bert really is innocent."

"Of hitting me," I amended. "That doesn't mean he didn't kill Harper."

"If Bert was the one to get her pregnant," Conchita mused, "it does give him a motive to want her gone before Carrie found out."

"*If* it was his," Ava added.

"But the murder and the intruder can't be unrelated," Eddie reasoned. "That would be way too much of a coincidence."

I shook my head. "No, you're right. I'm sure it all has to do with Harper." I paused. "But that doesn't mean they still weren't two different people."

"So who *do* you think hit you?" Ava asked, grabbing a croissant.

I sipped my latte, thinking about that. "I guess my money is on Tripp. He seems the most likely person to go bashing people around on the head. And I did see him at Carrie's once before when he thought no one was there—burning Harper's clothes."

Ava nodded. "So, you think Bert gets Harper pregnant, and Tripp finds out about it. He tries to blackmail Harper, but she refuses, and he kills her. Then he decides to blackmail Bert instead—"

"Which explains the money we found in his trailer," I added.

"—and he burns Harper's clothes because there was something about them that was his blackmail leverage, and he doesn't want to get caught now."

I nodded. "It all adds up."

"So why was he in Harper's room?" Conchita asked, eyes going back and forth between us again.

"Looking for more leverage?" Eddie offered.

I thought about that for a beat. "Then why destroy the leverage he had in the first place?"

"Good point," Eddie conceded.

We sipped our coffees in silence, realizing it did *not* all add up after all.

"You know, what about that sister?" Conchita finally said.

We all turned to look at her.

"Kellen?" I offered.

She nodded. "Maybe she killed Harper because she found out about the pregnancy."

"Just because she didn't want to be an aunt?" Eddie asked, shaking his head.

"No, but Kellen said Harper was always embarrassing the family. Maybe getting pregnant with a married man's child was the last straw."

"I don't know. I mean, a child out of wedlock is hardly the stuff of scandals," Ava said. "We're not living in the eighteen hundreds."

"Maybe *we're* not, but you should see the Bishops' place," I said, picturing the myriad of antiques. "Anyway, Kellen said her parents were scandalized by their daughter acting on a soap opera. If that's bad, living the way Harper sounds like she was would be even worse."

"Bad enough to kill?" Ava asked. I could tell she was still unconvinced. Then again, she'd yet to meet the ultra-blue-blooded Kellen Bishop-Brice.

"This all assumes that Kellen knew about Harper's pregnancy," Eddie pointed out. "If Harper was trying to keep it secret at the party, it's possible she didn't tell her sister."

"It's possible," I agreed. "But Kellen did sneak away to see her sister in private just before she died. And her husband said she was upset when she got home."

"You think it was because Harper told her about the pregnancy?" Eddie asked.

"I think we should definitely find out," Ava decided.

* * *

The gates at the Bishop estate were open today as I approached, so we skipped the intercom and drove directly up the winding driveway to the faux French château.

"Wow," Ava whispered beside me as she took in the expanse of green lawn, blooming foliage, and sculpted topiaries that sprawled on either side of us. "This place is serious money."

"Wait till you see inside," I told her, parking again near the towering fountain.

As I beeped my Jeep locked, my phone buzzed with a text. I quickly glanced at the readout. David Allen's number came up along with a short message.

Heard you had some excitement last night. You okay?

"Grant?" Ava asked hopefully.

I shook my head. "No. David Allen. Apparently he heard about the intruder at Carrie's."

Ava gave me a sheepish smile. "Yeah, sorry. That might have been my fault. I kinda told him this morning."

I gave her a raised eyebrow. "You talked to David this morning?"

She nodded. "Sure. We talk all the time. Mostly about you," she added with a wink.

"That's disconcerting," I mumbled as we approached the front door and I shoved my phone back into my purse.

My knock was answered by a different woman than I'd encountered on my previous visit. This one was younger and had a fair complexion and jet black hair, though she was dressed in the same old style maid's uniform in crisp black and white.

"May I help you?" she asked politely.

"I was hoping we could speak with Kellen," I said.

"Is she expecting you?" the woman asked.

"Not exactly." I cleared my throat. "But I was here before with Carrie Cross, Harper's friend."

While I wasn't sure the six degrees of separation actually explained my presence there, the fact that I was a repeat visitor must have convinced her I was on the approved persons list, as she stepped back, allowing us entry.

"If you don't mind waiting just a moment, I'll inform Mrs. Kellen that you're here," she said, closing the door behind us and giving a curt nod before she disappeared down a hallway.

We only had to wait a minute before Kellen herself appeared, her heels clacking noisily along the polished marble floor as she strode toward us. If she recognized me, she made no indication of it.

"Yes?" she asked in a clipped tone that immediately conveyed her belief that whatever the reason we were there, it was a waste of her precious time.

"Emmy," I supplied. "Emmy Oak. I, uh, stopped by with Carrie the other day to offer my condolences on the passing of your sister."

"Oh. Yes," she replied, her expression void of any emotion at the mention of her sister.

"I'm so sorry for your loss," Ava jumped in.

"This is my friend, Ava Barnett," I said, making introductions.

"How do you do," Kellen said automatically, though I noticed she simply nodded in Ava's direction in lieu of shaking hands. "Was there something I could help you with?"

A confession to her sister's murder would be nice. But I figured an accusation was a terrible icebreaker, so I went with the line Ava and I had come up with in the car ride over instead.

"I know Carrie was here helping Sandra plan Harper's memorial services yesterday. I thought I'd stop by and offer my catering services for the memorial as well." Which wasn't a total lie. If Kellen wanted to hire me, I certainly wouldn't turn down the work.

"Ah," she simply said. "Well, unfortunately Sandra is no longer with us, so the odious planning task has fallen to me."

She motioned for us to follow her as she turned and retreated back down the polished hallway.

"What happened to Sandra?" I asked her back as we wound past the oil paintings and antiques toward the great room.

"I had to let her go. This morning, actually. She was stealing from us," Kellen said, a sneer in her voice. "Can you imagine? After all we've done for her."

I wasn't exactly sure what that "all" encompassed, but apparently Kellen thought it deserved a degree of loyalty.

"Had she been with you long?" I asked, trying to reconcile the polite woman I'd met with Kellen's portrait of a thief.

Kellen shook her head as she led us to a grouping of club chairs near the fireplace. "Long enough. Anyway," she went on as she lowered herself into one of the chairs, "now I'm left holding the bag on this whole memorial."

"Well, hopefully we can be of help," I told her as Ava and I sat in a pair of chairs opposite her, the hard leather squeaking beneath me. "When are you planning the service for?"

"My mother and father will be arriving in a couple of days, so we'll obviously be waiting until then."

"How are they holding up?" I asked.

"They're devastated, of course," Kellen answered. She frowned at me, as if I'd asked a stupid question.

"Where are they traveling in from?" Ava asked.

"The Riviera," Kellen said, a note of pride in her voice, as if the location alone were a bragging right. "They own a vacation home there. They go every summer."

"It's barely spring," I noted.

Kellen frowned again, this time in obvious annoyance. "Well, they've been under extra stress this year. What with Harper's exploits. They went early."

"What exploits, exactly?" Ava asked.

Kellen turned her gaze to Ava. "I'm sorry—who did you say you were again?"

Clearly it was meant more as a dig to mind her own business rather than a genuine question.

But if Ava was insulted by it, she didn't let on, just shooting the same sunny smile Kellen's way as she answered, "A friend. And a fan of Harper's work."

Kellen snorted. "As if you could call what my sister did on that ridiculous TV show *work* compared to what the rest of us do."

"Yes, I believe Emmy mentioned your charity work," Ava said, impressively keeping a straight face.

"Philanthropy is a duty. My family has shouldered that duty for many years, and I'm proud to carry on that tradition."

"Did Harper leave any money to charity?" I asked, suddenly curious.

"Excuse me?" Kellen turned her attention back to me.

"In her will. I assume she had some assets?"

"My sister had nothing," Kellen informed me, her tone dry.

"Nothing?" Ava asked. Her voice held a note of disbelief as her eyes roved the opulently decorated room. "Surely she had some allowance or trust fund?"

"*Had* is the key word. My parents finally cut her off financially a few months ago."

"That seems harsh," Ava said. "What did Harper do that was so bad?"

"What didn't she do?" Kellen asked on a sarcastic laugh. "Anything that would cause the family embarrassment was like a fun game to Harper. But if you're asking what the last straw was, it was her DUI."

"I read about that," Ava said, nodding. "Last fall, right?"

"Yes. Well, I'm sure you did read about it. The press had a field day with that. Including the *Napa Valley Register*! Can you imagine how devastating that was for my father? All of his associates read the *Register*." She shook her head at the horror of it all. "Anyway, our attorney 'fixed' it for her, but my parents were done with her after that. They cut her off financially completely. Told her that she needed to grow up and start acting in a way befitting a Bishop."

"Grow up, as in quit acting and devote herself to philanthropy?" I clarified.

"Charity work builds character."

If Kellen Bishop-Brice was any indication, that statement was debatable.

"Kellen, what was it that you and Harper talked about the last time you saw her?" I asked, hoping to get to the point of our visit.

She blinked at me again, her eyelashes fluttering. "I-I told you. She came for Christmas. It didn't go well, and she left."

"I didn't mean then. I meant earlier this week. When you met her downtown."

Her skin went a shade paler underneath her expensive makeup. "W-what do you mean?"

"I mean, I know you saw Harper the day before she died."

"Th-that's preposterous."

"We have a witness," Ava said.

"A witness?" Kellen's pallor was practically ghostlike as she realized she was good and truly caught. How embarrassing. She licked her lips, eyes instinctively darting over her shoulder to her bookshelf, even though the only ones in attendance to witness her humiliation were Dickens and Shakespeare.

"Kellen, you did meet Harper, didn't you?" I asked softly.

"Alright," she finally said. "Yes. I saw my sister. There's no crime in that."

"Why did you lie about it?" Ava asked.

Kellen cleared her throat, clearly attempting to regain her composure. "We had things to discuss that aren't public knowledge, and I wanted to keep them that way."

"Like her pregnancy?" I took a guess.

Kellen closed her eyes for a moment, all composure gone, and I could almost hear the host of unladylike words running through her mind.

"What do you want?" she finally asked, opening her eyes back up and narrowing them at me. "Money? Is that it? You want to be paid off to keep your mouths shut?"

"N-no!" I stammered, caught off guard. "No, we just want to know what happened to Harper."

"Why?" Ava jumped in. "Has someone else tried to blackmail you?"

Kellen shook her head, her eyes flashing with fire. "Just my sister. Saying if I didn't help her talk to Mommy and Daddy about the pregnancy, she'd never forgive me."

"Is that what she wanted to meet about?" I asked. "Reconciling with your parents?"

"Reconciling with their money, you mean." Kellen gave that sardonic bark of laughter again. "Like I said, Harper had nothing. She was nearly broke. Her lifestyle far exceeded what she was paid on that little show of hers, even before they fired her. Without Mommy and Daddy to bankroll her, she knew she was in trouble."

I found the disdain in her voice hypocritical, considering she and her husband were currently being bankrolled by Mommy and Daddy too, but I said nothing, letting her go on.

"She knew they'd listen to me. She thought I could sell the idea of a baby, some happy family fantasy, and that would somehow magically change their minds about Harper."

"But you didn't?"

"Of course not. My parents are not sentimental idiots."

I could see how an accidental pregnancy, especially if it was a married man's child, wasn't every parent's dream for their daughter. But as I watched Kellen, I had to wonder how much of this disapproval really came from the Bishops and how much was just Kellen's.

"Surely the idea of an heir to carry on the family name would have been appealing?" I pushed. "At least a little?"

"Hardly." Kellen gave me a challenging look, like she knew I had no way of proving whether she was exaggerating or not.

"Did Harper tell you who the father was?" Ava asked.

Kellen shook her head. "No. And I didn't care to ask. Whatever degenerate she was spending her time with was her business, and I certainly didn't want to make it mine." She rose from her chair, her expression stoic. "Now, if there's nothing else, I'm sure you can see yourselves out."

* * *

"Suddenly I'm feeling lucky to have been an only child," Ava said once we'd left the Bishop residence and were back in my Jeep. "The love for her sister was downright smothering."

"Ditto," I agreed.

"But, I'm still not convinced she killed Harper just to avoid embarrassment."

"No," I said, going over what Kellen had said in my head. "But maybe it wasn't about that. Maybe it was more about the money."

"How so?" Ava asked as I pulled down the driveway.

"Well, Kellen said Harper was angling to reconcile with her parents."

"According to Kellen, her parents wouldn't go for it."

"Right *according to Kellen*. But maybe they would have. Maybe Kellen was afraid that a grandchild would suddenly change everything," I said, a theory forming out loud. "Kellen's been living off her parents' money, and her husband, Morgan, all but said she was just waiting for them to die so she could get her half of the inheritance."

"But with a grandchild now in the mix, she ran the risk of the inheritance being split three ways," Ava said, picking up my train of thought.

"Exactly," I said, nodding. "And who knows how much of their estate the Bishops might have willed to their only grandchild. It could have even been more than just a third. Maybe even the bulk of it."

"Only now with Harper gone, Kellen stands to inherit it all."

Ava and I both fell silent contemplating just how much that *all* would be. Judging from the mansion we'd just left, it was plenty worth killing over.

"But what about the blackmail?" Ava asked.

"What about it?"

"Well, I don't see Kellen blackmailing her sister."

"You're right," I admitted. Of all the rotten things I could imagine Kellen doing, that wasn't one. She'd said herself that Harper didn't have any money. "So who did?"

"I still like Tripp. He finds out about Harper's pregnancy and says he'll keep quiet about it if she pays him."

"Assuming it's Bert's and Harper doesn't want Carrie to know?" I asked, hating that every theory seemed to end in Bert being guilty.

Ava must have picked up my feeling, as she shook her head. "Or whoever the father is. I mean, maybe it was even someone else with more to lose than Bert. Harper could have been seeing any number of guys. I mean, who knows what she was doing three months ago?"

I froze, that last part of her statement making something in the back of my mind click. "Actually, I know exactly what she was doing three months ago." I turned to face Ava. "She was taking horseback riding lessons from Tripp Jones."

She blinked at me, the same realization hitting her. "No! You don't think Harper and Tripp…" She let the insinuation trail off.

I nodded, bobbing my head up and down so vigorously that my hair flopped in my face. "I think it's entirely possible."

"But he hardly seems her type."

"You haven't seen him with his shirt off," I told her. "If I wasn't halfway convinced he was a murderer, a guy with abs like that could be temptingly my type."

"Harper pregnant with Tripp's baby," Ava said, trying the theory on for size. "This is better than an episode of *Carefree Hearts*!"

"Or worse," I added. "Depending on your point of view."

Ava swatted me on the arm. "That show is awesome."

"If you say so." I grinned at her. "It does change things though. If Harper was pregnant with Tripp's child and not Bert's, Tripp would have had no reason to blackmail Harper over it."

"So who did?" Ava asked.

"And why?" I added.

"Exactly," Ava said. "And I think that's the key to this whole thing."

"So, how do we find that out?" I asked, thinking out loud.

"Grant didn't say if the techs found anything on Harper's phone?"

I shook my head. "No, but he probably wouldn't tell me even if they did find something."

"Well, maybe there was more to the message? Like, maybe something that would point to the blackmailer's identity?"

"You really think he'd sign it?"

"No," Ava said, pouting. "No, you're right. But maybe something about the drop-off location or the language. I don't know." She shook her head. "I just wish we could have seen it ourselves."

"Me too," I agreed. I paused, thinking back to what Carrie had told me about the message she'd seen. "You know, it might be a long shot, but it's possible maybe we *can* see it."

"How?" Ava shot a glance at me again.

"Well, I remember Carrie saying they only have two working security cameras. One at the property entrance and one at the front door. Carrie said Harper was on the front porch when she spotted her phone."

"You think maybe the camera picked something up?" Ava asked, her eyes lighting with enthusiasm.

I shrugged. "Like I said, it's a long shot...but it's possible."

Ava grinned. "Carrie's house is on the way home," she pointed out. "Might as well stop by and check it out, right?"

* * *

"Oh, hi, Emmy. I wasn't expecting you," Carrie said, as she pulled her front door open fifteen minutes later.

"Sorry. We should have called," I told her.

"No, no. It's fine." She paused. "I actually meant to call you. Nolan told me all about the attack last night. Are you okay?"

My hand instinctively went to the bump on my head, which thankfully the painkillers had mostly relieved. "I'm fine," I assured her.

Carrie shook her head. "First Harper and then the break-in. I'm not sure how much more I can take." The dark rings under her eyes told me she'd had as rotten a night's sleep as I had. She looked pale, and her naturally slim frame looked downright skinny today, her jeans baggy on her hips.

"I'm sure the police will find the intruder," I told her, trying to sound comforting.

Carrie nodded. Barkley yapped around our feet. "They were here again today. That detective."

I pursed my lips. I'd figured as much. "What did he say?"

Carrie shook her head. "I don't know. He talked to Bert alone in the den."

"And Bert didn't say what it was about?"

Again her head shook. "No. He said he didn't want to talk about it."

I'll bet.

Barkley jumped up against Carrie's leg, his boundless energy a stark contrast to how tired she looked.

"Sit," she told him halfheartedly.

He jumped more, yapping playfully at her.

She finally relented and picked him up before turning her attention back to us. "Can I offer you some coffee or something?"

"I never say no to coffee. But why don't you let me make it," I offered.

"I couldn't ask you to do that," Carrie protested, though it was about as halfhearted as her attempts to silence Barkley, her body seemingly void of any energy.

"You didn't ask. I offered," I told her with a smile. "Why don't you go sit on the terrace and get some sunshine, and I'll bring it out?"

Ava linked her arm though Carrie's. "Come on, I'll keep you company," she said.

I gave Ava a grateful smile as Carrie was reluctantly led outside.

Ava kept the chatter bubbly as they disappeared through the house, and I made my way to the kitchen, quickly putting Carrie's coffeemaker to work. I found a bag of pastries on the counter and added it to a tray with our steaming mugs before I carried it all outside to hear the tail end of their conversation.

"—so quiet here without Dante." Carrie sighed wistfully.

"Have you heard anything from Animal Control?" Ava asked as she set the tray down on a teak table on the patio.

"No. But Tripp told me that he was doing his best to get him released. I told him they just can't euthanize him for what he did. He's not a killer. He was just scared."

While I knew Dante hadn't purposely killed Harper, he was a wild animal, and clearly they were dangerous. But I kept that thought to myself.

"I didn't know if Bert was joining us," I said to Carrie, handing her a mug of steaming coffee.

"No. He's upstairs. On the phone with his lawyer. This whole thing is just so unfair. I just wish it was over." Tears welled behind her lashes. Barkley whimpered, nuzzling into her.

Ava took her hand and squeezed it tight.

I handed Carrie one of the paper napkins I'd placed on the tray, and she dabbed her eyes.

"Carrie, we actually came by because we wanted to ask you something about the night of the party," I said, sitting in the seat opposite her.

"Yes?" she asked, sipping at her coffee.

"When you saw Harper's phone that night—with the word *blackmail* on it—you said you were on the porch, correct?"

She nodded. "That's right. Harper had ducked out to get some air."

"And that's one of the few places where you said you do have a working security camera?"

She nodded again, a small frown forming between her eyebrows. "Yes. Why?"

"Well, do you think there's any chance the cameras might have caught a glimpse of Harper's phone?"

She blinked at me, the frown deepening as she thought. "I-I don't know. I never thought of that. It's possible, I suppose." She paused. "The police officers have already looked through all the footage though. It was one of the first things they did when they arrived."

I should have figured as much. However, there was a chance they might not have been looking for the same thing we were.

"Did they take it all, or do you still have copies?" Ava asked.

"We still have it," Carries said, nodding. "I mean, it's all digital. The police just copied files from our system, but we didn't erase anything." She paused again. "You really think there's something there that might help Bert?"

"I think it's worth looking," I told her, meaning it.

"The system is set up in the den," Carrie said, rising to lead the way.

Ava and I followed, leaving our coffee behind as we entered the house through the back door and made our way down the short hallway.

It was welcoming and cool after the heat on the terrace, yet it felt eerily quiet. I knew that Carrie had purchased it as an escape from the fast life in LA, but with the pall hanging over the place now, I wondered if she planned to stay on.

The den had a distinctly masculine feel to it, filled with dark woods and leather chairs in warm brown tones. The desk was immaculate—its top empty except for a sleek, slim monitor—the view to the hills beyond the estate was spectacular, and the absence of Barkley's hair told me he either wasn't allowed in here or their housekeeper did a mighty fine job.

Carrie sat at the desk and jiggled a computer mouse, the monitor springing to life.

Ava and I moved behind her to view it.

Carrie did a little clicking around, opening a program that linked to their security system. As she'd mentioned, it didn't look high tech, and by the slightly pixilated look of the software, I assumed it predated the app craze. But even if it was dated, it seemed to work, having logged footage of the night in question. Several files appeared with the date of the party on them. Carrie clicked on one, and a video player appeared.

From the angle of the footage, it looked like the cameras were mounted in the upper right corner of the eaves, facing the doorway, though the frame was wide enough to cover most of the front porch and a small swath of the driveway beyond. We watched several people come into view, entering the house one after another as the party got underway. Occasionally Carrie's face popped into the frame, greeting newcomers and ushering them into the house.

"What time did you see Harper go outside?" I asked.

Carrie shrugged. "I don't know. I didn't actually note the time."

"Let's just let it play then," Ava said, eyes on the screen.

We did, watching several more minutes of people arriving before the steady stream ceased. A few stragglers appeared, and then there was several minutes of nothing—no activity on the porch, all of the guests having made their way into the party.

Then finally Harper's dark hair appeared, her sequin clad frame moving into view.

"There!" Ava said, pointing at the screen.

"She must have ducked out to check her messages," Carrie said as we all watched Harper lean against the porch railing and pull her phone from her sequined clutch. She clicked and scrolled, though she was angled away from the cameras, keeping the screen hidden from us.

"That's weird," Carrie said softly.

"What? What's weird?" I asked.

Carrie swiveled in the leather chair to face me. "Well, I could swear that's not Harper's phone."

I felt my heart rate speed up. "Why do you say that?"

Carrie turned her attention back to the screen, frowning. "Harper had just bought the new iPhone. She had it in this really sparkly gold case." She pointed to the screen, where Harper was clearly holding a matte black phone. "That one is the wrong color."

"Maybe she just took the case off?" Ava offered.

"Maybe," Carrie said, but I could tell by the hitch in her voice that she wasn't convinced.

"Well, she's definitely reading something," Ava said.

She was right. We could plainly see Harper scrolling, her eyes narrowing as she took in the message on her screen. The trouble was, from our angle we had no idea what it was. I was beginning to think this whole thing was a bust.

"Oh, that's me!" Carrie said, pointing as her figure appeared on screen. "This is where I came to get Harper to meet my agent."

We watched as Harper's head snapped up from her phone and she spun around to greet the hostess. Her smile was as stunning as I remembered it, and she moved in close to give Carrie a hug.

"There!" I shouted.

In hindsight maybe a little too loudly, as Carrie jumped in her chair.

But when Harper went in to embrace Carrie, she'd had her phone in her hand still, the angle of the screen directly facing the camera.

"Can you back it up?" Ava said as Harper and Carrie stepped apart again on the video.

"I think so," Carrie said, pursing her lips together in concentration as she clicked a *Rewind* button.

"See if you can pause it when Harper hugs you," I directed.

Carrie nodding, clicking the *Pause* button a second later as the two women embraced.

I leaned in, squinting at the screen to get a better look at the phone in Harper's hand. It was blurry, but I could tell it was a text message, and I could just make out the words.

"How dare you blackmail me!" I read out loud.

"That's it!" Carrie said. "That must be what I saw."

"Can you see who it's from?" Ava asked, leaning in to squint at the screen herself.

I shook my head. "No, it's too small." I paused, something not feeling quite right. "But we didn't see Harper typing, right?"

"What?" Carries asked.

"We watched Harper get a message and read it," I said, my mind working over what I was seeing on the screen. "We didn't see her typing anything out."

Ava nodded. "Right. We would have seen her thumbs moving. Or her talking, at least if she was using speech to text."

"But she didn't do either. She just read the message." I paused. "Which means, Harper didn't send this message—she received it."

Ava blinked, and I could see her coming to the same realization I had. "'How dare you blackmail me,'" she repeated. "Harper wasn't *being* blackmailed...she was blackmailing someone else!"

CHAPTER FIFTEEN

———

"No," Carrie said, shaking her head. "I can't believe that. Harper wouldn't do that."

"I'm afraid it looks like she did," I said, pointing to the screen again.

Carrie bit her lip, warring emotions evident in her eyes. "She wouldn't," she repeated, but I could hear the statement losing conviction.

Ava put a hand on Carrie's shoulder. "I'm sorry."

So was I. Especially as I thought of what, exactly, Harper could have been blackmailing someone about.

Kellen had told us that morning that Harper was hard up for money. She'd been cut off by her parents, fired from her job, and just found out she was pregnant. I could see her being desperate for cash. Desperate enough to start an affair with Bert, just to blackmail him about it later?

Then again, hadn't Kellen mentioned Harper "blackmailing" her? She'd said Harper had told her she'd never forgive her if she didn't help her get back in her parents' good graces…but maybe Harper hadn't stopped at emotional blackmail. Maybe she'd asked Kellen for actual cash to keep quiet about something. I didn't know what skeletons lurked in Kellen's closet, but I did know embarrassment was high on Kellen's list of things to avoid in life. Had Harper threatened to reveal something embarrassing about the Bishop family if Kellen didn't pay up?

Of course, there was also my favorite suspect, Tripp. While it was possible Harper had gotten physically close to the cowboy when he'd given her riding lessons, it was also possible she'd gotten emotionally close enough to him to have found some secret she used to her advantage. Had she found out something incriminating about Tripp that he'd rather keep quiet? My mind went back to my conversation with Grant and the fact Tripp had been a suspect in a prior murder. Maybe Harper had found the evidence the police lacked to convict him and had blackmailed Tripp with it? Maybe the duffel full of cash hadn't been a payment *to* Tripp, but one he'd been preparing to give to Harper?

"...sure that's not her phone."

I realized I'd been so lost in my own thoughts that I hadn't been paying attention to the conversation around me. I tuned back in to find Carrie staring at the footage on the screen again.

"What about Harper's phone?" I asked.

"It doesn't look right," Carrie repeated. "I don't think it's even the right size. Her new iPhone was bigger." She swiveled in her chair to face me again. "I don't think that phone is hers."

"Could it be a burner?" Ava asked. She squinted at the screen. "Remember we thought that Tripp could have used a burner phone to make his blackmail requests so the calls couldn't be traced?"

"Tripp?" Carrie turned a confused look from me to Ava.

"Uh, yeah," I admitted. "We thought maybe Tripp was the blackmailer at first."

"But why?"

"Well, I, uh, saw him doing something. Something that seemed off."

"Off how?" Carrie pressed.

I hesitated to tell her, not sure if I was sharing sensitive information with the wife of a killer. But chances were it was all going to come out eventually anyway, so I quickly filled her in on seeing Tripp burn Harper's clothes in the fire pit and how Ava and I had happened to see a duffel bag full of money in his trailer. I did not elaborate on how we'd happened to be inside his trailer, but luckily, Carrie didn't dig, her blonde brows just pulling deeper and deeper into a silent frown as I talked.

"And you think Tripp might have had something to do with Harper's death?" she asked when I'd finished.

I nodded. "I think it's a possibility."

Carrie turned her gaze back to the screen, chewing on her lower lip in thought. "The police took Harper's iPhone."

That much I knew. I also knew they hadn't found any mention of blackmail on it, and now I knew why—she'd had a disposable phone.

"They didn't mention finding a second phone among her things?" I asked.

Carrie shook her head. "No. And Bert actually watched them pretty carefully. He would have noticed."

"Maybe she hid it," Ava said.

"But the police have been all through her room. I think they would have found it."

I'd been through there too, and I hadn't seen a black phone.

"Maybe…" Ava said, drawing out the word, "her killer took it off her after she died."

I raised an eyebrow her way. "Go on."

"If the killer was someone Harper was blackmailing, the last thing they'd want is for the police to find a phone with their number in it, right?"

I nodded. "Right. Especially if it had blackmail requests on it."

"You think the killer still has the phone now?" Carrie asked, her gaze once again pinging between us as we formulated our new theory.

I shrugged. "It's possible they destroyed it."

"Or, it's possible it's still hidden away," Ava added. "Like at the bottom of a bag of cash."

"You mean the duffel bag in Tripp's trailer?" Carrie asked.

Ava nodded. "What if Harper was blackmailing Tripp about something she found out during their relationship?"

"Possibly about his past," I added, thinking of his ex-girlfriend who'd ended up dead as well.

"Right. And, if Harper was using a burner phone, it's possible Tripp didn't even know who was blackmailing him!"

"Until he went to hand off the duffel bag of cash at your housewarming party," I said, nodding toward Carrie.

"Maybe that was the first time he realized Harper was behind it, and he got angry," Ava said, picking up the thread again. "Maybe they fought, and Tripp lost his cool. And he threw Harper into the horse ring."

I cringed, trying not to picture her body there.

"Then he takes the cash back home," Ava continued, "along with Harper's disposable phone that she used to blackmail him. Then, the next day, he burns the evidence in the fire pit."

"But he was burning clothes. Not a phone," I pointed out.

Ava shrugged. "Maybe they were all tied together somehow."

"Maybe," I said. While it was a good theory, I felt like something wasn't quite fitting.

"I think we should go talk to Tripp," Carrie said, standing.

"I don't know. He wasn't really in a talking mood the last time I approached him," I told her.

"He'll talk to me," Carrie said, determination in her voice. "If he did this to Harper—if even part of what you're saying is true—there's no way I'm letting him get away with it."

* * *

Rosebay Meadows hadn't improved since my last visits. If it was possible, in the pale afternoon light, it looked even worse. The grass looked taller, the odd slabs of pavement more cracked, and the smattering of dilapidated homes and trailers clinging to the hillside looked even more run down.

"This is where Tripp lives?" Carrie asked, winding her window up.

"At the top of the hill," I explained, slowing my Jeep as I pulled up the dirt road.

"I had no idea," she said, more to herself than us. Whether she had no idea her horse trainer wasn't as well off as she was or that some people actually had to live like this, I wasn't sure. But as I pulled to a stop outside Tripp's small plot of land, she let out a sad sigh before exiting the passenger seat.

As the three of us carefully stepped over the debris in the front yard, I felt my phone buzz in my pocket. I pulled it out to see another text from David Allen.

Looking for proof of life. And all the gory details.

I grinned before shoving my phone back into my pocket and making a mental note to text him later when I had time for details. I caught up with Carrie as she was banging her fist on the metal front door so hard that the sound echoed inside.

I shifted nervously from foot to foot, wondering exactly what Carrie planned to say.

When no one answered, she knocked again but had much the same results—an echo from the interior but no sign of an occupant.

"His truck's not here," Ava pointed out, nodding to the empty spot where it had been parked the day before. "Maybe he's not home."

Carrie pulled her phone from her purse and scrolled through her contacts, stopping when she got to Tripp's name. I heard it ring four times before a generic computer voice said to leave a message.

"No answer," she told us.

Ava stood on tiptoe and peeked in the front window. While there wasn't a whole lot to see through the grungy glass and tacked up sheets, she did come to one conclusion. "Lights are all off in there. I don't think anyone is home."

I took a step back toward my Jeep. "Well, I guess we can try coming back another time— Wait, what are you doing?"

Ava paused with her hand on the front doorknob. "What?"

"Are you trying to break in?" My gaze went from Ava to Carrie, and I stopped myself from adding *again* just in time.

But Ava shook her head. "No,"

"Good."

"I was just wondering if the door was locked."

"Ava, I don't think that's a good—"

But I didn't get to finish as she plowed ahead, twisting the knob in her hand and pushing the door open easily. She gave me an innocent look. "Well, what do you know?"

I rolled my eyes.

"He's trusting, for a criminal," Carrie mumbled.

"Alleged criminal," I added, suddenly feeling like it was a very bad idea to bring her here at all.

Ava pushed the door all the way open and stepped inside, Carrie right behind her. I hesitated a moment, but since I was already an accessory after the fact *again*, I followed them.

I glanced around and noticed some of the mess had been cleaned up. The interior felt different. Bigger. Like some things were missing.

"The pile of clothes is gone," Ava called from deeper in the trailer, standing at the bedroom doorway.

I moved beside her and surveyed the small back room. She was right—no clothing in sight. I would have thought it was laundry day, but also missing was his bong, boots, and any sign of his horse training equipment.

Ava lowered herself to the floor, looking under the bed. "The duffel bag is gone too."

"What do you mean, gone?" Carrie asked from behind us.

"I mean, it's not here." Ava straightened back up.

No clothes, no equipment, no money.

I met Ava's gaze as she voiced the same thing I was thinking.

"It looks like Tripp's skipped town."

Carrie's expression went from confused to angry, and she let out a couple of choice words that would never make it into a PG-13 movie. Suddenly I saw where she got that Stormy Winter's rage from on *Carefree Hearts*. "How dare he! He kills Harper and then runs!"

I wasn't sure both of those statements were confirmed facts, but I had to admit that him leaving in a hurry did not look like the work of an innocent man.

"We should probably get out of here," I said.

Before I could act, Carrie's phone sounded from her handbag, and she quickly retrieved it, swiping the call on.

"Hello..." Carrie answered, her voice still holding an edge from her tirade. She paused as she listened to the other end, her expression changing. "Wait—Bert, slow down. I can't understand what you're saying." She stepped out of the trailer.

Ava kicked a stray beer can before she and I followed, closing the door behind us. Just for good measure, I used the hem of my dress to wipe the handle for any prints we might have left behind as I vaguely listened to Carrie's side of her phone conversation behind me.

"No, don't say anything. I-I'll call Shuman. You just...don't say anything. I'll be right there." Carrie's voice was tight, and I could feel the sudden fear in it as she hung up.

"What's wrong?" I asked, taking a step toward her.

She carefully put her phone back in her purse. "It's Bert." She lifted her eyes to meet mine. "He's been arrested."

CHAPTER SIXTEEN

———

The Sonoma County Sheriff's office was located in Santa Rosa, housed in a large, imposing building made of glass and brick. The inhabitants of the building were about as intimidating as the building itself, a mix of stoic police officers wearing guns at their waists, dour faced residents waiting to air various grievances, and disappointed loved ones and "known associates" alike waiting to post bail for the incarcerated. Carrie pulled her purse close to her chest as we made our way through the lobby toward the front desk.

After getting the initial call about her husband's arrest, Carrie'd phoned her lawyer, who had immediately agreed to meet Bert at the county detention center. We'd left Tripp's trailer and driven back toward town, where we'd dropped Ava off at Silver Girl. Ostensibly, it was because she said she had some paperwork to do before going out dancing with Nolan that evening. But really, I thought maybe she felt as if she were intruding on something personal with Carrie and Bert.

Mostly because I felt the same way. I'd offered to take Carrie home and stay with her while she awaited news from their attorney. But despite the threat of press, she'd insisted on going to the sheriff's office to support Bert. As much as I feared her husband was actually guilty, I knew Carrie needed someone there to support *her*, maybe more than Bert did, so I'd accompanied her to Santa Rosa, where we were hoping Bert's lawyer had been able to arrange for bail.

I followed her across the polished concrete floor, noting the flyers taped to the rendered walls alerting us to the many organizations that could help prevent suicide, stave off addiction, and explain low cost medical care. I almost stopped to take a picture of the last one, but thought it in bad taste, all things considered.

Instead, I followed Carrie to a large counter with the window separating the uniformed officers from the riffraff—aka us. A tall man whose biceps strained the sleeves of his khaki uniform looked up and slid a glass partition open.

"Can I help you?" To be honest, his tone didn't suggest that he was particularly interested in our answer.

Carrie's voice trembled. "I'm here to post bail for my husband. He's been arrested." She whispered the words, surreptitiously checking over her shoulder, as if a member of the paparazzi were about to jump out from behind a plastic plant and snap a photo.

"Name?" the man, whose name tag read Jonah Smith, asked in the same bored monotone.

"Uh, my name or his?" Carrie asked.

Smith gave her a *well duh* look. "His."

"Right." Carrie licked her lips. "Uh, Bert Davenport."

At the mention of Bert's name, Smith's eyes suddenly showed interested for the first time since we'd walked up. "Bert Davenport? That wouldn't be the same Bert Davenport who played Little Bertie, would it?

"Um…yes?" Carrie said, clearly not sure if that was a good thing or a bad thing in the eyes of the officer.

"Well, I'll be." Smith cracked a smile. "Little Bertie from *Home with the Hendersons*." He was obviously a fan.

Carrie smiled. "Yes, that's right," she said.

He turned to a coworker one window over and tapped her on the shoulder. "Did you know that Little Bertie is in our cells?"

She looked fresh from the academy and barely legal to drink. She blinked at him. "Who?"

"Little Bertie!"

"Is he like a rapper or something?"

Smith scoffed. "No, no. He was on *Home with the Hendersons*! I used to watch that show all the time. Little Bertie had this catchphrase. Oh! What was it?" His fist tapped his forehead, as if that would help him remember.

"'You know it, Mama!'" I volunteered, giving him the cheeky wink made famous by Bert.

He grinned. "That's it! Geez, you reminded me so much of him when you did that."

Huh. I made a mental note to never do that again.

The female officer still gave him a blank look.

"Don't tell me that you've never heard of the show?" he pressed her.

She continued to stare, yet I did detect a hint of *you're a weirdo* lurking in her eyes.

He shook his head. "Never mind. Do we have a Bert Davenport here?"

She clicked a couple of keys at her computer. "Yes, but he's waiting to go in front of the judge for his bail hearing."

Smith nodded and turned back to Carrie. "You just need to go next door to the courthouse. They can help you from there."

Carrie gulped. "Thank you."

The courthouse's entrance was on the adjoining side street. I'd never been inside but wasn't surprised that the décor matched the station. The same hard plastic chairs, the same counter with the glass partition, and the same flyers on the walls. The only difference was the electronic metal detector we needed to walk through.

Carrie repeated the same process with the courthouse officer on duty—minus the Little Bertie fandom—and we found out that Bert was being arraigned down the hall. By the time we arrived at the designated courtroom, we caught Bert just exiting through the solid double doors.

He looked worse than I had ever seen him. His eyes were sunken, highlighted only by the dark rings that circled them. His shirt was untucked, his slacks rumpled, and his hair was almost standing on end, as if he'd been running his hands through it all afternoon.

Carrie raced toward him, throwing herself into his arms. "Oh, Bert!"

He held her tight, and as much as I could tell he was trying to be her rock, I could see the fear and uncertainty of the events that day had taken their toll on him. His posture held none of the bravado or confidence I'd previously come to associate with him. "It's going to be okay," I said softly, though the words held zero conviction.

I hung back, giving the couple a moment, but as soon as they stepped apart, Bert's eyes flickered over to meet mine. Carrie must have noticed, as she jumped in to explain my presence. "I was with Emmy when you called. She drove me here."

"Thank you for taking care of Carrie," he told me.

I'd admit I was taken aback. It was the most genuine thing I'd ever heard him say to me.

"Of course." I gave him a smile.

A gray haired man exited the courtroom carrying a briefcase and came up behind Bert, clapping him on the shoulder. "You okay, Davenport?"

Bert nodded. "Thank you. I didn't think the judge was going to agree to bail."

The man, who I took to be Bert's lawyer, shook his head. "They have a nice case—I'll give them that. But a lot of it is circumstantial evidence. I'll file motions to suppress the financial records as soon as I get back to my office."

"Financial records?" Carrie frowned. "What sort of records?"

But both men ignored her.

"You really think you can get them thrown out?" Bert asked.

The attorney nodded. "If not that, we can certainly discredit the witness who saw you together."

"Witness?" Carries asked, eyes going from one man to the other.

But again, they both ignored her.

"You go home and get some rest," the attorney directed Bert. "I'll be in touch."

With that, he clapped Bert on the shoulder again, then stalked purposefully down the hallway without any acknowledgment that Carrie or I might have existed.

Carrie bit her lip, her face pale, her eyes threatening tears, as they had been ever since she'd gotten Bert's call. As soon as the gray haired man was out of earshot, she turned to her husband. "What happened? What was he talking about with witnesses and records?"

Bert sucked in a long breath, his eyes darting toward me, as if not sure he wanted to discuss this in front of the caterer.

"Bert?" Carrie prompted. "What's going on?"

My heart went out to her. I had a terrible feeling I knew exactly what was going on, and I wished there was more I could do than be a shoulder to cry on as I watched the train wreck in front of me play out.

Bert sighed and sank down onto a bench along the wall. "It's all going to come out in court now anyway." He leaned his head in his hands, rubbing at his eyes. As if trying to rub away the current circumstances.

"*What's* going to come out?" Carrie asked, perching gingerly on the bench beside him. "Honey, talk to me?"

When he lifted his head, his expression was defeated. I wasn't sure what being arrested, processed, and fingerprinted by the police might feel like, but I could tell that even the short time Bert had spent in police custody had broken what little spirit he had. He suddenly looked like Little Bertie again—vulnerable, small, and about to confess to something Mama Henderson wasn't going to like.

"I'm so sorry, Carrie," he told her, his voice breaking on the last word. "The police know everything. I can't hide it anymore. It's all going to come out."

While part of me felt like an intruder in this private moment, the other part of me wondered if I was about to hear a murder confession. I stood next to Carrie, trying to be as unobtrusive as possible even while moving close enough that I didn't miss a word of what Bert was about to say.

"What's going to come out?" Carrie asked. I could see the fear in her eyes.

He shook his head. "Harper." He slowly met Carrie's gaze. "I've been lying to you about her."

I steeled myself, knowing what was coming next and dreading it for poor Carrie.

"You have?" Carrie's voice was small.

Bert nodded. "I was not giving her investment advice. There were no investments."

Carrie frowned. "Why did she say you were?"

Bert let out a slow breath. "She was covering up what was really going on."

"Which was?" I could tell Carrie halfway didn't even want to know by the hesitation in her voice.

I reached a hand out and put it on her shoulder for support, dreading Bert's answer.

He let out another deep sigh before answering. "Blackmail."

Wait—what?

"Blackmail!" Carrie said. She turned and shot me a meaningful look.

Bert nodded. "Harper was extorting money from me to keep quiet about…something."

"*You* were the person Harper was blackmailing?" I asked, trying to contain my shock.

Bert glanced up to meet my gaze. "Yes. I-I'm sorry, Carrie," he said, turning back to his wife. "I should have told you. I should have trusted you. I should never have lied to you."

"I-I don't understand." Carrie shook her head. "What was she threatening to do?"

Bert licked his lips. "She was threatening to tell you the truth."

"Me?" Again Carrie's gaze pinged to me, as if maybe I knew what Bert was talking about. Which, honestly at this point, I did not.

"Bert, what did Harper have over you?" I asked point blank.

He did a little more sighing, but I could tell any fight he might have had in him was long gone. "I'm broke, Carrie."

"B-broke?" She shook her head again. "No. You have investments."

"No. I don't. I lied about those. All of them."

"But you're so good with money. I mean, all the money you've invested for me…" She trailed off, realization hitting her mid-thought.

"You haven't made any investments for Carrie either?" I surmised.

He shook his head slowly.

Carrie blinked, and I could only imagine the thoughts running through her head. "Okay," she finally said, "then what have you done with the money I've given you?"

"It went to pay back loans." He clasped his hands in his lap, his eyes going down to them. "The truth is, I blew through any royalties I'd earned as Little Bertie years ago. I've been living on credit and loans. Borrow money from one place to pay off another." He paused. "I thought it was all finally going to crumble, when you came along."

"You married me for my money?" The hurt in Carrie's voice was crushing.

But Bert's head snapped up, and I realized he did have a little fight left in him after all. "No!" He shook his head vehemently. "No, that's not true at all. Carrie, I love you. With all my heart." His voice cracked.

As much as I hadn't been total Team Bert up until that moment, the genuine emotion on his face tugged at my heartstrings, and I was inclined to believe him.

At least about his love for my friend.

"I just...I needed a little time," he continued. "To get back on my feet. I just...I needed to put the creditors off a little longer."

"So all the money I gave you. It's all..."

"Gone," Bert confirmed.

Carrie took a deep breath, and I could feel her spine straighten, her nerve steeling as she processed this. "And Harper knew this?"

"Yes."

"How?"

Bert sighed. "She knew one of the guys who'd loaned me the money. I don't know how she put everything together, but she got enough out of him that she did. About everything—even the phony investments."

Carrie's jaw twitched as her lips formed a tight line. I didn't know who she was the most angry with—her lying husband or her conniving best friend. "So what did Harper want from you?"

"Money," Bert answered. "She threatened that she'd tell you everything if I didn't pay her."

"Did you pay her?" I couldn't help asking.

He nodded. "I couldn't risk losing you," he said, eyes on Carrie.

"How much?" I asked.

"Ten grand."

The same amount in Tripp's trailer.

Carrie sniffed. "You asked for $10,000 from me last month because you said you had a tip on some bonds."

"I'm so sorry I lied to you," Bert repeated. "I-I just couldn't bear the thought of losing you."

Carrie frowned, as if not sure what to believe now.

"The money you gave Harper," I cut in. "It was in cash. In a Links club duffel bag?"

Bert looked up and blinked at me, the surprise evident on his face. "Y-yes." He sucked in another deep breath. "Harper told me to meet her for dinner. The night before the party. We met up in town at Tyler's Place, and I tried to convince her not to do this. That if she needed money that badly, Carrie would be happy to give her a loan or something. That we could help her."

Carrie didn't look happy to help anyone at the moment, the frown on her face growing with Bert's story.

"But Harper didn't give in?" I asked.

Bert shook his head. "No, she just laughed at me. Said I was so naïve. She took the cash."

"And then what?"

Bert shook her head. "Then I thought it was over."

"But it wasn't?" I prompted.

"No." He did more headshaking, as if trying to shake away the whole thing. "No, she asked for more. The night of the party."

"She texted you for it?"

Bert frowned. "No. She asked in person. She cornered me at the party. As I was going upstairs. She said she wanted more."

The scene I'd witnessed between them. I'd misinterpreted the entire thing all along. Harper hadn't been talking about sleeping with Bert—she'd been threatening him.

"Did you pay her more?" I asked.

"No. I told her the truth—that I simply didn't have any more." He turned to Carrie. "I thought it was only going to be a one-time thing, but she wasn't going to stop. She was going to keep asking for more. Putting me further in debt. She was going to lord this over me forever."

"Then what did you do?" I asked, slowly, fearing the worst.

But Bert simply said, "Nothing. Then she died."

Well, that was awfully convenient timing for him.

If Grant knew all of this—about Harper's blackmailing and Bert paying her off—I could see why he thought Bert might have taken matters into his own hands to make Harper stop. I had a feeling Bert was telling the truth about how desperately he loved Carrie and how much he didn't want to lose her. But that was what worried me. Desperate men did desperate things. I was less convinced that he was telling the truth when it came to exactly how Harper had ended up in Dante's pen.

"You hate me now, don't you," Bert asked Carrie.

Her expression hadn't changed, the frown still etched on her forehead. She sucked in a deep breath, and I could feel her making a decision in that moment.

"No," she finally said. "No, I don't hate you. I-I'm disappointed."

Bert nodded, eyes welling with regret.

Carrie sighed and stood. "Come on. Let's go home."

CHAPTER SEVENTEEN

———

Since I'd driven Carrie to the station, and Bert had arrived by squad car, I offered to drive the couple home. The silence was deafening and awkward, as Carrie's face was in a perma-frown, staring out the passenger window, and Bert was slumped in my back seat. I finally turned on the radio, just to fill the air with something other than tension, letting mindless pop songs take over.

By the time we finally arrived at Carrie's place, the sun was beginning to set behind the hills, dappled beams of fading light flashing between the tall oaks. I pulled to a stop beside Nolan's sports car, and as Carrie and Bert got out, I gave her a quick hug and told her she could call me anytime—day or night—if she needed to talk. She thanked me before leading Bert into the house, though I could tell her mind was a million miles away. Probably going over every conversation she'd ever had with her husband and picking it apart for the half-truths and little white lies that were woven into them.

I slipped back into my car, grateful to be alone with my thoughts as I pulled down the winding drive and pointed my Jeep toward the orange and pink colored hills of Oak Valley.

Even if my thoughts inevitably went right back to Harper's death.

I was 50-50 on Bert's innocence where killing Harper was concerned, but he'd felt brutally honest with the rest of his confession. And while it had been a lot to take in, one detail had stuck with me—Harper had approached him in person. She hadn't sent her blackmail threats to him via text. Which meant the message we'd seen her get the night of the party had been from someone else.

Bert hadn't been Harper's only victim.

So who else had been? And had *they* been the one to finally reach their breaking point and kill Harper?

I was contemplating that thought as my phone rang through my car's Bluetooth system. I swiped it on and immediately heard Ava's voice fill the interior of my car.

"Crisis, code pink," she said.

Panic surged in my belly. "Crisis? What happened?"

"I have nothing to wear."

I rolled my eyes in the dim light. "Do *not* do that to me today. Not knowing what to wear on a date is not a full blown crisis."

"That's why I coded it *pink* and not red," Ava explained. Then she paused. "I'm sorry. I'm guessing things did not go well with Carrie this afternoon?"

"As well as can be expected," I informed her. "Bert's attorney was able to get him out on bail. Though just how innocent he is remains a question." I quickly filled her in on his courthouse confession and my realization that Harper had been blackmailing not one but two victims. Or possibly even more.

"Wow," Ava said when I was done. "I did not see that coming. I mean, I fully thought Bert was having an affair."

"Me too," I admitted. "Though I'm honestly not sure if it's better or worse for Carrie."

"Poor thing." I could hear the genuine compassion in Ava's voice. "Okay, now my closet crisis does seem a little petty."

I grinned. "I'm sure you have something that will wow Nolan. What about that pink dress…the one with the spaghetti straps?"

"You don't think it's too casual?" she asked, and I could hear rustling as she dug through her options.

"I think it's very chic."

"He's taking me to Single Thread before we go dancing."

I did a low whistle. "Wow. First Silvio's, now Single Thread. He knows his fine dining." I shoved down my jealous appetite.

"I know. Not really a casual chic kind of place."

"What if you pair it with those drop earrings I saw you working on last week? Maybe a couple necklaces and the right pair of heels would amp it up?"

I heard more rustling. "Okay, yeah. That might work. And it does show off just the right amount of cleavage."

"Right amount for what?" I joked.

"If you have to ask, you don't want to know," she teased back. "You know, it's kind of ironic."

"That guys like cleavage?"

"No!" Ava laughed. "I was thinking about Bert again. I mean, ironic that he was so into playing Lord of the Manor at the housewarming party—looking down his nose at us—when he was actually flat broke."

I nodded to myself. "Well, isn't that always the way? People tend to point out in others the very things they hate most about themselves."

Ava was quiet for a moment.

"You still there?" I asked, hoping I hadn't lost my Bluetooth connection.

"Yeah, just contemplating that and what it says about me. I called my landlord cheap today."

I couldn't help but laugh. "Let's go with thrifty."

"Sounds much better," she agreed. "Thanks. Hey, I gotta go, but I'll call you with deets later."

"Have fun tonight!" I told her.

"Trust me—I intend to," she assured me before hanging up.

I grinned as the call dropped, thinking if Ava was *thrifty*, what did that make me? What was it I saw in others? Well, lately I saw potential murderers everywhere I looked—Bert, Tripp, Kellen.

I tried to put that thought from my mind as I wound toward home.

By the time I pulled up to the winery, the sun was just a dim red glow on the horizon. I noticed a few cars in our lot and felt hope surge that maybe we had a good tasting crowd that evening. I locked my Jeep and put on my best hostess face as I pushed through the winery's main doors to take stock of our tasting room.

Jean Luc looked busy, with at least half a dozen people at the bar, swirling our reds in their glasses and sipping from small pourings of Chardonnay and Pinot Grigio. A few people in suits and pencil skirts had pushed two tables together, a couple of open bottles on them, clearly enjoying an after-work release. I was about to introduce myself to them and chat them up with the charming history of our little vineyard, when a patron at the bar caught my eye.

Morgan Brice was hunched over the bar top on his stool, his eyes darting back and forth, his right hand twirling his wedding band around in a nervous twitch. When he spotted me, he popped up from his seat, abandoning his half full glass of white, and quickly closed the distance between us.

"Emmy," he said urgently. "Your wine steward said you weren't here."

I cringed, hoping he hadn't called Jean Luc a "wine steward" to his face. The Frenchman took the title of *sommelier* very seriously. "I just got in," I told him. "Was there something I could help you with?"

"Kellen said you were at the house today," he said, his tone low and urgent.

I nodded. "I was. I, uh, stopped by to offer my catering services for the memorial," I told him, going with my previous half-lie.

"Kellen was quite agitated this afternoon," Morgan went on, his eyes darting left and right. "You didn't tell her, did you?"

"Tell her…?"

"About my visit to see you. That I—" He paused, leaning in and lowering his voice. "That I told you she'd met with Harper just before she died."

Oh. That. "Kellen did mention having spoken to Harper. But your name never came up," I said truthfully.

Morgan visibly sighed in relief. "Thank you. I mean, not that Kellen or I have anything to hide, but you know. I'm not sure she'd appreciate me…"

Ratting her out behind her back?

"…advocating on her behalf."

I stifled a snort. "I understand."

"It's just she seemed so agitated this afternoon. So upset. I-I just wanted to make sure it wasn't something I'd done."

"Maybe the grief is just hitting her," I said. Or guilt. But I didn't think that thought would do anything to calm Morgan's nerves. "It must be overwhelming having to plan the memorial now as well."

"No, Sandra's taking care of all that," Morgan said, shaking his head.

"Oh. Kellen told me she let Sandra go this morning," I said, wondering if maybe matters of the household staff were beyond his purview.

"What?" His head snapped up. "Why on earth would she do that?"

I pursed my lips, suddenly feeling like I was in the middle of a domestic scene that was none of my business. "I-I'm not really sure. You should ask her. I think she mentioned something about Sandra stealing things…" I trailed off, hoping he'd let it go and go home to his wife.

But instead of the indignation Kellen had displayed at being robbed by her staff, Morgan sucked in a gasp, his face going pale. "Oh no," he said on a long breath. "No, no, no, no." He suddenly looked unsteady on his feet.

"Are you okay?" I asked, steering him toward an empty table and pulling a chair out for him.

He fell into it with a less than graceful plop, his expression still looking like he'd seen a ghost. "No one was supposed to notice," he mumbled, more to himself than to me.

"Notice what?" I asked gently, sitting beside him.

He shook his head. "Poor Sandra. She doesn't deserve this."

"Morgan," I said slowly, "what do you know about Sandra stealing from you?"

He shook his head, seemingly coming out of his shocked stupor and turning to me. "She didn't steal anything."

"But someone has," I said, watching his expression.

He nodded slowly. "She'll divorce me. No one was supposed to notice," he repeated. "She wasn't supposed to notice. She'll divorce me for sure."

"Divorce you?" I asked. "You mean Kellen?"

He nodded again. "If she finds out, she'll divorce me. Then what will I do?" He blinked rapidly, staring into the space behind me.

"Morgan, did *you* steal something?" I surmised.

He closed his eyes and whimpered, as if I'd delivered him a physical blow.

I put a hand on his arm. "Morgan?"

"Yes." He finally opened his eyes to meet mine. "Yes, it was me. But it wasn't really stealing! I mean, the items I took. They would have been hers anyway. You know, when the Bishops passed. It would have been hers."

"Hers? You mean, Kellen's?"

He shook his head. "No. Harper's."

Puzzle pieces finally began to click. "Harper asked you to take things from her parents' house."

"She knew I didn't have any money of my own," he explained. "It was the only payment I could think to give her. And she knew exactly what the items were worth. Exactly what she wanted as payment."

"Payment. Morgan, was Harper blackmailing you?"

He nodded slowly again. "I was weak," he said softly. "Too weak to resist her beauty. And she knew it. I never meant for it to happen!" He turned to me, as if pleading his case. "I love Kellen. Honestly I do. But Harper was just so…so beautiful. So seductive. So impossible to resist."

"You slept with her?"

"Yes." The word was choked out on a sob that he quickly covered with the back of his hand. "Kellen was at a charity gala, and Harper was in town for the weekend. She asked me to meet her for drinks. I know that I should have been stronger. I should have resisted. But…Harper knew just how to hit my weak spots."

"When was this?" I asked.

Morgan sniffed loudly. "I don't know. She was in town taking some sort of riding lessons for a role. Maybe three…four months ago."

I felt my spine stiffen. "Three months ago?"

Morgan nodded, seemingly oblivious to the significance of the timeline. "We both agreed it would be a mistake to tell Kellen, and I thought that would be the end of it."

"But it wasn't?"

"No. No it wasn't." He sighed deeply, twisting his wedding band again. "When Harper found out she was being written out of her TV show, she came to me. She said she needed money. I told her I didn't have any—she knew that! She knew Kellen and I live by her parents' generosity."

"But they'd cut *her* off."

"They had. Unfair of them, if you ask me. But no one ever does," he mumbled.

"So Harper asked you to steal from them?"

"It was just going to be little things," he repeated. "And really, they should have been Harper's anyway. It wasn't really stealing. A small painting here, a rare book there. I swear I didn't even think anyone would miss them!" he pleaded again.

"Or that Sandra would be blamed," I added.

His pallor went sickly pale again. "No. No, she doesn't deserve that." He sighed deeply. "Please don't say anything to Kellen," he said, his voice so low it was almost a whisper. "I-I'd like to tell her myself."

"Of course," I agreed. Honestly, the last thing I wanted to do was be the bearer of that news. Though, I wondered just how clean Morgan planned to come with his wife—about the missing items or about the affair that had prompted their need as well?

"Thank you," he said, rising from his seat. "I think I should go home now."

"Can I ask you one more thing?" I asked as I walked him to the door. "Did Harper send you a text the night she died? Asking for more?"

Morgan frowned. "No. I mean, yes, Harper did text me sometimes. She…" He licked his lips, choosing his words. "She was very specific about her requests. But the last time I heard from her was days ago."

"You're sure?" I pressed. If Harper hadn't been extorting money from Morgan that night, and she hadn't texted her threats to Bert, that meant there was still another blackmail victim out there.

"Positive," he said. Then he mumbled a halfhearted goodbye before he shuffled to a sleek black Mercedes that perfectly represented the lifestyle his in-laws had provided him.

I stood in the doorway of the winery, watching his taillights glide down the oak lined drive, wondering just how desperately Morgan Brice wanted to keep that lifestyle. Desperately enough to lie to his wife and steal from her family, that much was clear.

His affair with Harper fit the timeline for being her baby daddy. What if Harper realized she wasn't going to be able to keep quiet about Morgan's moment of weakness forever? Would Morgan have taken matters into his own hands?

As much as I could almost feel his desperation, I had a hard time picturing the sniveling kept man killing the woman he clearly was still enamored of.

But if Kellen had found out Harper had been sleeping with her husband—if Harper had possibly even told her the truth about her unborn child's paternity—I could well see Kellen coldly and calculatingly getting rid of the sister she'd always resented without breaking a manicured nail over it.

CHAPTER EIGHTEEN

———

After seeing Morgan off, I made the rounds of the guests in the tasting room—introducing myself, making sure everyone's glass was full, and offering to have Jean Luc arrange for cases to be delivered should they wish to take advantage of our on-site discounts. By the time I'd hit everyone, I could feel the exhaustion of the day setting in and my stomach starting to growl protest of missing lunch.

Luckily, as I made my way down the hall to the kitchen, the delicious scents of garlic and rosemary beckoned to me, promising that Conchita had something delightful up her sleeves.

Only as I walked into the kitchen, I realized I was not the intended recipient of the heavenly scents.

Grant sat at the counter, Conchita busy fussing over him. Again.

"Good evening, Emmy!" She carefully placed a plate of her Simple Salmon with Sherry Potatoes in front of him. An uncorked bottle of Pinot Noir stood beside it, allowing it to breathe.

"You know, if you keep feeding him like this, he's going to keep showing up," I joked.

"Oh, now wouldn't that be a pity." Conchita gave me a knowing wink.

Grant grinned. "I, uh, just stopped by for a moment, but Conchita insisted I stay for dinner."

"I'll bet she did," I mumbled, shooting her a look.

Luckily—or possibly by design—her back was to me as she pulled some rolls from the oven.

"How could I say no?" Grant shrugged, looking anything but innocent.

"He couldn't." Conchita set the rolls on a plate and shoved it toward him. "It would have been rude. And our detective is not rude."

"*Our* detective?" I asked.

She wisely chose to ignore me. "Now, I have a cheesecake in the refrigerator for dessert, and I'm sure you can take care of the wine." She nodded at me while removing her apron. "I must go. *Jeopardy!* is about to start."

As she bustled from the room, Grant gave me a sheepish look. "I have a feeling she's setting us up."

I had a feeling he was right.

I answered him with a grin. "Is it working?"

He chuckled. "Quite possibly. The night is young."

Oh boy.

I cleared my throat, pouring us each a glass of Pinot before sitting on the empty stool beside him.

"So, you just stopped by, huh?" I asked.

He picked up his fork, stabbing into the salmon with it. "I did. Wanted to check in on you after last night."

My hand immediately went to the bump on my head. "Thanks. But I'm good."

"You sure?" he asked. Then he surprised me by reaching his fingers out and gently brushing the hair away at my temple. "It looks like the bruising is worse."

I licked my suddenly dry lips. "Uh, yeah. It looks worse than it is."

His fingers lingered in my hair a moment longer before he finally nodded and pulled them away. "That's good." He paused then added. "You're vibrating."

"What?" I asked, hormones making my brain hazy.

He nodded toward my back pocket. "I think I heard your phone vibrating."

I blinked, realizing he was right. I pulled my phone out, glancing at the readout only long enough to see it was David Allen again before swiping to ignore.

"Sorry," I mumbled. I picked up my glass, sipping to cover the heat still surging through my body at his touch.

"So, how was your day?" Grant asked, stabbing another bite of fish.

"Busy, thanks to you."

"Me?"

"Yes, you." I swiveled on my stool to face him. "You arrested Bert."

"Ah." He nodded. "You heard about that."

"You could say that." I dug my fork into the salmon and took a bite. The subtle, refreshing flavor of the fish blanketed my tongue, and I took a beat to savor it before resuming conversation. "You really think Bert killed Harper?"

"I really think the evidence points that way."

"That was a careful answer."

Grant's mouth curved up in a half smile. "Look, it's not my job to pass judgment on guilt or innocence. That's for a jury. My job is to collect enough evidence to facilitate an arrest."

"Which you did."

He nodded, turning back to his meal.

"Bert mentioned something about financial records being introduced as evidence. Was he talking about his or Harper's?" I asked, wondering just how much Grant knew about Harper's extortion racket.

"I can't comment on that," he said around a bite.

"The discrepancies you talked about in Harper's bank accounts," I said, hoping to bait him. "They're because she was blackmailing people for money. Like Bert."

Grant took a beat before he nodded. "I know."

"Did you know he wasn't the only one?"

His dark eyes cut to mine, and while his expression was neutral, I'd swear the little hazel flecks in them kicked up a notch. "Is that so?"

I paused, wondering if I was hurting Bert or helping by sharing what I knew. But at this point, anything in Harper's life that created a shadow on someone else could only be a positive thing, right?

"There was her brother-in-law, Morgan Brice, too. And someone else."

"Someone else?" he asked, his expression giving nothing away as to how much of this was news to him and how much he already knew.

I nodded. "I-I'm not sure who. But I saw a message on her phone from one of her victims. And it wasn't Bert or Morgan."

Grant's eyes narrowed. "On her phone," he repeated.

"Yes, but not the one you have."

"Clearly." The hazel flecks kicked into high gear again, suddenly making me feel guilty even though I was perfectly innocent. Well, at least in this case.

"It was a disposable phone. We saw it on the surveillance footage." I told him how we'd found the video and seen the text that Harper had gotten on the phone that Carrie swore was not her regular iPhone. "Which is why nothing showed up on the phone your guys were processing," I finished.

He nodded, taking it all in. "Why didn't you tell me all of this?"

"I'm telling you now," I pointed out.

He shot me a look.

"Okay, okay," I said, throwing my hands up in surrender. "I should have told you about the burner phone as soon as we realized it. But it's not like you can do anything to trace it anyway."

"That's not entirely true," he corrected. "It won't be registered to an owner, but every phone has a serial number attached to it, and there are records kept by its service provider. If Harper used a credit card to purchase it or bought it somewhere with security surveillance where we can see her purchase, then we can find the number associated with the phone and access those records."

"Wow. I'm impressed."

The corner of his mouth curved up in a grin. "Turns out I'm not as incompetent as you thought, huh?"

"I never thought you were incompetent."

"Just wrong?" he baited.

"Just…sometimes blinded by the evidence."

He narrowed his eyes at me, contemplating that one. Though the half smile remained, so I figured I wasn't on too shaky ground anymore.

"So you think you can trace who sent Harper that message?" I asked, feeling hope that we might uncover Harper's other victim…and possibly her killer.

He nodded. Then he set his fork down and slipped off his stool. "I think there's a good possibility." He moved to put his jacket on. "I'd like to get a look at that security footage again first."

"Wait—you're leaving now?" I hated the note of whiney teen in my voice.

He must have noticed too, though his reaction was more amusement. "Apparently my evening just got busy, thanks to you," he said, using my line from earlier.

"But I have cheesecake," my inner teen whined again.

The grin curved both corners of his mouth this time, as he leaned in close. "That wasn't the dessert I was interested in anyway."

Heat surged through me so fast, it curled my toes.

I barely had time to get ahold of my hormones before he planted a quick peck on my cheek and stepped toward the door.

Though, before leaving, he paused in the doorway. "Keep the doors locked, and stay safe tonight," he said.

I nodded dumbly, my hormones still rendering me mute.

He shot me one last devastatingly sexy grin and walked away.

I heard a wistful sigh. It might have come from me.

I shook my lust off and pulled myself together, clearing our plates. I'd just finished the dishes and was pouring myself another glass of Pinot, when my phone buzzed with a text.

I swore if that was David Allen again…

Only, as I glanced at the readout, I saw this time the message was from Ava.

I sipped from my glass, not sure I could stand hearing how fabulously her dinner and dancing with a celebrity was going while I was contemplating an evening alone with a bottle of wine and a cheesecake. But curiosity finally won over—hey, if I was going to spend the evening doing a single, I might as well live vicariously, right?—and I swiped the text open.

I know who killed Harper. Meet me at Tripp's trailer.

I froze, staring at the words on the screen, my heart rate picking up.

Had Ava had a sudden revelation at dinner? Or maybe Nolan had said something over drinks that made everything fall into place. Tripp's trailer…had she realized something we'd missed there that afternoon? Something that definitively pointed to the cowboy as the guilty party?

I set my wineglass on the counter.

Is Tripp guilty? I texted back.

I waited, feeling anxiety build in the pit of my stomach as I stared at the screen.

One minute. Two.

Five minutes later, she still hadn't responded.

I bit my lip. Maybe she couldn't text back right now. Maybe she was already driving up to Tripp's place with evidence that he was a cold blooded murderer.

I picked up my phone.

Be right there, I told her, grabbing my purse and hightailing it to my Jeep.

* * *

The sun was a distant memory as I hit the winding dirt road of Rosebay Meadows. Clearly no one had bothered to install streetlights out there, and the hulking shadows of abandoned shacks and dimly lit trailers hunkering down in the inky blackness created an eerie scene. If there were ever a moment when I believed in creatures of the night, this was where I imagined they hung out to plot their evening escapades. Even the trees looked sinister in the sliver of moonlight peeking through their twisted branches, as if their long limbs might reach out and grab at me a la Snow White's haunted forest.

I pulled to a stop beside Tripp's trailer, noting his truck was still absent. I didn't see Ava's car either, but it was hard to make out distinct shapes in the dark. I turned off my engine and grabbed my phone.

I'm here, I texted to Ava.

I waited a beat, but no answer came back.

But as I glanced out my window toward the trailer, a flash of something inside caught my eye. Like the beam from a phone app or flashlight. I shook my head as I saw it again, moving around at the back of the trailer where Tripp's bedroom was located. Had Ava decided to do some more *not*–breaking and entering?

I shoved my phone into my pocket and got out of the Jeep, locking the door behind me as I quickly jogged the few paces to the door of Tripp's place, trying to ignore the chill in the air. I rapped softly on the door.

"Ava?" I called in a mock whisper. "It's me."

I didn't hear an answer, but the beam of light flashed at the back window again.

I put my hand on the doorknob and slowly turned it, pushing inside. "Ava?" I called again.

The main cabin was dark, and I blinked, trying to get my eyes to adjust to the absence of light. Table, chairs, a pile of cardboard boxes. It seemed undisturbed since that afternoon, but everything felt a little creepier in the dark. The bedroom door was closed, but I could see light beneath it.

"Are you back there?" I asked, taking a step toward the rear of the trailer.

I thought I heard a muffled response, but it was hard to make out. As my eyes began to adjust, I slowly took small steps toward the closed bedroom door then gingerly pushed it open.

What I saw on the other side had my breath hitching in my throat.

"Ava!" I cried.

My best friend was sitting on Tripp's bed, her hands secured behind her back with a piece of rope, feet bound together, and a bandana tied around her mouth. Her eyes were wide and rimmed with tears, and she was shaking her head at me.

"Are you okay?" I asked, rushing toward her and pulling the bandana from her mouth.

"Emmy," Ava croaked out as soon as her mouth was free, "don't. It's a—"

"Trap," came the conclusion to her thought.

Only it didn't come from Ava's mouth but from a low, menacing voice suddenly at my ear.

CHAPTER NINETEEN

———

I froze, feeling my breath come fast as something hard and cold pressed into my side.

"Sit," the voice commanded, accompanied by a strong hand grabbing at my upper arm and shoving me toward Ava.

I stumbled, catching my balance as I hit the bed and spun around to face our attacker.

His blue eyes were twinkling with mirth and something distinctly more sinister as his full lips curved into a wicked smile accentuating the dimple in his left cheek.

"Nolan," I breathed out, my gaze going to the gun in his right hand. His left held a phone, the light shining into the room in an almost blinding beam as he played it over first me then Ava.

"Emmy." He nodded my direction. "So pleased you could join us this evening," he said, his voice as pleasant and evenly modulated as if I were simply over for a cocktail and not being held at gunpoint next to my best friend, who'd been bound and gagged.

"Wh-what's going on?" I asked.

"Come now, Emmy." Nolan tsked between his teeth. "Surely you don't expect me to believe the dumb blonde act?"

I was loath to admit that in this case it wasn't an act.

"You sent that text? From Ava's phone?" I asked, my eyes on the one in his hand, which I realized now was in a pink case with the Silver Girl logo on the back.

He shrugged. "Well, as you can see, Ava is a little tied up at the moment." He grinned at his own terrible joke, though the smile held more menace than humor. "So, I thought I'd help her out by issuing you an invite to our private little party."

I glanced at Ava. Her lips were pursed into a thin line, and I could feel the anger radiating off her. Clearly this was not how she'd seen her night going.

"I don't understand," I told him honestly.

"Don't you?" he took a step toward us, the gun moving that much closer. "Well, let me recap the evening for those viewers just tuning in," he said, sending a sarcastic wink Ava's direction. "Your little friend here is a sucker for a charming compliment, and you are a sucker for a sob story. Some of my finest acting, this was not, but you both were an easy audience." He gave a mock bow.

I realized he was more than just cocky—he was arrogant *and* unhinged. And, as the gun bobbed up and down in my direction with his movements, I realized he was also likely a murderer.

"You killed Harper," I said slowly.

"See? I knew you weren't such a ditz." He grinned at me, though it was hardly a compliment.

"You threw Harper into Dante's pen and watched while he crushed her," I said, trying not to picture the scene.

Nolan nodded slowly, and I could see the emotion behind his eyes. Though it wasn't the grief he'd put on for us before, but something akin to pleasure that sent a chill up my spine.

"So simple, really," he said. "Of course, she struggled a little, but the vain thing only weighed a hundred pounds. And with those ridiculously high heels, she was off balance already. Really, I don't know how you ladies get around in those."

"You let that poor horse do your dirty work," Ava spat out beside me, the contempt clear in her voice.

Nolan shifted his gaze to her. "Darling, don't be disappointed. There's plenty of dirty work left." The gun rose, pointing squarely at Ava's head.

Fear clutched at my chest. "Tell me how you did it!" I blurted out, trying to divert his attention.

His eyes flickered to me. "How?"

I nodded vigorously. "Yes. How did you lure her to Dante's pen?" I asked, hoping to play on his own vanity to buy time. "It must not have been easy."

The gun lowered a tad. "Well, I wouldn't call it hard either. In fact, it was Harper's idea to meet in private in the first place."

"So that you could deliver her blackmail payment," I said, realizing I was staring at Harper's final victim.

His mouth curved into that wicked smile again. "So you know about that too, do you? See, I knew you knew too much."

Honestly I hadn't known nearly enough.

My eyes shot around the interior of the trailer, mostly still shadowed. Dirty magazines, a pile of sheets, a couple of empty beer cans. Nothing that screamed weapon or escape route.

"You were one of Harper's blackmail victims, weren't you?" I asked.

"One of?" Nolan threw his head back and laughed. "Well, well, well, our little Harper had quite a racket going on."

"So you didn't know about her brother-in-law or Bert?" I asked, eyes cutting to Ava. If one of us could distract him, it was possible the other could grab the gun. Or at least slip out and get help.

Unfortunately, Ava's eyes were still firmly on Nolan, shooting angry daggers in his direction.

"Good heavens," Nolan said, tsking his tongue more. "Do tell—what did Harper have on our Little Bertie?"

I almost hesitated to say, but anything that kept him talking and not shooting was a positive at this point. "Bert was in debt. He was using Carrie's money to pay back his creditors and lying to her about investing."

Nolan laughed out loud. "Oh, Bertie. I give the old boy credit—he had me fooled with his incessant chatter about foreign markets."

"I would guess you had him fooled as well," I said.

"I had you *all* fooled." His eyes cut to Ava, a smirk on his lips now. "Didn't I, darling?"

Ava's lips curled into a snarl, and I put a hand on her leg to try to calm her. As angry as she was, the last thing we needed was to push Nolan over the edge.

"What did Harper threaten you with?" I asked, trying to divert his attention from my bestie again.

He tore his gaze away from Ava and back to me. "Only my career!" he answered hotly. "My fans, my art, the image I've spent years cultivating!"

"I don't understand," I said, feeling like a broken record where that phrase was concerned. "Harper had already been fired from *Carefree Hearts*. Was she saying she'd get you fired as well?"

"Worse," he spat out. Then he pulled in a long breath, seemingly trying to get control of his clearly tentative hold on his emotions again. "She threatened to go public with something that would have ruined the image of Dr. Drake Dubois forever."

I had to admit, I was intrigued. "What was it?"

He paused, and for a moment I wasn't sure if he was going to spill it. Finally he said, "Let's just say I did some questionable art-house films early in my career that were not in the best of taste."

I frowned, trying to read between the lines of the flowery language. "Wait—you starred in pornos?"

Ava gasped beside me.

He narrowed his eyes. "I was young. It was good money. And the director promised me it would lead to more mainstream roles."

If he'd believed that, he was dumber than I'd pegged him for. "And Harper found out?"

He nodded. "She knew as well as I do that our core audience is Middle America. The Bible Belt. Women who would never look at Dr. Dubois the same way again."

I wasn't sure if he was giving women enough credit. It was, after all, the twenty-first century. And while his core audience might not be the adult film watching crowd, I had a feeling most of those Bible Belt dwelling Middle American women weren't totally ignorant when it came to what happened in the bedroom.

"Surely something like that wouldn't scare away all of your fans, right?" I said.

But Nolan shook his head. "You don't understand. Our producers know their audience. *Well.* And they don't like to take chances. If something like this were to come out, I'd be written out of the show in a heartbeat." He pointed the gun at me, waving it like a teacher would a ruler at a child who was slow to catch on. "You do know why Harper was written out of the show, don't you?"

I shook my head, eyes cutting to Ava. She was the soap fan. But even she shrugged.

"Her DUI. Producers thought she was too much of a risk for the show's image after that. A wild card."

In their defense, they were probably right, given the extortion that followed.

"No way was I going to let them do that to me." Nolan drew up to his full height, straightening his spine. "Not to Dr. Drake Dubois!"

"So you agreed to Harper's demands," I said.

He nodded. "Although the threats were anonymous at the time. I had no idea it was Harper." He gave a self-deprecating laugh. "Though I should have. She was, after all, in the best position to recognize my anatomy from those early films."

"Wait, are you saying you and Harper…" I trailed off.

Nolan shrugged. "You saw how beautiful Harper was. And I wasn't joking when I said she loved men. All men. Her costar included, as it turned out."

"You were sleeping with Harper!" Ava blurted out. If it was possible, she suddenly looked even more furious.

Nolan nodded. "I'm sorry to say that it's true. I fell under her spell. Oh, in my defense, she was quite good at casting those little spells of hers over men. Even the great Dr. Dubois was not immune."

I was beginning to wonder if he was aware he was not living in an episode of *Carefree Hearts*.

"And then Harper betrayed you," I said softly. It seemed to be a theme in her life.

"Yes." Nolan stretched his neck, as if he needed to relieve tension.

I took the brief second of his distraction to feel beneath the bed with my feet. Dust, some item of discarded clothing, papers of some sort. I stretched my ankle out, keeping my eyes securely on Nolan's face to prevent him from looking down. My big toe connected with something smooth and cool. Glass.

The Jack Daniel's bottle.

I sent up a silent thank-you to the gods of slobs, inching my backside just the slightest bit forward on the right side to stretch toward the bottle as I tried to think of how to keep Nolan talking.

"You were the one who sent the text to Harper the night of the party," I said. "Saying how dare she blackmail you."

Nolan nodded. "Like I said, I had no idea it was Harper then. I just knew I wasn't going to keep paying that extortion forever."

"Forever?" Ava piped up. "It wasn't the first time?"

Nolan shook his head. "No. The first demand for money came a few weeks ago. In hindsight, the timing should have given me a clue. It was just after we all found out Harper was being written out of the show." His sneer turned into more of a grimace as he relived the scene in his mind. "She was quick to pick up a new career, wasn't she?"

"How much did she ask you for?"

"Ten grand."

It seemed to be her magic number.

"She told me to leave the cash in a duffel bag in an empty studio at the lot," he went on. "At the time, I honestly thought it was one of the crew or some greedy security guard. But I figured a one-time payment was cheaper than a scandal."

"Only it wasn't just the one time."

His eyes hardened, his classically chiseled jawline tensing. "No. She demanded more."

"She texted you again," I guessed.

"Yes. She sent it before we left LA. Told me to have cash on hand for my weekend in Wine Country. Then once we arrived, she sent one saying that by the end of the party, everyone in the room would know my dirty little secret if I didn't bring another payment to the horse stables."

"Did you?" I asked. I could feel my foot connecting with the top of the whiskey bottle, slowly rolling it toward the edge of the bed.

"Yes. But I wasn't about to let her get away with it that time. I realized she wasn't going to stop, that she could drop a text again any time she wanted. So I waited. Watching from the shadows as my blackmailer approached."

I could almost picture it—Harper in her sparkling dress, slinking up to the stables, thinking herself so clever to have milked her prey for cash once again. Maybe she'd even been dreaming of the designer handbags or Italian leather heels she'd purchase with it all. Never suspecting that her victim was about to turn killer.

"And that was when you realized it was Harper," Ava added.

Nolan nodded. "I'd only planned to confront the blackmailer. Tell him it was over—that if they want me silent about their identity, they'd leave me be."

"But then you saw it was her. The woman who had pretended to love you."

"She did love me!" he spat back, anger rising in an instant, contorting his face from the handsome TV star to something out of a horror movie. "She did! It was real! You hear me?"

"O-of course it was," I said quickly, fear and adrenaline surging as fast as his anger had, sticking in my chest like a lump. I glanced to Ava. I could see her lower lip quivering, the fear taking hold in her too.

Nolan's grip on his sanity was tentative at best.

And we were on borrowed time before it snapped completely.

I licked my lips. "So what did you do?" I asked softly as I felt the whiskey bottle slowly roll out from under the bed.

"What did I do?" he asked. "What did I *do*? I killed her! I grabbed her from behind and threw her over the fence. And I watched that magnificent creature crush the life out of her."

I winced, as if I could almost feel the physical pain of the blow myself.

"And then you went back to the party as if nothing had happened," Ava said, her lips still quivering. "Went back to flirting with me."

He paused in his tirade. "I had to. You were my alibi, my dear. You and your blind fandom, you wonderful idiot."

If he hadn't had us at gunpoint, I'd be tempted to smack him for insulting my friend that way. As it was, I put my hand on her leg again for support, hoping she felt the solidarity.

"And you kept your lunch date with her the next day," I said, wriggling my toes again, hoping to stall for just a few more minutes. How on earth was I going to get the whiskey bottle from the floor to my hands to somewhere close enough to Nolan to cause any damage before he got a shot off, I had no idea.

Nolan nodded. "I'd seen you talking with that detective," he told me. "I felt like you were close. I wanted to know what the police where thinking, and Ava felt like my best way to stay in the loop. Make sure they weren't looking in my direction."

Which they weren't. And still wouldn't be, I realized with a sinking feeling.

"That's why you made a date with me the following night too?" Ava asked, her voice still radiating hurt.

"Of course," he said simply.

"The one where you came home to find me knocked out," I said, putting it together. "But it couldn't have been you sneaking around in Harper's room at Carrie's house that night. You actually *were* with Ava."

He nodded. "I was. Right up until we arrived at Carrie's house and saw someone with a flashlight in the upstairs window."

"So someone else hit me over the head?" I asked.

Nolan chuckled. "While I could let them take all of the credit, the truth is as soon as I rushed upstairs and saw *you* lurking around, I knew I was in trouble. You just couldn't mind your own business, could you?"

Trust me—in that moment I really wished I could.

"So you hit her?" Ava breathed. I could see her going through the events in her mind—including the deceit he had employed on her that night.

"It was just supposed to be a warning. Enough to get her to keep her nose out of Harper's business. I knew the more she dug, the closer she'd get to the truth."

"And to you," Ava added.

Nolan nodded. "She'd been at the house asking questions about blackmail, and then I find her snooping around the guest rooms? I knew she was looking for Harper's second phone."

We'd been right. Harper's killer had taken it. "You have it?" I asked.

"*Had.* It's long gone now."

Rats. "So you hit me on the head that night then pretended to have found me that way?" I asked.

"Now *that* was some of my finest acting work." He preened as if one of us might give him a gold statuette for it.

"Then who was it I saw going through Harper's things in the first place?"

Nolan shrugged, palms up. "Search me. But if *I* were floating the police a theory, I'd point the finger at the cowboy."

"Tripp?" I asked. Honestly, he'd have been my first guess at the time too.

Nolan nodded. "The way I see it, Tripp killed Harper, stole her blackmail proceeds, then skipped town."

While I knew he was making up a story, I could see some truth in two out of three of those statements.

"Only, you two girls come snooping around his trailer. *Again*—"

I cut a questioning look to Ava.

Nolan must have seen it too, because he said, "Oh yes, Ava told me all about that too."

Ava mouthed the word *sorry* in my direction. I sent her a smile. How could she have known?

"—and Tripp decided you had to go before he disappeared forever," Nolan continued his narrative. "So he shot you both."

He raised the gun, pointing it directly at Ava's head.

Panic rushed through me. It was now or never.

In one quick movement, I reached down and grabbed the whiskey bottle, screamed to draw his attention, lunged toward him, and swung with all I had. The bottle collided with the side of his head, and shards of broken glass shattered over us both.

He yelled as blood gushed from a cut to his temple, and he shifted focus, turning the gun in my direction. I instinctively raised my arms, ready to protect myself from a bullet, when Ava pulled both feet up and kicked out against his body.

He surged backward, slamming into the closed bedroom door.

I reached for his right hand, aiming to wrestle him for the gun in his stunned state. But before I could make a grab for it, the back of his left hand connected with my cheek. Stars flitted momentarily in my eyes before I landed on the vinyl floor with a thud.

Before I could get my bearings again, I felt his fist grab at the back of my shirt, lifting me up and shoving me into the wall, where I collided with a poster of a girl in a bikini.

My head was taking a beating, and the room was a little fuzzy, but I sucked in air, trying to remain steady on my feet as I spun around to face him again. Only before I could do more than cry out, his fingers wrapped around my throat. I gasped for air as he squeezed, his face contorted with rage. Darkness threatened the outer edges of my vision, but I hung on to consciousness, my hands flailing in front of me, scratching at his face.

"Emmy!" Ava cried behind me. I heard a thud as she wriggled off the bed and fell to the floor, hands still tied behind her back.

"Quiet, you moron!" Nolan yelled to her.

I didn't like his tone at all, so I brought my knee up between his legs. As I connected squarely with my target, Nolan groaned. His grip on my throat loosened, and I gulped in a big lungful of air.

Unfortunately, he was quick to recover, reaching out with the back of his hand again and giving my other cheek a swat that had me crumpling to the floor beside Ava.

"Are you okay?" she asked, inch-worming herself to me.

"Enough!" Nolan yelled.

I blinked, looking up to find him towering over us, gun in hand, a trail of blood running down the left side of his face. He was breathing hard, spittle forming at the corners of his mouth as he panted.

"Enough of all of this!" he yelled, his voice getting louder and more maniacal with each word. "I'm ending it now, and there's nothing you or anyone else can do about it—"

The last word froze on his lips. I watched as his eyes rolled back in his head, his hand holding the gun go limp. A second later his body melted to the floor like it was made of rubber, barely missing us as he crashed-landed on the hard vinyl.

I blinked, looking from Nolan's prone form to the doorway.

To find David Allen standing there, a heavy dumbbell in hand, raised above his head like a baseball bat that had just hit a home run to the back of Nolan Becker's head.

CHAPTER TWENTY

———

The events of the next few hours were a blur of tears, relief, medics, and police officers. As soon as David had secured Nolan's gun, untied Ava, and ascertained that neither Ava nor I had any life threatening injuries, he'd promptly called 9-1-1. As he'd given a shortened version of events to the dispatcher—who promised every kind of help at her disposal was on its way—Ava had used her former bonds to tie up Nolan. While she'd said it was in case he regained consciousness, I had a feeling it was at least partly revenge, by the way she pulled the ropes extra tight.

I wasn't sure how long the three of us sat there waiting for the authorities, the mixture of panic, relief, adrenaline, and shock rendering us largely mute and physically weak. But I did manage to get from David that after not getting any response to any of his recent texts to me, he'd started to worry. He'd driven up to Oak Valley to check on me, where he'd arrived just in time to see my Jeep speeding in the other direction as I'd hurried to answer Ava's call.

On instinct, he'd followed. He said he would have intervened sooner, but he'd lost sight of me just before the turnoff to Rosebay Meadows and had spent a few minutes driving around the surrounding streets before finally finding my Jeep parked at the top of the hill. He'd arrived just in time to hear Nolan screaming at Ava to be quiet.

I told him his timing had been perfect.

A police officer was first to arrive on the scene, filling the sleepy road with flashing red and blue lights and sirens, and several other emergency response vehicles quickly followed. They split the three of us up—paramedics descending on Ava and me, and uniformed officers pulling David aside to get his story.

Once my injuries had been assessed as just nasty bumps and bruises, I gave my version of events to at least three separate people, detailing Nolan's confession and David's heroic arrival. By the time I was finishing the third round, Nolan had regained consciousness and I heard him being read his rights as he was handcuffed to a gurney and loaded into the back of an ambulance. I didn't think I was being too mean that I hoped he recovered fully and quickly so he could stand trial and feel the full force of justice.

"Emmy?"

I turned from the sight of Nolan being wheeled away to find Grant striding purposefully toward me, a frown etched on his face.

"Emmy, are you alright?" he asked, suddenly at my side. The hazel flecks in his eyes were running a mile a minute, and his eyebrows were drawn in obvious concern.

I nodded, trying to put on a brave face. "I'm good."

His eyes roved my person, not showing any sign of relief at my words. "You don't look so good."

"Gee, thanks," I said, trying at humor.

His eyes met mine. "You sure you're okay?"

I felt tears prickling at my eyelids, but I blinked them away, nodding. "I'll be fine. Thanks to David," I added, giving credit where credit was due.

"Yeah, I heard he was the man of the hour." Grant's face was a blank, though his tone didn't seem totally pleased.

"He's not going to be in any trouble, is he?" I asked. "I mean, for knocking Nolan unconscious?" I peeked around Grant's frame to where David was shifting nervously from foot to foot beside a uniformed officer. Then again, David never looked too comfortable in the presence of law enforcement. Considering he made his living off of illegal card games, I could hardly blame him.

"No. It's being considered self-defense. Or in this case, defense of others. No charges will be brought."

"Good." I nodded. "Does he know that?"

That did elicit a small smile from Grant. "I might make him sweat it for a couple more minutes."

I gave him a playful swat on the arm.

He chuckled in earnest before asking, "So think you can tell me what happened?"

I sucked in a breath, feeling a little stronger now that he'd lightened the mood a bit. "I think so."

"And don't leave anything out this time," he warned, giving me another knowing smile.

I didn't, giving him the full, unedited version of events, including filling in all the missing bits of incriminating activities Ava and I had engaged in to get to that point. I'd like to say they'd all helped lead me right to the killer's identity, but the honest truth was I'd been as clueless as Ava when it had come to Nolan's real personality. That was one thing I had to hand to him—he'd been a heck of a good actor. Unfortunately, the only people who would be appreciating his skills now would be the population of the California penal system.

By the time I was done with my narrative, I was mentally and physically drained, and Grant had a deep frown etched on his face. I could tell he was trying hard to stay in Cop Mode and treat me like any other witness. But as I finished with how Nolan had been pointing his gun at me just before David burst in, Cop Mode melted and Grant pulled me in close for the tightest hug on record.

Not that I minded. If I'd have had my way, I would have stayed locked in his warm, safe arms like that forever.

As it was, it was over much too soon. He pulled away, his intense gaze meeting mine.

"Don't do this to me again," he said, his voice low and husky. "My heart can't take it."

I swallowed hard, trying to decipher if he feared an actual heart attack or was developing real feelings for me. And wondering which was more dangerous.

"I won't," I promised.

He narrowed his eyes, his mouth curving up ever so slightly at the corners. "Liar."

I couldn't help but laugh. "Okay, on my honor, I promise I will *try very hard* to stay out of harm's way."

"I guess that's the best I'm going to get out of you, huh?" He grinned in earnest.

I matched it, nodding.

He leaned in and gave my lips one feather light kiss, causing my body to have an instant hot flash.

I was still reveling in the sensation when he pulled back.

"I have to process this crime scene you've created," he told me.

I might have whined a little.

He grinned in response. "But I'm going to have Officer Green make sure you get home safely."

"Sure you don't want to see to that personally?" I asked. "You never know what trouble I might get into on the way home."

He chuckled again. "Trust me—I would much rather be going home with you."

Oh boy. There went that hot flash again.

"But," he continued, "I promise you this—I am taking you on a *real* date soon."

"Oh?" I asked, liking the sound of that.

He nodded. "Uh-huh. As I recall, a *real* date is just the two of us, out for dinner, preferably at Silvio's."

I couldn't help the smile spreading across my face. "That's some attention to detail, Detective Grant."

"That's kind of my job, Ms. Oak," he replied, giving me a wink before he waved over an officer in a brown sheriff's uniform.

After instructing the man to drive Ava and me home and see us safely inside, Grant leaned in and gave my lips one more deliciously too-short kiss before pulling himself back into Cop Mode and joining the swarm of officers inside Tripp's trailer.

* * *

"So Nolan had been lying to us all along," Carrie mused, shaking her golden locks back and forth in bewilderment at how her former friend could have been so deceitful.

"Then again, so was Harper," her husband, Bert, reminded her.

I didn't point out that he hadn't been completely honest throughout either. Mostly because it was rude to insult your host.

It had been a week since Nolan's arrest, and the tabloid press had finally settled down enough that Carrie and Bert had been able to leave the house without being accosted by paparazzi. They'd invited Ava, David, and me over for drinks to thank us for helping to clear Bert of all charges as well as enjoy an early spring evening on their patio near the fire pit.

"I can't believe that I fell for Nolan's charm," Ava said as she grabbed her glass of Oak Valley Chardonnay, supplied by yours truly. "I feel like such a fool."

"There's no way you could have known," I told her, trying to soothe her wounded ego.

"Well, I can tell you one thing—I'm off actors *and* doctors for good!" she said.

We all laughed, and I thought I detected David looking pleased beside her.

"You know," he said. "I knew I recognized Nolan when I first met him. And it wasn't from his *TV show*."

I shot him a look. "Oh no. Don't tell me you've seen his *other* films?"

He did an innocent palms-up thing. "What? I'm not allowed to have a healthy libido?"

I sipped from my glass, the subject of David's libido not one I wanted to delve into. "Anyway," I went on, "Grant told me that Nolan made a full confession at his arraignment, and he's entered a guilty plea."

"He'd have a hard time claiming not guilty after what he told us!" Ava noted.

I nodded. "True. And I think he's banking on the judge going lightly on a celebrity."

Carrie snorted. "I hope not! That man deserves everything that's coming to him."

While I had to agree, I knew a reduced sentence in this case likely meant life in prison rather than the death penalty— and neither one sounded like a picnic to me.

"With charges of homicide, as well as the kidnapping of Ava and assault to both of us, I'm pretty sure he won't be seeing the outside of a cell for a long time," I assured her.

"You realize that's twice I've been the white knight coming to your rescue," David told me with a wink.

"And I thank you," I told him, meaning it. "From the bottom of my heart."

My sincerity must have caught him off guard a little, as his usual sardonic smiled faltered. "Well, just promise to keep me in the loop next time."

"How about I promise there will be no next time instead," I said.

David let out a bark of laughter. "I'll believe *that* when I see it."

I opened my mouth to protest, but Carrie's new housekeeper, Sandra, arrived then from the kitchen with a tray of fruit and cheese in hand.

Turns out that when Carrie had gotten Bert home, she'd contacted Sandra about the memorial arrangements again only to find out that Sandra had been fired from the Bishops' employ. Carrie had immediately offered her a job.

Never mind that Kellen Bishop-Brice had offered to rehire Sandra again once Morgan had made his confession about where their *unnoticeable* little treasures had been going. Carrie offered to match what the Bishops had paid Sandra, and Sandra had figured that working for Carrie versus Kellen was a no brainer. At least that was what she'd told me when she'd answered Carrie's front door that afternoon.

According to her, apparently Kellen had not, as Morgan had feared, been angry enough to divorce him. She had decided it best "not to bother Mommy and Daddy" with the knowledge of his thefts, instead sweeping it under the carpet in true blue-blood manner. Whether Morgan had confessed to just stealing or the entire crime of having cheated on his wife with her sister as well, I didn't know. Though I could guess that one of those sins would be more easily forgiven than the other.

As we nibbled on the artisan cheese and sipped our wine, Ava piped up beside me. "Did you ever hear back from Animal Control about their plans for Dante?"

Carrie nodded. "Yes! Actually Tripp was able to convince them not to put him down."

"Oh, that's wonderful!" Ava said, clapping her hands together. "Is he back home?"

"Oh no," Bert cut in. "No, we've learned our lesson." He shot a loving glance toward Carrie. "Wild animals are not for us."

"At least no more wild than this guy," Carrie joked, giving Barkley's head a pat as he snoozed at her feet in the soft grass. "No, we sent Dante to a wild horse sanctuary up near Redding. He'll be well cared for and happy there."

"Oh, that sounds lovely," Ava agreed.

"Speaking of Tripp," David cut in. "Did we ever find out what it was he was burning in the fire pit here?" He gestured toward the cozy blaze beside us, staving off the early evening chill as the sun set.

I nodded. "The police picked Tripp up shortly after Nolan's arrest. He was heading toward Reno."

"With the duffel bag full of cash," Ava added. She knew because she'd been with me the morning after, when Grant had come over and told us all about it.

"So he *was* running," David deduced.

"Yes, but not for the reasons we guessed. It turns out," I started, retelling the story Grant had given us, "Tripp *had* been sleeping with Harper. At least, three months ago he had been. She'd dumped him as soon as her riding lessons ended, and he hadn't seen her again until she showed up in Sonoma for Carrie's party. Tripp spotted her downtown with her sister, Kellen, just like he told me."

"However, he'd left out the part where, after Kellen left, he'd approached Harper and they'd renewed their acquaintanceship…back at his trailer," Ava added. "If you know what I mean."

"Then," I continued, "he said that the following day, Harper showed up at his trailer again, this time asking him to hang on to a duffel bag for her."

"The money you gave her," Carrie said, turning to Bert.

Bert had the good graces to at least look sheepish.

"Tripp claims he didn't know what it was, but Harper said she needed to keep it safe somewhere."

"Only, then Harper died," David supplied.

"Right. That night. And, naturally, Tripp got curious and looked in the bag. Once he saw it was full of cash, he panicked. He said he was worried that with his past history—"

"Being arrested for the death of his *last* girlfriend," Ava added.

"—that the police would immediately start looking in his direction as Harper's killer. And now he had a mystery bag of cash."

"If I were Tripp, I think I'd be feeling nervous too," David admitted.

"Ditto," I agreed. "He said he went through his trailer and grabbed anything that tied him to Harper. Including a couple items of clothing that Harper had left behind."

"So, it *was* Harper's clothes he was burning here," Carrie commented, gesturing to the fire pit again.

"It was. He figured even if the ashes were found here, it would point to a killer in her social circle and not at him. Only when he realized later that someone had broken into his trailer—"

Ava did some innocent whistling.

"—he became paranoid again. He snuck into Carrie's house to go through Harper's things and make sure there was nothing that pointed to a connection between them."

"Which is when you found him," Bert said.

I nodded. "I guess my arrival scared him away."

"Too bad it hadn't scared Nolan away as well," David said, referring to the conk on the head I'd received that day.

"Truly," I agreed.

"But if Tripp was innocent of killing Harper, why did he run?" Carrie asked, sipping her wine.

I shrugged. "According to Grant, Tripp's fear and paranoia got the best of him. He thought he'd take the money Harper had left behind and go start over somewhere new."

"Not like he was leaving a lot behind," Ava noted.

"Did Grant bring any charges against him?" David asked, swirling his wine in the bottom of his glass before downing the last sip.

I shook my head. "Tripp didn't know where the money had come from, and he wasn't the one who extorted it from Bert in the first place. Really, the only crime he committed was breaking in here that night—"

"Which we're not pressing charges for!" Carrie piped up. "How could we when he saved Dante?"

"—and destruction of property," I finished. "But burning a couple of silk charmeuse blouses isn't a crime."

Ava winced. "Maybe it should be."

I grinned. "At least he left her handbags alone," I reasoned.

"And the money?" David asked. "In the duffel bag?"

"It was returned to Bert," Carrie said.

"Correction," Bert piped up. "It was returned to *Carrie*." He shot her another sheepish grin. "Where it belongs. From now on, Carrie is in charge of this family's finances."

Carrie put a hand on her husband's arm. "What's mine is yours," she said softly.

The two shared a look, and I suddenly felt like we were third, fourth, and fifth wheels. Clearly she'd forgiven her husband, even if she was too savvy to ever quite forget.

"Well, I hope it puts a dent in your financial problems," Ava added, grinning at the couple with just the slightest hint of envy in her eyes.

Carrie nodded. "It will help. And we've decided to downsize a little and live a bit more frugally until all the debts are paid off."

"Oh, I hope that doesn't mean you'll have to sell this place," Ava said, glancing around at the beautiful acreage.

"I don't have the heart to do that," Carrie admitted. "Especially not now that Sandra's working here. Actually, we thought we'd hang on to it and rent the rooms out as a B&B. If we can entice enough Wine Country weekenders to use it, the extra income will go a long way to getting us solvent again."

"That is a fantastic idea," David Allen said, pouring himself another glass of Chardonnay. I could see the wheels turning in his head, his own mother's estate lying dormant at current.

"Isn't it? It was Carrie's idea," Bert said, putting an arm around his wife's shoulders. "Beauty, compassion, and brains—how did I get so lucky?"

"Well, at least somebody's love life panned out," Ava said, and I could tell she was still thinking of Nolan.

"Cheer up," Carrie told her. "Our first weekender is coming at the end of the month." She got a mischievous gleam in her eyes. "Lord Shamus Whelmsbottom."

Ava gasped. "The baronet who lost his fortune and became a private eye to track down his long lost sister who ended up in a coma after Stormy Winters pushed her down a flight of stairs?"

"The one and only!" Carrie told her.

David snorted and leaned in to me with a mock whisper. "She does know these people are all actors, right?"

I waved him off. "As long as Lord Whelmsbottom isn't a homicidal maniac, let her have her fun."

David shook his head as he sipped his glass of wine. "Well, what I want to know is, whose baby was Harper pregnant with?"

I shrugged. "That we may never know. Harper had been seeing Tripp, Nolan, *and* her brother-in-law, Morgan."

"One thing Nolan had been apparently honest about was Harper's love of men," Ava mused.

Carrie shook her head, a sad look on her face. "I guess I never really knew her."

I put a hand on her arm and was trying to come up with something comforting to say to that when Sandra walked up again, this time with a tray of chocolate cupcakes that instantly served to lighten everyone's mood.

Sandra passed them around, but when it came to me, I politely refused.

Carrie turned a shocked expression my way. "Emmy Oak. I have never seen you turn down dessert before."

I felt a blush creep into my cheeks. "They look lovely, but I've actually got to get going."

"So soon?" Bert asked, and to his credit I actually detected a note of disappointment in his voice. I was beginning to think I might have had the man pegged wrong. Or maybe Carrie was just becoming a good influence on him.

"Sorry, but I have a…prior engagement."

"This wouldn't happen to be an engagement with a certain detective, would it?" Carrie asked, a note of teasing in her voice.

Even as the heat in my cheeks burned, I felt a smile growing on my face along with it. "Possibly," I hedged.

"He's taking her to Silvio's tonight," Ava told them.

"Wow," David said, an unreadable expression behind his eyes. "Things must be getting serious."

I waved him off. "It's just a date."

At a fancy restaurant. With a hot guy. Who was an excellent kisser.

"Well, have fun," Carrie said as I got up and grabbed my purse.

"Oh, trust me," I countered, feeling that smile turn into a full-fledged cat-that-planned-to-take-the-canary-home grin. "I intend to."

ABOUT THE AUTHOR

Gemma Halliday is the #1 Amazon, *New York Times* & *USA Today* bestselling author of several mystery and suspense series. Gemma's books have received numerous awards, including a Golden Heart, two National Reader's Choice awards, a RONE Award for best mystery, and three RITA nominations. She currently lives in the San Francisco Bay Area with her large, loud, and loving family.

To learn more about Gemma, visit her online at
www.GemmaHalliday.com